A New Day

Foothills #4

Carrie Thorne

Thorny Books

A New Day

Foothills #4

Carrie Thorne

ISBN 979-8-9867090-0-0

Dedication

For my mother. The best friend a daughter could ask for. Supportive in everything I do, including being beta reader #1. Thanks, Mom!

1

Audible

*Y**ou were working long hours, and I needed a little release, that's all. Mariella meant nothing to me. Babe, I miss you so much—*

Haley pitched the phone across the cavernous ivory living room. True to form, the phone hit the curtain—thanks to her shitty aim—and slid safely to the floor. Didn't even crack the screen.

Shoulders slumped, her throwing arm nagging from a useless tantrum; she slogged across the frigid tile to grab the dang thing. Glaring at the traitorous device, she deleted the stupid email. And blocked the sender.

Ten years. Ten years she'd given to that creep. Eight years of marriage. They'd been so young. So foolish.

And come on. Long hours? She wrote her blog from home. If he'd needed any "release," all he had to do was knock. Or at least have the decency to dump her first.

And it wasn't just Mariella. Not that she had proof, at least not in the vivid way that she had with Mariella. That revolting vision was imprinted in her brain. Red lace. Big tits. Enthusiastically bouncing on top of her husband. In their bedroom.

Monthly girls' night always involved excessive quantities of appletinis and sex tips. And, okay, maybe she was being paranoid, but it always seemed like those tips were awfully specific. Now she knew.

It wasn't paranoia.

And they'd teased her for being a prude. With a snort worthy of a prized bull, she stomped across the room and plopped onto the stack of cardboard boxes. She wasn't a prude. She was normal.

Sleeping with your friend's husband was not normal. Nate had accused her of cheating weeks prior, in one of his many lame-ass excuses when he got caught, claiming a wife couldn't be so disinterested, or so hard to please, unless she was getting it elsewhere.

Ha. Didn't occur to him she was *disinterested* because she wasn't attracted to him anymore? That she was sick of being treated as a... a... a *thing*, a showpiece, a housekeeper, rather than as an intelligent, independent woman? That she could only take so many digs before she realized this wasn't what she'd hoped? And she'd been considering couples' therapy.

A vigorous knock at the front door interrupted her pity-fest. No one knocked as aggressively as her mother. Dear Patricia did nothing mildly. Haley almost envied her mother's fierce personality. Almost.

Thanks to a judge with keen insight that finalized her parents' divorce, when Haley was suffering in silence while enduring puberty, figuring out boobs and periods and zits on her own, Haley was placed with her father. Miracle of miracles. Drake was a good dad. Not great, but there had been love.

"Hello, Mother?" she said as she pulled open the extra-wide, extra-thick front door that had cost more than her blog earned in a year. With a sweep of her arm, she welcomed Dr. Mallory into her home for the first time. And last.

Patricia breezed past her and tensed her shoulders, her platinum hair not daring to shift out of place as she eyed the paltry stack of Haley's belongings. Haley had insisted they liquidate everything, especially the house they'd lived in not even two years, and a quarter of that was spent liquidating while moving at a snail's pace through this mess of a divorce. Every time she thought she was free, he'd find another hurdle to slow the process. She didn't want to spend months arguing over who owned the Waterford crystal glasses or the bone china that she'd detested from the moment Nate had insisted they add the finery to their wedding registry. Yet, that is exactly what had occurred.

"Haley, dear. How are you holding up?" Haley almost sighed and went in for a possibly maternal hug. Nope. Not Patricia's style. Patricia didn't even seem to catch the hint that Haley was drowning in need for simple affection. Nothing new, from her mother or her husband. "You must be so distraught."

"Actually, I'm glad it's finally over. I feel... relieved. Foothills sounds like the change of pace I need."

"Well, I suppose Foothills could use another woman with excellent taste. You can commute to Seattle. I know a few people you can call for help to find a prime location to open an interior decorating firm." Patricia's calculating eyes were alight with her own brilliance. "We could carpool together every day. I have no doubt you will want to work the extra hours, anyway, like I do on surgery days."

"Mother, I'm not sure that running an 'interior design firm' describes what I do. My blog is steady and my share of our assets should be enough to keep me comfortable."

"You must have a long list of clients here in San Francisco. You'll be able to acquire a whole new clientele in Seattle, but—"

"Mother, it's a *blog*. Freelance at its best. All those photos were from my friends' houses. I didn't finish college and don't know the first thing about starting a brick-and-mortar business. Nor do I want to." Nate's studies had come first. But she'd made the most of it. Of the loneliness during his long hours. Of ensuring they had a meticulously run home and social standing.

Her home decorating blog had been for her alone. It was more successful than she had anticipated, but she'd had unlimited use of Nate's income to do regular remodels to keep her designs fresh. And elevated social status decried upgrading homes every few years.

Patricia pulled her bug-eyed sunglasses back down and stalked to the front door. "Well, load up your boxes. Our road trip will be such a fun adventure. I wish you could have kept the Porsche, but I suppose the Land Rover is more practical for the trip." She almost shrugged, but her stiff shoulders couldn't quite make the movement convincing. "Our first night is at a winery in Sonoma."

"I'm sure it will be great." She'd only seen her mother during summer and winter breaks as a teenager, and even less frequently over the last decade. The mother-daughter trip to move her back home had been Patricia's idea. Having gone through several divorces herself, Patricia seemed almost sympathetic.

Touchdown Fire, this is it, San Francisco Fire wins the Super Bowl. What a play. Forty-yard pass nearly intercepted, Halseth snatches the ball and spins, making the final push into the end zone and... oh man, did he just—

Finn shut off the rehash. *Get over it.* He clenched his jaw, grinding his molars until he heard a crunch. His knee throbbed just watching the latest over-played recap. Best fucking game of his life. But not even the adrenaline of the

TD could mask the pain as his knee bent ninety degrees in the wrong direction.

Two surgeries later, months of physical therapy, and he was almost back to a decent sprint. Not that any team in the NFL was going to touch him again. Twenty-eight wasn't old, but it was for a wide receiver with an unstable knee.

He headed for the stairs, but halted when Pops strolled in the front door. The scent of smoked salmon wafted off him, honey and salty and soothing and familiar. Hmm, smoked salmon today. Pops had nailed the smoked meats and cheese recipes, carving out a unique niche in Foothills.

Not Finn's thing. He'd rather handle the front end of things. So far the arrangement had been working great, his sister in the kitchen where Mom used to reign, and Evan nudging Pops gradually out of the smokehouse and into the office.

"Hey, Finn. You okay?"

"Yeah. Of course." Finn grabbed the rail to the stairs, hovering as he waited to hear the lecture Pops had undoubtedly been holding on to for months now.

"Great. That's great. Things still going okay behind the bar?" Nearly matched in height, Finn shared his father's broad, athletic build, chocolate eyes that crinkled when they smiled. And, although Scott's hair was dappled with gray, it was as thick as Finn's chestnut.

"Actually, yeah. I like it."

"That's what I hear. Some of the regulars tell me you're a natural."

He ran a hand through his hair, ruffling the defiant cowlick. "I don't know about that, but it suits me."

"Great." Uh-oh. Never a good sign when Pops was in bobble-head compliment mode. "If you need me to jump in and take on more so you can look for a coaching position or, you know, something that suits you better, just say the word."

"Sure." Nodding again, he stepped up to the next stair.

"Okay then."

Finn stepped up a few more steps.

"Hey, Finn?"

Chuckling, Finn turned and leaned against the rail. "Yeah, Pops?" Lovably nosy, Scott's crinkly eyes creased more heavily today. Pops scratched his fingers through his salt and pepper hair, grinning as he said, "I'll quit harassing you in a minute. I worry."

"I know, Pops."

"I haven't seen Trace around much. You two doing okay?"

Finn shrugged, a familiar hollow gnawing in his gut. "I guess."

"I know you guys have a history. It made sense you'd reconnect when you got back to town, but, well..."

"I know, Pops. It seemed like the right thing to do when I came back. But, well..."

"It's okay to take a break, let her know you weren't ready."

"I'll talk to her." Knowing Trace, she'd be understanding. Maybe they'd chat when she got back from her big trip.

When he'd come back to Foothills a few months ago, she'd stopped by to see how he was doing. She'd been checking in on his mom regularly anyway, so she'd waited until he'd been home a few days before interrupting.

He dashed the rest of the way up the stairs and tossed on his running clothes. He pulled on his knee brace and headed for the backdoor. He almost made it, when his watch chirped with an incoming call. Huh, speak of the devil.

Stepping outside so his dad and sis wouldn't hear, he answered, "Yeah?"

Trace's sweet voice vibrated through the tiny speaker of his smartwatch. "Hi, Finn. I'm flying out in a few days. I was hoping we could talk before I go?"

"Sure. I'm heading out for a run." He could already hear the guilt oozing through her voice, but she wouldn't do it over the phone.

"Are you working tonight?" Yep. He knew exactly why she wanted to meet up.

"Yeah. I want to get in a run first, so, uh—"

"Of course. No problem. I won't keep you. Can I bring over coffee in the morning?"

"Sure."

"You okay?"

Of course he was okay. He'd been *fine* for weeks now. His dad, his sister, his little brother. Maybe they weren't yet. Mom's presence still coated every square inch of the family home. They all missed her like a missing limb. Fuck, it didn't take a therapist to figure out his first knee surgery failed because his heart was too damn broken to let the rest of him heal. "Yeah, I'm fine."

"Okay. See you in the morning," she closed with a regretful brightness in that unshakable pleasantness.

He looked to the forest beyond, the orange glow of the sun threatening to knock him down with a scorching summer heat if he didn't get his ass in gear. "See ya."

"Okay. Later." She hung up. He almost wished she'd get it over with on the phone, but she'd want to do it in person. To make sure he was actually okay. As if coffee and pastries would soften the blow.

They'd been hot and heavy in high school, never apart. When he'd come home to Foothills after... everything, reconnecting had seemed obvious. He stretched out his stiff limbs and took off down the road at an easy pace, not wanting to re-ignite the swelling that had nagged at him for a solid week after he'd run on the bum knee too hard a few weeks back. Foothills needed a gym. He was a sprinter, dammit, and his knee didn't tolerate this sort of shit anymore.

By the end of the two-mile loop, about all his joints could handle today, the sun had warmed the cedar boughs that canopied the last of his path. Pungent, the earthy scent welcomed him home. He swung open the front door, kicking off his shoes. They landed with a spin in the basket. After wiping the briny layer of sweat from his forehead before it dripped into his eyes, he skated across the linoleum floor to the foot of the beige-carpeted stairs.

Zoe, his little sister and bossiest of the Halseth clan, pierced the air with her shrill voice. "Don't you think about taking all the hot water."

He stopped mid-step, hovering before daring to climb the next step.

Like a cranky apparition, she popped out from the pass-thru to the kitchen. She held her coffee a few inches below her lips and glowered through the steam. "Finbarr Halseth. If you take another thirty-minute shower like you did yesterday, I'm going to kick your ass and you can do all the cooking tonight, as I'll be too frozen to move."

Finn angled his head and looked down at her. "I'm so sorry, your highness. My physical therapist thinks hot water will help relax my muscles. Unless *you* want to tend bar *and* man the kitchen tonight?"

She glared into her coffee, then back at him. "Just no jerking off in there."

From deep in his throat, his laugh echoed out loud. "Never. But I am investing in a lock for my bedroom door and will be perfectly willing to tell Pops about Josh Stevens and the car incident."

"You wouldn't," she growled, expression pure pout, her brown eyes heavy with menace.

"Then let me take my damn shower."

"Fine," she muttered, spinning around on her heel and heading back for the kitchen.

Still chuckling, he hobbled up the stairs. He dropped his clothes on the bathroom floor and turned the faucet to steaming. Flipping back the blue flowered shower curtain, he stepped over the beige bathtub wall and into the shower.

Ahh, he sighed as the hot water drenched his skin. As soon as he got downstairs, he was propping his knee up with a big-ass icepack until he had to leave for work. Aiming the showerhead as high as it would go, he ducked his head and let the water stream down his body.

Grabbing his cock, he relaxed in the steam of the shower, tracing his thumb over the shaft... then remembered his sister's threats.

Fine. He missed living alone. With an unlimited budget and on-demand hot water.

Finn shut off the water and stepped out, his knee a bit looser than it had been that morning. Day by day, he regained mobility. He pulled on a pair of jeans and a *Halseth's Smokehouse and Pub* black t-shirt, then hobbled half-speed down to the kitchen for a cup of coffee and a long ice on that knee before his shift started.

Trace would be up early with apology coffee and pastries for them both. Bright eyed and bushy tailed to put him at ease, even for the somber occasion. Finn's alarm squawked rhythmically, shattering the tranquility of the sun-drenched morning. Hauling his ass out of bed, he limped across the bedroom and silenced the alarm. The first few steps were always the roughest before things loosened up.

He'd have to look for a place with enough room to add a gym or something; he was going nuts in the cramped space, his equipment boxed up in the garage. Pops was in better shape than he was these days, but Pops had full access to the high school gym as the football coach.

The moment he reached the bottom step, the doorbell rang. Like clockwork. He unlocked the front door and greeted his coffee date.

Standing adorably sincere in pink capris and a black summer sweater, Trace held out a travel mug she'd brought from home. He smiled and accepted the ordinary brew. She knew he wouldn't have wanted the fancy shit from the coffee stand that was laced with sugar and sweetness.

"Good morning," she said. Without a hint of make-up this morning, she looked so much like the girl he'd loved so long ago. Clenching tight in his chest, his heart contracted in anticipation of another blow.

"Morning. Come on in." He led the way through the entry to the kitchen. "Warm out there?"

"It's pleasant. Want to sit outside?"

He nodded, opening the slider and motioning for her to go out first and choose her seat. No way in hell he was having this conversation in the middle of the family kitchen. Evan would already be at work, but Zoe and Pops would be able to hear every damn word if their bedroom windows were open. Oh well. Save him the explanation when they interrogated him later.

Trace followed the winding gravel path through shrubs overgrown with blooms every color of the rainbow that his mother knew by name and personality to the small table in the middle of the rose garden. Damn, he ought to get out here and prune. Brenda would be so disappointed in the overgrown mess now that she wasn't here to tend to it. Not that anyone shared her green thumb, but he'd look it up and see if he could figure it out.

She set out a paper bag on the table. "Mom sent along a dozen of your favorites."

He peeked in the bag, the savory scent of cheddar and bacon croissants almost tempting his stomach to accept food. Rolling it shut again, he set it back so he could see her. "Thanks."

They sat in silence for a bit, the morning breeze fluttering the leaves around them.

By the time he reached the midway point in his coffee, he realized she was struggling to find the right words. Okay, he could handle more small talk. "So. When do you leave?"

"Saturday." She crossed and uncrossed her ankles, not quite facing him.

"All packed?"

"Yes." She smiled finally as the awkward melted to normal. "You know me. I started packing the moment I got the offer." Yeah, she'd have been ready weeks in advance. "Finn. I, um, was hoping we could talk about something."

"Sure." Here we go. Just rip off the damn band-aid. It had been too long, anyway. Their little experiment had been a stinging example of how you can't go back.

"When we... I mean... wow, this is hard." She drained the last of her coffee and set the flowered mug on the table between them. "Do you ever think we rushed into getting back together?"

Staring blankly into the overgrown ravine beyond, he shrugged. "Yeah. Probably."

Her shoulders relaxed. "I mean, I was so excited that you were back home, but hated why. At first, I thought you needed time to adjust. Not that I expect you to feel even remotely normal yet; you have so much to process. But it's been months and things haven't changed."

"I know."

"When we were kids, I think we were only apart when you were at away games. I don't know what I was expecting this time around. Something along those lines, I guess. But I've hardly seen you. You didn't even know what day my flight leaves, and certainly haven't offered to drive me to the air-port."

"I can take you to the airport."

"That's not what I meant." She sighed, leaning her elbows onto the table between them.

Recognizing she needed more, he turned toward her. "Look, Trace, I know what you meant. You're right. I'm not the guy I was. We're not the people we used to be. We were pretty great in high school, but a lot's happened since then."

She lit up as he said the words she must have been chewing on for days. "Exactly. I mean, when I get back, we can talk more and see where we're at. But, well, I don't want to be apart all summer, both of us thinking we need to keep this going. I know the timing is terrible. You're still grieving your mother and floundering from leaving football and coming home. I also think that's part of the problem. You don't need one more thing on your plate, and I think that's what I've been. One more ball in the air."

Actually, he was a pretty damn good juggler. But she might be right. Maybe after he settled in, got his own place, found his routine, the spark might re-ignite. Doubtful, but possible. "Thanks for being there for me through all of this. You're right. I don't have the capacity to be involved right now. You deserve someone that can prioritize *you*. And that's not me. I love you, just not the way I did before."

Air flowed easily in and out through her lungs, and he watched as she sat up, that gentle smile widening to amused. "You're such an ass."

"What?" He sat up straighter, laughing in utter confusion as she smiled while seeming to insult him.

"Here I am, dumping you, days before I skip town, while you're going through the worst grief. Don't let me off the hook way so easy." She nudged him under the table like she had in the old days to let him know she was messing with him. "Can you at least pretend to be furious with me? Yell and throw things?"

He chuckled with her, then adopted a comical glower. "Dammit Trace. Don't crush me like this, you heartless bitch." He nudged her back. "There, is that better?"

She laughed and sat up higher, contorting her amusement with an angry face. "Screw you, Finn."

"There. Now we can call it a real break-up." Smiling, he stood and held his hand out for her.

Trace accepted and let him pull her up, but she dropped his hand and wrapped her arms around him in a bear hug. "I am going to miss you."

Hugging her back, he rested his cheek against her wild strawberry blond hair. "I'll miss you too. Enjoy your adventure this summer."

She pinched his side and pulled away. "I'll call you when I get back. Stay out of trouble."

Strolling down the garden path, a swing in her hips, he watched his oldest friend walk out of his life again. They'd always be friends, but the wave of relief rushing from his lungs told him they'd made the right decision.

2

Line of Scrimmage

"Now that you're home, we will expect to see you for family dinner the first Sunday of every month. Grady has insisted we alternate, so I am sure you'll want to be included in the rotation, when you feel ready to entertain." Patricia held her hand on the car door, the sun's rays casting a blinding reflection on her platinum hair. "Your stepfather refuses to miss football, lord knows why, so you'll want to get your cable hooked up before they start airing anything."

That was lucky. She wouldn't want to miss any Fire games. "As I lack a TV, furniture, dishes, and cookware, it may be sometime before I entertain. But I'll be there." Haley climbed back into the driver's seat. "Thanks for coming to get me."

With a single nod of approval, Patricia lifted her suitcase and stalked into Mallory Mansion.

Haley shifted into gear and headed toward home. Although a small town, crossing Foothills' sprawl was a bit of a trek thanks to large land parcels. Abutting a national park to the north and a national forest to the east, its residents were made up of those that sought the beauty and solitude of raw nature.

Her home lacked the expansive views or rambling trails like so many Foothills homes, but it was comfortably nestled in the forest on the outskirts of downtown. The two-acre property was as serene as she remembered. Settled just off the road in a mature neighborhood, it could easily be a showpiece, with its sharply angled roof in the alpine fashion, natural brown cedar siding, and the sort of entry that cried out for brightly colored shrubs and porch rockers.

Not that she had any of that yet. The driveway was rough with potholes, the porch covered in nearly a decade of leaves, the shrubs overgrown, and the trim no longer the cheery blue she remembered.

Yet she felt a long-awaited, almost foreign sense of normal wash over her.

Opening the car door, she stepped onto the gravel drive and looked up at her new home. Old home. The home she'd grown up in. She could picture Grady and Ryder sprinting in the front door after a long day at school, dumping their homework under the entry table and racing upstairs for a much-needed break from the many activities Patricia kept them all involved in. Haley would still be in her ballet tights and leotard under her flowered dress, chasing behind her half-brothers for a break of her own.

Until the day her dad came up to her bedroom and dropped to the edge of the bed, burying his head in his hands. *"Hale, your mother and I are getting a divorce."* Her heart had shattered. Leave her brothers? Her friends? Foothills?

Tears flooding over her cheeks, she'd begged. *"Dad, I don't want to go. I like it here."*

"Home will always be here for you. This was your grandparents' home. My first home. One day, it will be yours again." His gruff voice still rattled about in her mind.

What would he have said, seeing her wasting her life away with Nate? Being the perfect housewife neither Patricia nor he had raised her to be? He'd intended for the move to help her to fulfill her own dreams. Not that she had ever been interested in glam and status, but she'd been good at it.

Sliding the key into the lock—well, jamming it through the pollen-encrusted receptacle of a deadbolt—she entered her home. Haley was immediately knocked back by the foul scent of a death.

Ew, she squealed, dancing up and down, never feeling like quite so much the spoiled city girl she'd become as she laid eyes on nature's housewarming gift. Smack dab in the middle of the great room floor was a raccoon in full rigor mortis. *Uck, disgusting.* She pinched her nose and glanced around for signs of carnage, but it was just the one body. And one was more than enough.

The slate tile of the foyer was hardly visible through the inch-thick layer of dust, almost slippery as she walked over it in her Frye booties. The stairs to the right were fuzzy with cobwebs coating the carpeted steps. A dilapidated cardboard box sat on the landing halfway up. To the left, the dreaded raccoon carcass had taken up residence where a coffee table should be in the middle of the great room. Near him, the river-rock fireplace extended floor to ceiling with a time-shined hearth where she used to warm her back on cold mornings, but was now littered with dried leaves. On the opposite side of the immense room, the kitchen was in no better shape, with outdated pink tile that was marbled white and brown with dust. Above, the timber beams were sturdy, the ceiling an eggshell white and stain-free.

The inspector she'd sent out had ensured the bones of the house were in great shape. The plumbing had been questionable from years of disuse. So, she'd had the plumbing tuned up, electricity certified, and HVAC updated before daring to move in. Months of waiting for home, liquidating her former life, and cutting off all ties to her social circle.

Sighing with her whole body, she accidentally inhaled odor-of-raccoon again. The house needed a lot of... love.

And, apparently, an exterminator to figure out how the hell the raccoon had gotten in. She dashed out to the garage and came back with the splinter-handled shovel they'd used to fill chuckholes back in the day. When Patricia was at work, because that sort of thing should be hired out. For all Drake's snobbery, he had at least grown up in the rural town and appreciated the merits of manual labor.

Damn, she'd missed Foothills. Nate had been snootier than Patricia, and lacked the feminism. His wife was not to cook or clean. He could provide all the means, so she might... what? Sit on her ass and wait for him to get home?

Certainly not to hit the gym, as muscles weren't feminine. Nor raise children, not until they were at least thirty-five or forty. Shopping. Days at the spa. *Argh*.

Forcing her eyes open and refraining from squealing like a terrified rodent herself again, Haley scooped up the stiff carcass and backed carefully out the front door. Shovel extended as far from her as possible, she looked around for a garbage can.

No can. Crap, she forgot about setting up the garbage service. Crap, internet. Paying bills shouldn't be left to the little missus; too complicated for her inferior brain.

How had she let herself slip so far into the perfect life *he'd* imagined for her?

She set down the shovel. Its stiff body rolled off the blade and onto the ground. Cringing, she almost pitied the poor thing with its mouth frozen open, its little fingers open as if someone had walked in on its private moment. Under the massive Doug fir at the far side of the property, she dug a deep hole and rolled its mangy carcass into the grave.

Her phone buzzed in her pocket. Holding it with her fingertips, in case a fragment of dead raccoon germs had magically flown onto her hands, she held the phone away and read the message from Grady.

Welcome home, Sis. Settling in okay? I know you said no, but please consider staying with us until the house is habitable?

She had missed her brothers. Nate had always been so busy with work, and didn't like her traveling without him, so she hadn't come home much over the last few years. She texted back, *Thank you for the offer, but I need this. Dead raccoons and all.*

I get it. If you need anything, supplies, breakfast, a vacuum, extra arms... exterminators, let me know, ok?

She messaged back. *I know. Thank you. Bring me dinner tomorrow? And a vacuum would be the best housewarming present ever.* She dropped the shovel back in the garage and eyed the kitchen and living room. Yikes. Going to be like a night in a haunted house, without the ghosts. Hopefully, Mr. Raccoon had gone peacefully.

Absolutely. Hope you don't mind, I let Trace know you were coming home.

Aw, of course he did. *I'm so glad you did. Send me her number?*

A moment later, her phone buzzed with the number. Fifteen years. Joined at the hip through eighth grade. Surely there would still be that connection? She needed that connection. Staring at the screen, she let the anxious palpitation beat a few times, then hit Send.

"Hello?" A sweet, feminine voice lilted on the other end.

"Hey, Trace. I'm back."

Giggling in her delightfully soprano voice, her childhood best friend woo-hoo'ed. "About damn time. I can't believe it."

"Grady gave you a heads up?"

"Yes. You have a good brother. I'm so sorry to hear about the divorce, but I'm thrilled you're home. I missed you."

"I'm sorry I wasn't the pen pal I promised to be." It had been so lonely, moving so far from her friends and family. And she'd tried so hard to fit in. Foothills to Beverly Hills at age fourteen. Ouch.

"Me neither. You ended up in ritzville and I got a boyfriend and was convinced the world turned only for us. No wonder we didn't keep in touch."

"I'd forgotten about that. I think the last email I'd gotten from you was a picture from homecoming freshman year, you in your fire-engine red dress with quite the hottie on your arm."

"And you sent that one of you in the Vera Wang homecoming gown."

"Ouch. Let's not dwell. I'm turning over so many new leaves, remembering what I liked about me. My cheating bastard ex-husband and charmed life was..."

"Not you. We were always halfway up a tree or making mud pies. I can't imagine how rough that transition had been."

The damn waterworks threatened with fiery pressure behind her eyes, but Haley hadn't shed a tear in years, and when nothing came, no relief from the pressure, she feared she had forgotten how. Or maybe her body knew Nate wasn't worth it. "Chocolate pie instead of mud is a bit more my therapeutic dessert these days."

"Me too. How about I come over Wednesday morning and bring coffee and breakfast? I don't know if Grady told you, but I'm leaving in a few days for the summer. I'll be back end of August, and when I get home, we can stay up all night, watching movies and talking about boys and eating popcorn."

"He did tell me. I'm bummed but I'm glad to hear you're going on an adventure. We'll catch up over coffee. And consider yourself fully informed, the house is unfurnished and covered in dust and dead rodents."

"Attractive. I'll bring a picnic blanket and we can sit outside."

"See you soon."

They disconnected and Haley shoved the phone in her back pocket. The old Haley was always at the top of a tree, covered in mud. After ballet and martial arts and basketball and even science club. Finding the old Haley again might be a worthy adventure.

By the time she carted all five boxes of her belongings into the house, the shadows had grown long and her arms and back ached. And her tummy growled. She flipped the switch in her desolate bedroom, a single bulb on the ceiling fan lighting up, but not without a few crackling flickers. Humph. Pulling her phone out, she searched for delivery.

Crap. First world problem. No delivery service in rurality. Not even pizza. Grumbling, she shoved her phone back in her pocket, grabbed the keys, and ventured out in search of food.

Main Street was bustling for a Monday night. Larissa's Diner was as cheery as the day she'd left, but sadly closed for the evening. The bank hadn't changed a bit, but was dark now that business hours were over. She'd avoided Tracey's Apparel like the plague as a child, but it sounded fun now. Coffee shop on every corner, where it had only been every other corner back in the day. Some things changed. A few new shops, restaurants, and inns added character.

She was relieved to find no big-box retail had taken over. Essentially the base camp for dozens of mountain adventures, the town still held that artsy-tourist vibe.

Ahab's was packed and looked too crazy for a quiet dinner alone, but she knew it was the hub where the cool grownups had hung out. Naturally, that hadn't included her parents. Amber streetlights, updated since she'd last been here, flickered on as she scanned the streets. Sutherland's Hardware was closing up for the evening. Good to know they were still around. She'd be investing a hefty sum there as she fixed up the house.

Maybe Pippa Sutherland was back in town? Or her older brother, Asher. Haley had always had a huge crush on him.

Like all the other girls at school. Not that she was looking for a relationship of any sort right now. Ouch.

Ooh, a hole-in-the-wall pub. That was new. The narrow cedar structure with black trim and a sky blue old-fashioned door said cozy was its goal. She parked out front, checking in the mirror to be sure she didn't look as if she'd spent the last week on the road, nor buried a dead raccoon in her backyard a few hours ago.

When she stepped onto the sidewalk, she could already smell the yummy scent wafting out. The rustic blue door opened, and a smiling couple exited the restaurant, gazing at each other, walking hand in hand. Happy and adorable. Jerks.

She shifted her purse over her shoulder and stepped inside. The mouthwatering scent of smoked meats and cheeses, homemade sourdough, and fresh brews filled her anticipating tummy. Famished, she nearly orgasmed at the impact of the savory smell.

Not too many tables, but filled enough to feel loved, the place was cozy without being cramped. Behind the register, at the edge of the bar that dominated the main wall, a collection of t-shirts and ball caps were neatly folded for sale, both themed with the restaurant's name in block lettering, and others that had clever sayings and "Foothills" emblazoned across the chest or back. Below the register, a refrigerated display case was filled with smoked meats and cheeses from the pub, some of Grady's Black Op beers, and a collection of cookies from Trace's mom's bakery, were labeled for individual sale. Warm and fuzzy at the familiar touches, Haley felt at home already.

The bar itself was a gleaming polished wood, the center of which was home to a half dozen taps. Corrugated metal siding with an iron-finished pipe footrest made up the base of the bar, twelve black leather bar stools were filled with ten happy diners.

As she moved to claim the corner spot at the edge of the bar, a roguishly deep voice radiated out from the kitchen, the vibration sending shivers over her skin as if priming her for something scrumptious. The body that followed triggered an unconscious dopey-grinned hair flip. Tall, freaking built with a black t-shirt hugging powerful shoulders... pecs... abs... *hmm, nice view*. Forcing her eyes north, her gaze landed on the face.

Oh. That was nice too... she could hardly follow her own train of thought. Chiseled jaw, gooey chocolate brown eyes, trim brown hair with a feisty cowlick that spiked his hair up in front. Really familiar, but so out of context she couldn't place him. Must have gone to school together. Regardless, she could sit and stare at this guy all day. He hadn't even looked at her, and she could feel his hands clutched on her hips, tugging her against him, his supple lips trailing over her collarbone, like a private fantasy.

Still frozen in place, she about melted to the floor when he finally looked her way. "Hey," he called over the customers he'd just finished serving. "Grab a seat wherever you'd like."

Remembering he wasn't a figment of her imagination, that she was hungry—and not just for those biceps—she snagged one of the last seats. He snagged a menu from the unattended hostess' podium and met her across the bar.

"Thanks," she whispered on a controlled exhale. Her pulse pounded through her limbs, straight down to her core as she accepted the menu and met his gaze.

Finn clenched his jaw tight, keeping his feet planted firmly on the ground and his brain focused on keeping his cock from saluting the gorgeous brunette in front of him. What the hell was wrong with him? Like a fucking adolescent without a smidge of control over the unruly appendage.

Behaving like the grown up he was, he kept his eyes on hers. He absolutely did not notice that her lace-trimmed tank top hugged some spectacular breasts, hinting at a subtle shadow of cleavage. Did *not* notice how those lips were strawberry edible. Hair pulled back in a messy knot, her jeans and button-up top were wrinkled, like she'd had a hell of a day.

"Get you anything to drink?" he asked.

She paused, holding her breath for a moment, then laughed. "God yes. I don't even know what I want. Beer. Something that'll bite me back and remind me I'm still alive."

He practically groaned at the vision that invoked. "I gotcha. One sec."

Punching a few codes into the computer, he closed out the checks for the pair of retired loggers in front of him. Ken and Ron were here every Monday, while their wives went to their book club. He slid their checks across, and nodded. "Stay out of trouble."

Grabbing a glass from under the bar, he filled a pint with the hoppiest IPA on tap.

Tara slid up to the computer next to him and punched in an order. The server was always so dang peppy. Well, she had twenty-one-year-old knees and a high ponytail that spun all night as she walked. He assumed it must generate enough electricity to keep her going like an overly caffeinated barista. "Hey, I heard you and Trace broke up. What happened?"

And she hadn't yet learned that some things were not appropriate to bring up at work. Not that they socialized outside of work. But she was nice and a damn good worker and always meant well, so he let it slide. "Some things don't work out." Worse, he'd been single a grand total of ten hours, and word had spread.

"I'm sorry. Zoe says Trace was your high school sweetheart and had figured you two would get married now that you're back in town. How romantic, to reunite after all those years apart? I always wanted one of those second chance romances, but I'd have to have a decent first chance first." Her ponytail nearly smacked him in the face as she turned to grab a trio of menus and a cluster of silverware wrapped in black cloth napkins.

"Really not looking to talk on it," he muttered.

She batted apologetic eyelashes at him before bouncing across the room to welcome the newcomers.

Crossing back over to the hottie at the end of the bar, he flipped a cardboard coaster like a coin so it landed face up and set the beer on it. "See what you think of this one."

Sapphire blue eyes dancing in amusement, her gaze didn't leave his as she took a testing sip, licking her lips and smiling as the hoppy brew slid down her throat. She glanced at the tap. "Black Op? I'm embarrassed to admit that I haven't tried it yet."

He nodded, quickly disappearing to fill an order, and was back in a flash. "The best. I can't say Foothills is such a small town that I know everyone, and I've only been back in town a few months, but I've never seen you around." *Dumbass.* He used to be decent at meeting women, but he was epically drowning in lame with this one.

"I just moved back into town. Today, actually." She gestured to the wrinkled clothes and her eye twitched comically.

"Hence the need to get bit?" *Not helping.*

The corner of her mouth quirked up. "Yes. My house is not exactly in shambles, but I already had to bury a dead raccoon, I have no furniture or even dishes, and will be sleeping in my brand new sleeping bag on carpet that has not been vacuumed in over a decade."

He knew exactly where she could sleep, much more comfortably tonight. *Shit, never mind,* he remembered his own less-than-ideal living situation. Not that she would, or should, take some stranger up on *that* offer after knowing them for thirty seconds. "At least the raccoon was dead when you buried it."

A slap-happy, snorty chuckle loosened her tight shoulders. "Too true." Leaning her elbows on the bar, she glanced down at the menu, then back up at him, the corner of her mouth turning up in a flirty smile. "I'm so hungry, but I still can't use my brain. What's good?"

Swallowing, he crossed his arms, trying to remember... well, remember anything when she looked at him like that. Like he was the best thing on the menu. "Either the summer salad with smoked salmon, or the sausage sampler with side of cheese soup if you're more for comfort food tonight."

"I'd love to try the sausage." She took a long pull from her glass and licked her lips.

Holy shit. She wasn't exactly making a move, but something about the way she talked, the way she looked at him when she said it, shot straight to his... okay, she was fucking hot and was licking her lips while asking to taste his sausage.

Rather than typing her order into the computer at the bar, he hollered it at Zoe as he passed the kitchen and stepped outside for a breath of fresh air. What had happened to him? He'd been dumped a matter of hours ago. Then a few minutes of a normal interaction with a beautiful woman, and he was brewing some sort of horny panic attack.

Fuck, this time last year, he'd have gotten her number and promised to swing by when he next passed through town. And then his life had been turned upside down. In so many ways.

3

Huddle

"You know what you need, Haley? You need a rebound. Some fantastic sex with no strings attached." Trace shoved in her last bite of pastry and waggled her eyebrows.

Slapping her knee, setting her coffee down before she spilled it all over her lap, Haley's laugh erupted at the suggestion. "Wow, I missed you. We've been back together, what, twenty minutes? And you're already making me laugh."

When Trace had walked in her door, they'd jumped up and down and hugged and cried like the dorks they'd been so long ago. No weirdness, they dove right in like no time had passed.

Trace rolled her eyes, grinning wickedly. "I'm not kidding. You're this bungled mess of repression and vivacity. Take all the time you need to find yourself again, but I'm thinking a little fun will help."

"Hmm. Fantastic sex." Haley scanned the forest ahead. "I'm not sure I remember what that's like. It's been over six months since Nate even looked at me. And probably even longer since I looked at him." They sat on Trace's picnic blanket on Haley's flagstone patio, comfortable despite the loose gravel and twigs digging into their butts, as she had yet to invest in a broom. "I've had about every STD test done in the book. Clean slate."

"See? You need great, safe sex to get your mind off of cheating-bastard Nate. You've got your work cut out for you fixing this place up, but you'll need other outlets. Not that I'm one to talk."

"I'll work on that."

Trace raised her coffee in salute. "Consider it your assignment for the summer. When I get back, I'd better hear some salacious stories."

Laughing her ass off, Haley air toasted, her coffee sloshing from the motion. "I'm not sure about salacious, but I will do my utmost. And same goes for you. I mean, I'm assuming you're single as you sound like you are."

"Sadly, yes. I think I'm pushing you to have a carefree rebound because I suck at relationships. I think my expectations are always too high."

"That's not a thing. Expectations, yeah, watch out for those if you expect someone to be what *you* want them to be. But, well, and this may sound crazy, but I worked my ass off to keep Nate happy, all the while ignoring myself. Maybe you shouldn't settle for anyone that doesn't raise you up, make you feel more yourself, while not sacrificing your own happiness."

Trace shifted her wild strawberry blond waves out of her face as the breeze kicked up. "I think I just want to be swept off my feet."

"Then consider your assignment to be open to a ravenous sweeping."

Draining the last of her coffee, Trace shrugged. "I will do my utmost. Now, Foothills doesn't have great selection, but Grady knows everyone and should be able to give you the run-down of eligible bachelors."

"I'm not asking my brother to help me with a hook-up." Imagine Grady's face? He'd been a great support since she'd first called to say her marriage was over and that she was coming home, but this would be out of his comfort zone.

"Fair point."

Swallowing the last of her cheesy pastry, Haley rose to her feet and held out a hand for Trace. "Come on and tell me how awful my house looks."

Giggling, Trace accepted the hoist up. "The patio has promise." They walked in the sliding glass door that led to the great room. Dusty, mucky, grimy. "I can see where you've got work to do."

"I have carpet installers coming tomorrow with samples and to take measurements. After coughing up dust balls accumulated from two nights of sleeping on the bedroom dust bowl of a carpet, I prioritized flooring." She went to slide a box out of the way, but her low back spasmed in the movement. Groaning, she grabbed the aching muscle but threw out her shoulder in the process. "This remodel, or even cleaning stuff, isn't for wimps. I'm so sore. I've never cleaned like this before. Scrubbing tile and showers and toilets and even walls... That shit's harder than it looks."

Trace nodded, looking around at the shining kitchen tile, tidy fireplace, and not-dusty floors. "Seriously? I mean, it's a lot all at once, but have you never...? Oh, wait, you probably had *staff.*" She drew out with a pretentious nasal accent, then giggled it off. "I know you had money growing up, but that asshole you married must have been loaded."

She shrugged, but it pinched her neck and she winced. "Pretty much. Half the reason for my parents' divorce was Dad's promotion, so my inheritance alone, I was set up for life. Now Nate and my finances are so convoluted with our combined investments and accounts, dragging this divorce on so much longer than it should."

"I'm so sorry. When will it be finalized?"

"Six weeks and two days. But who's counting?"

"Do you have to fly down there?"

"Well, if all goes smoothly, no. But I have little doubt we'll need to meet with the mediator again, so probably. I mean, every time I think we have it all nailed down, he counters. When you balance out my inheritance but I never worked because he needed a wife to entertain and 'support him,' then Nate's income and our mutual investments, the house, I'd rather just call it even. I could get nasty about him, well, sleeping with everyone, but I just want it over."

Hobbling into the kitchen, Haley tossed their garbage under the sink.

Trace threw her head back in laughter as she watched her friend. "This house is so different from what I remember. But you're just the same."

"The same? What about all that repression you just pinned on me?"

"Okay, so the same under that stifling outer layer. You're snarky and dive into a problem without fuss. You won't nickel and dime or gripe and groan where you could and probably should. And this disaster of a house. For a woman that spent the last decade 'entertaining' and 'supporting,' you've taken on a huge undertaking that few professionals would even consider. And, you'll probably make a profit on it. I saw your blog; you must have a huge following."

Haley scowled, looking down at her two-hundred-dollar yoga pants and equally pricey t-shirt, her chipped toenail polish. "Maybe."

"And you've shed the role of society wife so smoothly, finding that feisty girl you used to be."

"Ugh," she groaned, leaning against the countertop. "It's not tough to shed something that was never *me*. Every damn dinner party, I'd be a wreck beforehand. Everything had to be perfect.

"It was so weird. Within days of informing Nate that we were over, right about when the sight of him naked with my 'best friend' in our bed was not so vivid in my memory, this flood of relief washed over me. I figured I would be broken, but I felt so... *alive*." She gazed out the window, at the wildflowers spread over the unmowed yard that mingled amongst the blades of grass. A breeze kicked up, and the entire field swayed with it in a dexterous tango. "I can't believe how fast I felt the buried Haley coming back to life, like she'd been screaming to get out all along. Nate was shocked; not used to me flipping attitude."

"I'm so sorry you had to go through all that. Selfishly, I'm thrilled you're back. When Grady called and let me know you were hurting and needed a friend when you got home, I did a little dance and cheered." She chuckled, her eyes following Haley's to the field outside, then shook her thought away. She looked over to the massive, gleaming stainless-steel fridge. "That's a fancy thing."

Haley pulled on the long handles, cool heavenly light casting over them. "Patricia's version of a housewarming present. I could have gone without the LED lighting and 'smart' adjustments, but it was very thoughtful, and I am grateful. Apparently, a matching dishwasher, oven, and wine refrigerator are on the way."

"Wow, that's pretty generous. She must actually have missed you."

"Or she's buttering me up for something. Although she was disappointed that I am neither surgeon nor astronaut, and am no longer the society woman of her dreams, but I am at least a 'designer' with a respectable social media following that will make an adequate showpiece for her."

"Ouch."

Shrugging, a sharp pinch in her shoulder reminded her not to move so abruptly. She admitted, "That's Patricia. But she seems to be behaving herself. Not that I wasn't inundated with relationship and career advice on the drive up from San Francisco."

Wincing, Trace sealed her eyes shut. "It's amazing she didn't damage you permanently." She opened her eyes again and leaned on the counter next to Haley. "I can't believe you're finally back, and I'm leaving. I already like you as much today as I did fifteen years ago. After you left, I was so lonely."

"Who did you hang out with in high school? I had to start all over again, but you should have at least had Pippa and Freya and some of the other girls from the old neighborhood?"

"It was tough, as I wasn't close with anyone else in our year. And, then, well, I got a boyfriend and didn't really want anyone else. Pippa and Lincoln finally got married."

Checking her watch comically, Haley said, "Precisely as planned."

"And Asher is engaged to her best friend, Sophie. They're really cute together."

"Damn, there goes my rebound plan." She winked. "I've actually spoken to Sophie on the phone already. She's my new accountant at Grady's recommendation, and I have an appointment with her tomorrow."

"Sophie's awesome, so we'll let her keep Asher. It's a small pond around here, but you'll find someone."

"I don't want to find someone, but I am on board with your safe rebound sex idea. I didn't date much until Nate, and, sadly, have never been with anyone else. First semester at college and, as they say, that was that."

"You must have loved him at some point."

"I loved how he put me on a pedestal." Ouch. That sounded so much worse than she'd imagined.

It was true though. She'd been the woman Patricia and Drake had made her to be, shaking fingers at her barefoot cartwheels in the grass in her homemade cutoffs, putting her in more and more lessons to make her stronger, better... poised, successful, elite. And that had so quickly morphed into unflappable, uppity, and obedient.

Shaking away the regret, Haley was determined to never let go of herself ever again. No matter what. "While we're cruising through memory lane... You ever think about tracking down your high school sweetheart? See what he's up to? Maybe find one of those second chance romances?"

Trace shrugged. "Been there, done that. I want to be *noticed*, to be swept away in bliss, and I don't think he's in a position to do much sweeping."

"Well, maybe when you get back." She completely understood that one. Nate hadn't *noticed* her in years. Not that she'd taken much notice of him, either. There were moments she feared she really wasn't any good at sex, but even in the worst of times, she knew it was environmental. Depression or anxiety or just a shitty marriage, but she knew she was still a passionate person, somewhere deep down.

Then, wow, that bartender the other night. Yeah, she'd *noticed* him. And, maybe it was that she was getting downright desperate, but she felt like he'd *noticed* her, too. Those eyes on her. She felt like sleeping beauty waking up from a century-long slumber. Or, at least, a hell of a sex slump. Would tonight be too soon to return for another bite?

"I should be getting back right around when your divorce is finalized. Maybe we can celebrate singlehood and you can tell me all about your summer romance."

Chuckling, Haley nodded. "Fling, yes. Romance, no. Something light and fun. No more demanding men that will put their dick wherever they'd like and blame you for it, then buy you flowers and tell you how much you mean to them."

Tossing her arms around Haley, Trace hugged her tight. "Make that a summer rebound. No strings, no expectations."

Nodding, Haley smiled. "It's a date."

Trace laughed all the way out the door. She hopped in her car and waved as she drove away.

Haley was bummed to lose her for the summer. But, in a way, she craved the time to figure things out for herself. New leaf. New worries. New Haley.

Turning, Haley chewed her cheek, debating the focus of today's efforts. Fixing up this house could cover her blog for the next decade. Maybe she'd add a vlog. Never really her thing, but it would bring in some extra cash, and provide some useful tips for DIYers. And hopefully help build up the following she would inevitably lose, switching from expensive designs to practical remodeling and décor.

Her brain flashed randomly, for the umpteenth time, to the bartender from Monday night. Odds were, someone that appealing was spoken for, but a good starting point.

Things with Nate had been stale for so long, but she'd never lost the longing. Exhausted as she'd been the last few nights, falling asleep imagining the bartender doing... well, many things, had been a lifesaver. Haley from three months ago wouldn't have slept a wink, worrying about the next day's agenda.

Maybe she'd hit Sutherland's Hardware again. She'd already bought out their stock of cleaning supplies. Tomorrow. She had so much more cleaning to do, she whimpered as she opened the door to the garage and eyed her massive pile of cleaning supplies. Crap, she needed to pick up a garage door opener, too.

Soaking the mop with hardwood solution, she dug in. Through layer upon layer of dust, she found a rich, walnut tone. From entry to kitchen and into the bathroom, she had most of the downstairs shining. And before sunset, too.

Neck aching, shoulders throbbing, forearms vibrating and numb, she wiped a layer of dripping brine from her brow. Looking down at her hand, she found the sweat was black from all the grime she'd erased that day. Great. No longer on the floor or counters, but now caked onto her skin.

As the sun set, she cleaned her way in and out of the shower, and dragged her heavy limbs back in. Flipping the faucet to piping hot, she struggled to remain standing. She was sore all the way down to her toes. Was that even a thing?

"Pops? You up here?" Finn climbed the attic ladder, grimacing when he knocked his knee into the pathetic excuse for a rail, his vision darkening at the red-hot zap of pain from the impact. He quickly masked his reaction and popped his head through the opening. His dad was standing with his hands on his hips, glaring at the mess.

"Yep," the old man called back. Well, not that he was old, but he was *his* old man. Not yet fifty, he was healthy as a horse and could probably still out-throw him on the field. Ran circles around the high school football team he coached.

"What are you up to?" When was the last time he'd been up here? If the musty scent weren't enough, the clouds of dust that filled his nostrils was telling that not even Mom had made it up here in a while. Hell, she'd been tired before she was even diagnosed last year.

There were so many dusty old boxes. Christmas decorations, Easter, Halloween. Clothes that may come into style again one day. Generations of family photos.

"I packed up a box of your mom's books, and thought I'd store it up here. But..." He stood in the center of the chaos and scowled. "Well, I don't think there's room."

It was lucky the ceiling below wasn't bowed under the weight of everything. "Maybe it's time to start donating." He pulled open a plastic tub, the lid cracking in his hand. On top, he found a crocheted Christmas tree skirt on top, some plastic ornaments below. "Are you ever going to use this stuff?"

"Well. No. But, then I got to thinking, maybe you and Zoe and Evan might want some."

Finn lifted the lid off a weathered cardboard box that crumbled in his hand. Maniacal laughter echoed out, piercing his ears as a plastic witch with striped socks offered him a trick or a treat. "No. I really don't want this. I mean, yeah, we should save out a few trinkets for shits and giggles, remember Mom's quirky humor every year. But even she didn't have enough room for all of this. I don't think I've seen some of this stuff since I was a kid."

"That's what I thought."

"Pops?" Finn held his breath, afraid to ask the next question. He leaned his shoulder against the crossbeam next to him.

"Yeah?"

"Why don't we do a major cleanout. Each take a corner of the house to clean out Mom's stuff that none of us will make use of." It was time to move forward. If Pops wasn't ready, he was good with that. He'd be supportive.

Pops nodded, his few wrinkles darker than they'd been yesterday. "Let's pick up some moving boxes." Scott Halseth wouldn't want to dawdle. Not his style.

"I can hit Sutherland's and pick up supplies." Finn nodded toward the steps. "I'll follow you down."

Pops snorted. "You barely made it up here. I'll hang out at the bottom to catch you."

Rolling his eyes, Finn snorted back, "Laugh now. You can't tell me you're not getting a bit of arthritis in those joints."

"You kidding? I'm too damn young for that crap." Pops whacked him on the shoulder and shimmied down the sharp steps like an agile kid. Showoff.

Sitting over the gap, feet dangling, Finn gripped one hand on each side and dropped to the floor below, landing with the bulk of his weight on his good leg, the impact jarred from his heel to his molars. Popping up, he smirked playfully and returned the whack on the arm. Hoisting up the drop ladder, he raised it back into the ceiling.

"I'll be back." He grabbed his keys and was out the front door before either of them had a chance to second guess the decision.

He climbed into his Shelby, the rumbling purr of the engine almost taking the edge off of whatever was digging at him. Almost. Pops seemed totally on board, but was he pushing the issue?

4

Cadence

B reathing in the fresh, new carpet air, Haley halted mid-inhale, hacking and coughing out the fumes that singed her nose hairs. Damn, that was downright noxious. Even after opening every window in the house wide open, her vision was still blurred as her eyes tried to flush it out.

Yet it was an improvement from the thick layer of dust that still coated her sinuses.

She grabbed her purse and headed into the garage, which was now fully functional thanks to the garage door opener she'd installed while the flooring crew was doing their thing. For all her designs before, she hadn't installed much. Her arms still trembled from the exertion and her shin throbbed where there was likely a permanent indent, but she did it. And it felt so freaking good.

Maybe she was tooting her own horn a bit soon, but she was pretty good at this stuff. Watch out Bob Vila.

She hopped into the Land Rover, tossed her purse onto the passenger seat, cranked up the stereo, and slipped on her aviator glasses. As Grady would say, *Where we're going, we don't need roads.*

Chuckling, she thought how much fun she'd had yesterday, the adventure of getting to know her family all over again. Grady and Claire had brought breakfast sandwiches and stayed until dusk, buffing and polishing. She and her brothers had been close as kids, but it had been tough so far apart, all of them too busy through school to visit much.

And Claire. She was so normal and goofy and down to earth. So good for Grady, who took himself way too seriously. Used to anyway. Actually, seeing how he had dug his heels in and decided to be the man he wanted to be, was damn inspiring.

After they'd left, she'd hardly slept, wired after spending the day visiting with people she was completely herself with. Not just because she could, but because they brought it out in her.

And, despite her muscles screaming at her, she felt so… alive. Naturally, muscles were important for basic functioning, but to be able to feel them again? Fan-freaking-tastic.

High on satisfaction, or perhaps carpet emissions, she drove straight to her favorite pub, knowing it wasn't just the food she was looking forward to. Parking was at a premium in town tonight; she was lucky to find a spot around the corner. Checking her reflection in the mirror, she smoothed a few unruly eyebrow hairs, ran her fingers through her hair, and checked her teeth were free of lunch debris.

After a much-needed shower, she'd tossed on a simple cream-colored sundress and low boots. A little boho with a hint of edge, she'd always liked the look. It didn't hurt that Nate hadn't liked it one bit. Too short, too hippy, and too many eyelets.

One of her quiet rebellions. She was never going to be the picture-perfect show-wife again, but she still liked to feel pretty. For her. Maybe she'd add a style page to her blog and pull in more revenue.

The moment she stepped into the pub, she instantly relaxed at the mouthwatering scent on the air. Not interested in the quiet table in the corner, she sought an open stool at the bar. Appearing in the doorway from the kitchen, her favorite part of the pub was still laughing from some shared joke with the cook, or so she assumed, as he backed out of the kitchen, rich laughter warming the air, his grin still genuine as he turned and delivered plates to a pair of customers at the bar.

Catching sight of her, he halted, crossing his arms over his chest, a slow smile forming just for her. *Pitter patter*, her pulse tap-danced a hearty rhythm that spun her imagination for a dizzying twirl. He motioned to the end of the bar and rubbed his towel over the surface so it was fresh and clean for her.

Without any input from her brain, she floated over. Spinning a coaster like a top, he slapped it down and slid it to the spot he'd cleared.

"Hey." He grinned, resting his hands on the bar in front of her. Damn, she wanted to trace the lines that defined his arms. Did he spend all day at the gym?

"Hey," she answered, the corner of her mouth tugging up like a fish on a hook. Worth every nibble of the bait.

"Welcome back. Bury any dead animals this morning?"

"What? Oh." She chuckled softly. "No, thank goodness. I don't think I'll ever figure out how he got in. I have clean floors and functioning appliances now, so things are looking up."

"Floors and appliances, huh? Not so much on the furniture?"

"Not so much."

"Beer?"

"Please. Same as last time if you've got it."

Stepping back, he moved to the taps.

The server helping the table behind her smiled as she passed. "I love those boots."

"Thanks."

With a wink, the server sashayed past, her ponytail keeping a metronomic rhythm with each sway of her hips.

Her favorite bartender returned a moment later with her beer, setting it on the coaster and sliding it toward her. "This one's a little hoppier. Let me know what you think." Hands resting on the bar in front of her, he gaged her reaction, the corners of his yummy lips turned up in anticipation.

She took a testing sip, the bubbles filling her mouth and buzzing down her throat. "Even better."

"The guys at Black Op Brewing make us try out their creations before they bottle and send out for mass production."

"What a chore," she teased. She'd have to convince Grady to let her in on the early tasting crew, as part owner of the hippest microbrew in the region.

"Didn't exactly have to twist my arm." He grinned again. Even his smile was irresistible, slow to form as if carefully considered, and he didn't care to focus on anything but her. A slight bend in his nose from an old injury and that unruly cowlick at his hairline told of a daring side that sent a thrill shuddering under her skin. "You hungry tonight?"

Yes. Starving. Be my rebound? "Um, yeah. That smoked salmon salad sounds amazing."

"Good choice."

"Hey, you mind if I get some work done?" She pulled her laptop from her purse and held it up.

"Make yourself at home. Please." He backed up a step and turned, gliding to the computer to punch in her order. The man even moved beautifully, as if his hips, his core held all the power, every movement deliberate but graceful.

She set out her laptop and pulled up the draft of her next blog post. The text was nearly finished, but the photos were tough. Grime. Muck. Dust. Too bad she didn't think to snap one of the dead raccoon. Maybe she'd add a funny cartoon to offset the bleakness of the scene.

As she neared the bottom half of the beer, having put mental blinders on to avoid watching the sexy bartender at work *all* night, she made acceptable progress by the time her food arrived. Toasted walnuts and goat cheese dotted the top of the spring greens and smoked salmon, finely chopped red and yellow tomatoes made the meal a work of art in the white square bowl.

Flying over the bar, a rolled-up t-shirt rocketed toward the bartender. Seemingly unaware, he calmly tucked his water under the register and snatched the package from the air in an easy movement. In one fluid motion, he tucked it under his arm. Another came hurtling toward him from the server that had tossed the last, and he caught it just as effortlessly.

"Your spiral's coming along Tara." He grinned at the server, then passed the shirts across the bar to the young couple that had just paid their tab.

Huh. Something familiar about that. He turned and headed into the kitchen. The back of his t-shirt caught her eye. In block lettering, HALSETH crossed the top, extending shoulder to shoulder.

Oh shit, she nearly choked on the salmon, catching it in her throat before she completely embarrassed herself. Haircut, beard shaved, and totally out of context, but he was a regular in her fantasy life. No wonder she'd been so instantly interested. How had she missed it before? Trace was right, she absolutely needed a rebound.

He reappeared a moment later, carrying a plate of burgers in each hand. After he delivered the meal, he returned to check on her. "How's the salad?"

Biting her cheek to mask her blushing grin, she endeavored to not sound like a number-one-foam-finger swinging, face-painted fanatic when she said, "You're Finn Halseth." Not that she wasn't a huge fan, but, wow, how would she have guessed her favorite athlete would be serving her drinks in her minuscule hometown?

"That's me." He looked at her funny, like he wasn't sure what she was getting at. Or dreading what she knew. More of a wary smile than the flirty grin he'd granted her with all night.

"Sorry, I don't mean to rat you out if it's secret or anything. I'm a huge fan. I, uh, I just moved up from San Francisco."

He breathed a sigh of relief. "Me too. A few months ago." He crossed his arms over his chest and leaned against the bar in front of her, relaxing back into the slow smile that sizzled right down to her toes. "You don't know how many people begin that sentence with some graphic description of my knee bending the wrong direction last February."

She winced. "Yeah, that didn't look comfortable. That must suck. You played some great football for the Fire for, what, five, six years? And people remember you for the injury? At least they're remembering that last play. Pretty epic way to retire."

Still smiling, he nodded. "Yeah, I suppose so. Got my super bowl ring on crutches. Not sure yet that it was worth it, but that was a hell of a game."

From the kitchen, a woman with similar chocolate eyes, sporting a threatening glare for Finn, cleared her throat. "I said, order up."

Feigning an apologetic wince, he backed up a few steps and turned to grab the plates from the woman that had to be his sister. As he worked the busy pub, Haley forced herself to buckle down and finish the post. She liked to be consistent, treating it like a scheduled program rather than a hobby. It helped build a steady following. And, well, it was her sole source of occupational income.

He appeared a few moments later to return her credit card. His mouth opened and closed like he was about to say something, but he held his breath, and then said. "Have a good night."

T hat's the best he could come up with? Not long ago, it didn't take more than a wink and he had a date. He glanced down at the slip she'd signed in a casual, readable script. *Haley Salsborough*. "Drive safe, Haley," he pathetically added.

Her lopsided grin still lingered as she rose from the stool and slung her purse over her shoulder. "'Night," she whispered, barely audible. The pretty sundress she wore swung with each step. Damn, she was curvy in all the right places. He held his breath, arms folded over his chest as he watched her walk out the door. Should have asked her out.

Dammit, no. Trace was right. He wasn't in any condition to pursue a relationship.

The very concept sounded terrible right now. He was just getting his shit together. What did he have to offer a woman, when he couldn't even handle himself? Even the little experiment getting back together with Trace, who knew him well, or at least, she used to, had gone terribly.

Appearing in the kitchen doorway, Zoe raised a taunting eyebrow at him. "Hey, bro," she said, grinning mischievously.

"Zoe." He nodded, then moved to take another order.

She was still standing there when he turned around. "I think you were flirting."

"I'm allowed to flirt with a beautiful woman now and again. I'm single. Besides, she's from San Francisco and a fan. I don't exactly have many of those anymore."

"Are you interested because she's attractive or because she's an adoring groupie fawning over the great Finn Halseth?"

"Hey, I don't do groupies." He chuckled at the double entendre. He didn't *socialize* with diehard fans that had deeper intentions, and certainly hadn't *done* any in a damn long time.

Zoe's smile fell, her eyebrows heavy. "I don't think you need your heart broken again. Your career, then mom, then Trace... be careful, okay?"

"I'm not looking for anything. But it's nice to be noticed." So manly. Didn't bother claiming that he was fine. She wouldn't believe him anyway.

Tara swished past, pausing to whisper audibly to Zoe, "I think he needs a fling. Nothing serious, just a good lay."

Rolling his eyes, Finn crossed his arms and backed up a few steps.

Zoe nodded, conspiracy glinting in her dark gaze. "Good plan. Either that or he can buy us a bigger hot water heater."

Flashing the pair a wink, he spun around and caught up on greeting his latest customers.

5

Motion

Finn smashed his foot into the pile of rocks at his feet, splaying gravel across the parking lot. Fucking sunny day. The chipper blue sky laughing in his face. Shitty way to start the damn day.

"Hello, Finn? It's Jay Walker from Minneapolis." Exactly the call he should have been dying to get, and the throat punch he'd expected it to be.

Swallowing a suffocating lump that lodged in his throat, he croaked, "Yeah, Jay. I know who you are. How're things in your neck of the woods these days?"

"Great. Beautiful day here."

Come on, get to the point.

"What I called for, Finn, is, well, we'd like to have you come on out for an interview. If all goes well, maybe talk you into a contract for an assistant coaching position. I'd love to see you whip some shape into our receivers." The Midwest vowels drew out with each word, not a hint of pretension in his tone.

"That, uh, yeah. That would be great." Goddammit.

"Wonderful. How about we fly you out, show you around and see what you think?"

"Sure, sure I can do that." No he couldn't. Or wouldn't. But should. Opportunity of a lifetime, for the second time in his career, and the idea of it tied his stomach in knots.

"Great. I'll have my assistant call you to nail down the dates and send along an itinerary."

"I'll look forward to hearing from them."

Pops had walked in seconds later. "Was that a call on a coaching position?"

Finn nodded, his molars ground so tight he couldn't answer.

Smile reaching his crinkly eyes that had seen so many sunsets over the field, so many games himself and then as Finn's coach until college, and now as the high school coach, Pops dropped onto the stool and bumped his elbow into Finn's side. "Why don't you look more excited?"

"Dunno. A lot to take in, I guess. Just an interview."

"Don't want to get your hopes up? I get it. I thought you'd said you hadn't sent out any resumés yet?"

"I didn't. Coach Lund had asked if I minded if he gave out my number. Knowing Kit, he didn't wait for them to ask, but offered it out to anyone willing to listen."

"Doesn't matter how they tracked you down. The fact that they reached out? Come on, you must already have the job, they're just waiting on the formalities. Bet they already have the contract drawn up."

"He implied as much." His teeth still gritted together, he nodded. "Think I'll get some fresh air. Let it soak in."

"Of course. If I can do anything to help, you just let me know. Brenda would be so proud, her son, the professional football player *and* coach. Imagine, in a few years? You may get your own team." Pops beamed enough for both of them.

Nodding again, worrying his head might wobble off from all the agreeability, Finn backed out of the kitchen. Tossing on his nearest pair of shoes, he took off.

Not knowing where he was driving, not caring, he followed the road down the slope to the bottom of the hill, ending up at Riverside Park. He slammed the car door behind him. Fuck. Expanding his chest to draw air in, he let the oxygen fuel his brain, easing his turbulent thoughts.

The high elevation atmosphere was thin and dry, but as soon as he entered the trees surrounding the river, a humid breeze revitalized the air. Not many people out today. A group of teenagers was goofing around upstream, so he wandered downstream.

For a few hundred feet, he wandered under the dappling canopy until he reached a small clearing, and was startled... no, completely awestruck, by the furious woman on the beach. A rock the size of her palm in her hand, she tossed it up and tested its weight before launching it across the river. It cracked against the tree on the opposite side.

"Nailed it," she whooped as she jumped up and down. Haley Salsborough. Her hair was pulled back in a thick ponytail. Although artfully ripped in a clever pattern, her ankle-length jeans were clearly designer, accented by a blue t-shirt that moved like water over her skin and leather sandals that laced around her ankles.

He stood back, watching her crazy routine. Face scrunched in a livid scowl, she'd pick up another rock. When she deemed the rock acceptable, its weight in range and her target isolated, she launched it across the river.

As she reached for a fourth, he stepped closer. "Hey," he said.

She flinched briefly, but shook her head in surprise as she realized it was him. "Hey," she said, her scowl lightening to the feisty lopsided smile she'd entreated him with the other night.

"Didn't like that rock, huh?"

Wiping her hands on her jeans, she shook her head and said, "Nah. Too many rocks on this side. I'm trying to distribute them more evenly."

"Very thoughtful of you. I mean, look at this park. Hideous."

She glanced around theatrically. "What's with all the cheery pink flowers and artfully filtered sunshine?" Pausing, she stepped a few feet closer. She had to have caught the clench of his jaw, adding, "Sometimes this town is a little too lovely."

He stepped closer, but didn't get as close as he'd like. "Don't I know it. Days like today? I could use some bay area fog."

"And mist to wick away a foul mood. Although, I did miss the snow." She cleared her throat and strolled to the log that served as a park bench.

"Yeah. A little clean slate over the ground is nice." Unable to resist, he sat next to her. "Did you work it out?"

"What?"

"Whatever was driving your rock-throwing rampage? Those were some impressive shots."

"Thanks. That was the point, actually. I, uh, I don't remember the last time I threw rocks."

"Most grownups would probably say the same, if they even thought about it."

She glared across the water. "I suppose so."

He followed her gaze across the water. A leafy tree, one he probably knew the name of at some point, lie angled over the water, its leaves bouncing as the whitecaps high-fived each time they passed underneath. Deer tracks dotted the coarse sand on the narrow beach, probably out for a drink earlier this morning.

"I, uh, I have an interview," he blurted out, his brow scrunching as he realized he'd said it out loud.

"That's fantastic." She grinned and nudged his shoulder with hers. "For what? Where?"

"Assistant coach at Minneapolis."

"Holy crap, good for you." Sapphire eyes darkening, she studied his reaction, her gaze resting on his jaw, trailing along the clenched edge before meeting his gaze. "You're not excited."

"I don't know," he said with a shrug. "I mean, it's a great opportunity. One I really shouldn't turn down. Buddy of mine says Dallas has me on a short list, too."

"I'm not questioning. I get it. I mean, I've never had a job interview in my life. But, I understand not knowing if you want something or not." She shook her head, closing her eyes and smiling. "Okay, I'm not making sense."

"Yeah, you are. It's like I'm on the edge of a cliff and someone's extending their hand to rescue me," he trailed off, not sure of how to explain without sounding totally nuts.

"But you're not sure you want to be rescued?"

"Yeah. If I don't have a clue what I'm looking for, how can I feel relief from an offer I'm not sure I want? Of course, I haven't gotten any actual offers yet, so I'm getting ahead of myself, anyway."

"Why don't you check that hand out? See what it has to offer, then decide if you want to accept help? You can always say no."

Finn rubbed a hand through his hair, his cowlick splaying the front of his hair wildly. "True." He leaned toward her, nudging her side. "Or I could throw rocks at the problem."

Her eyes rolled, but she melted at his sweet acknowledgement of the moment shared. Rising to her feet, she held out a hand. The corners of his lips lifted in an easy smile.

Heat flooded through her at the contact, filling a piece she had felt was missing, but couldn't have been sure until that moment. Raw, fierce lust. A longing to pull that hand closer and see what it felt like on her body, skin against skin.

His eyes flashed with an intensity, an amusement as his smile grew into a grin.

At the shore, she begrudgingly released him and picked up a grapefruit-sized rock, smooth and cool in her palm. She set it in his hand. "Give it a try," she urged.

His lips turned up in a sweet smile before he tossed the rock in the air once, catching it with a give to compensate for its weight. Like an archer in the stars, he drew his throwing arm back and counter balanced the pose with his other hand before thrusting the rock forward.

The stone cut through the air with an audible whoosh, soaring across the river before it cracked against the same tree she'd been aiming for, then ricocheted off and splashed into the water.

"You could have been a quarterback," She nodded with appreciation.

He rested his hands on his hips and grinned again. "Could have, but anyone can throw. Not so many can run like hell, snatch a flying sack of pigskin traveling at fifty-plus miles an hour while their feet are a few feet off the ground, then land on their tippy toes, juke their way through the pack, and run the length of the field without getting caught."

"Those quarterbacks sure are a bunch of slackers. Not like those modest wide receivers."

Broad shoulders steady, hands resting on his hips as if he was comfortably watching the game from the sidelines, he flashed her a wink that melted straight down to her panties. "Sorry. Pops and Evan were both quarterbacks, so I learned early on you have to keep those egomaniacs in check. Zoe and Mom preferred to play as linebackers. I'm pretty sure that was Zoe's favorite, so she had an excuse to knock us on our asses."

"Aw, cute. The Halseth family scrimmage in the backyard must have been so much fun."

"Yeah, we had good times." His grin persisted, but grew distant.

Haley picked up a rock the size of her fist and tossed it in the air like Finn had, but with much less facile. Accidentally dropping it would lessen the badass look of it. She drew her arm back.

Finn cleared his throat, hesitated, and said, "You have a hell of a throw, but mind if I show you something?"

"I could be offended, but, well, I would love to throw like a pro." She raised her eyebrows.

He put his hands on her hips and steadied her perpendicular to the river. Stepping up close behind her, he moved his hands to hers. "Back like this." He gestured, guiding her arm into position.

She was tempted to move her hips out of position, knowing he'd steady her again. But, well, she really did want to improve her throwing, in case she ever got the opportunity to throw something at Nate's face.

"The power comes from your hips and shoulder. Your wrist is the level, not the hammer."

The air lightened as too much oxygen fueled her lungs as he touched her and used a reference she would appreciate. Her form threatened to falter as she filled her senses with the moment, but she swallowed the distraction and stabilized her core as he coached her along.

"Alright, now let's see it." He stepped back, his voice laced with the same lightness that lifted her.

Repeating the process as he'd shown her, she pitched the rock again. Didn't quite hit the tree, but close. Better, the rock blasted past and crashed in applause as it knocked a few branches before dropping to the ground in the shrubs beyond.

"Nice." He grinned as he returned his eyes from the landing site and settled on her.

She shrugged, but couldn't have masked the naked joy if she'd tried. "Whether you want to or not, you are a hell of a coach."

"Your throw was already pretty damn good, I was just looking for an excuse to touch you." He grinned, shifting his weight to the other foot.

"And I wasn't objecting." She picked up another rock and pitched it across the river. "You know, I used to be athletic. It's been so long, I forgot the thrill of pushing the limit. Aside from wanting to chuck one of these at my ex's face, I came out here for fresh air, then found I needed that release."

"I know what you mean. One of these days, my knee is going to let me sprint again. I'm getting there, but I can't tell you how much I miss running full throttle."

Not so literal, but yeah, she could. "I miss doing a lot of things full throttle."

"I don't mean to be nosy, but you mentioned an ex. Sounds like that was for the best?"

"Oh my god yes. I just wish I'd woken up and left sooner."

"I'm sorry. It's hard to see through the fog when you don't realize that's not all there is."

The ache that had brought her here returned, turning her legs to thick mush. "Especially when it seems mild at first, and before you know it, you're suffocating in it."

He scowled and shoved his hands on his hips, walking halfway up the beach and stopping again. "Or everyone seems to think you're lost in it, but you find it a refreshing mist."

Moving up the beach, Haley grabbed her jacket and stopped in front of Finn. "I like your metaphors," she said with a grin, beyond tempted to wrap her arms around his waist and bury herself against him, knowing the connection might settle them both.

He rubbed his hand over his hair, flashing her that easy smile again. "Same. Are the rocks more to your liking now?"

She nodded, unable to look away. "Much more even. I think I'll head home and see if my head's clear enough to finish my latest post. What about you? Better?"

His hands rested on his hips again, his gaze searching the other side of the river. "I will be." As she strolled away, he added, "Haley?"

"Yeah?"

"We've got a new IPA you should try. Good one that bites you back."

Grinning, she said, "Can't wait to try it. You work tonight?"

"Tomorrow."

"See you tomorrow."

6

Offside

B eaming at her success, Haley closed the file and snapped shut her computer. Vlogger extraordinaire. Look out Chip and Joanna... without Chip. Now she had to work up the courage to post it.

Changing into fresh jeans and a breezy blouse, she found her favorite heeled boots and even touched up her eyeliner, reapplying her strawberry guava lip gloss. Not that she was dressing up to have dinner alone, sort of. Again. She wasn't sure if flirting with the bartender counted as a dinner date.

Divorce was a lonely business. She'd already roped Grady and Claire into inviting her for dinner several times since returning. Patricia was busy six nights of the week, of course, as her neurosurgical practice and philanthropic efforts came first.

Not to mention, Haley was still recovering from their girls' trip. There had been several attempts at praise, which were awkwardly delivered but well meant. Whatever weirdness she'd had with her mother over the years, she could tell the uptight woman was trying, and almost felt sorry for her. Patricia continually seemed to trip over herself, reeling as she recalled how to dethrone herself.

She dropped her keys in her purse and swung open the door to the garage. It was oddly relieving to come and go as she pleased. No husband to question her, as he couldn't possibly fathom why she would want to take a walk in the park on a drizzly day. No staff to inquire after the menu for the week or if Mr. Salsborough's suit was pressed to her liking.

And no one to ask how Haley Salsborough had become a regular at the pub and why she grinned the whole way out the door.

Her phone buzzed with a call from a number she didn't recognize. San Francisco number. Could be her lawyer. Or the bank. Or... well, not a friend, as those had all slept with Nate and should know they'd better piss off or she'd bite their heads off.

Fine. Picking up the phone, she answered, "Hello?"

"Please don't hang up." His grating tone set her teeth on edge.

"Nate. You can't call me. Don't make me put something in writing."

"Hear me out. I miss you. This new house is bleak without your creative touch."

"Fuck off." She pulled the phone from her ear to end it.

"Wait. There's an offer on our house."

Dammit, she'd been waiting on that. "That's great." She wanted every last tie to that despicable man severed.

"Actually, we have a bidding war. The realtors included samples of your blog in the pamphlet."

"Wow, that's fantastic."

"I miss you, Haley."

Hang up. Hang up now before you say something stupid. "Not enough to keep your dick in your pants. Oh, wait, I'm sorry, that's right, it was because you missed me so much that you fucked all my friends." *Too late.*

"As if you were a saint that cherished our marriage. You can't tell me you weren't banging my partner. I didn't believe him when he told me, but he knows a lot about you. Even that birthmark on your—"

Click. She hung up before he could say anymore. What a slime-bag, sleaze-bucket, lying son of a bitch. Pinning it back on her? Claiming he missed her? Her attorney had put out enough fires thanks to Nate's pathetic excuses to turn things around on her.

Fuming, she slammed the car door shut and stormed out. Ripping open the car door, she chucked her purse inside and knocked her head into the steering wheel.

Ow. Shifting into gear, she backed out of the drive.

Dammit, Nate. She was not about to let him ruin the life she was building for herself. Just a few more weeks. How had she let herself—

No. Don't do it. He's the narcissistic asshole.

Shaking off the vile encounter, she headed for Halseth's. If Finn's arms didn't distract her from her shitty phone call, nothing would.

The guy was a puzzle. How was a former professional football player tending bar? Duh, she smacked herself on the forehead.

Ow. Again? She really needed to get a grip.

His name matched the name on the door. Halseth's was either his place or his family's. Couldn't be his; it was way too established to be new. He can't have been home more than a few months.

Downtown Foothills was packed for a weeknight. It was a cozy small town, where everyone knew everyone, but the tourists almost tripled their population on weekends in skiing and hiking seasons. Since her return, she'd found its tourism load had increased the population by at least another third, even on weekdays. Parked across the street, she hopped out, smoothed her jeans and checked that her top was nonchalantly half tucked.

One last seat at the bar. Not at her usual corner, but right in the middle by the taps. Well, that was okay. She'd get to watch those corded arms working all night.

From behind her, that heavenly voice vibrated the air, sending a thrill down her spine. "Hey," Finn said.

Turning on her stool, she discovered him spinning a tray in his hand, an apron filled with notebooks and checks stuffed in the pockets. "Hey," she whispered breathlessly. "Busy in here. I didn't know you waited tables, too."

"Not usually. Tara called out sick. Our other server and bartender are both busy tonight. Evan, my little brother, is out of town. My dad worked his ass off all day covering for Evan. Zoe's overworked in the kitchen and our back-up chef just arrived. I have no idea what's with the midweek rush tonight. Something about an adventure tour that recently added Foothills to their itinerary. And half the damn town is ordering takeout tonight. So, I am working double duty."

Another group walked in. Snagging a trio of menus, Finn greeted them and quickly cleared a table that had just emptied. Without pause, he breezed into the bar and poured a few drinks. Two orders up, he delivered dinners.

Behind the taps, he poured another round for the folks at the end of the bar and asked, "Want to try that IPA?"

"I'd love some... but would you rather have a hand? Not that I've ever waited tables, but I have eaten out a lot. Not much of a resumé, but, quite frankly, I have nothing else to do tonight."

He paused, the beer he was filling overflowed. At the chill, he set down the overfilled glass and wiped the spill with the bar towel at his side. "You kidding?"

"No, really. I need a distraction."

"Rough day?"

"Divorce sucks. Seriously, my soon-to-be-ex called and pissed me off. Accused me of... anyway. Not relevant. I need something useful to do. And hard."

He visibly winced. "I'm so sorry. Are you sure? I mean, you're here to relax."

She nodded with renewed enthusiasm, refusing to let Nate ruin her night as he'd clearly intended. "Seriously. Please. I'll just stew and replay that stupid phone call in my head over and over. And that will lead to flashbacks of his cheating ass banging my 'best friend.' Sorry, wow, I didn't mean to throw all that at you."

"No, I'm sorry. What an asshole." Finn nodded his head toward the side of the bar. She grabbed her purse and followed him over. "Hang on." He popped his head in the kitchen and shouted, "Can one of you guys cover the front for a few? I found help and need to bring her up to speed."

Movements as smooth as her brother's, Zoe slipped off her chef's apron and picked up a notepad. "Gotcha." If she was puzzled at Finn's choice of sub, she didn't let it show past a quick grin and a wink before she disappeared.

Finn tipped his head toward the back, grabbing a black Halseth's t-shirt off the shelf as he passed the register. Following him down the hall past the bathrooms and into a breakroom, Haley swallowed her last-minute anxiety. She hadn't worked a real job a day in her life.

Ouch, she sounded so pathetic.

Nope. Not dwelling.

But what if she messed everything up and they lost business because of her?

The room bordered on cramped and was little more than a heavy-duty wooden desk with equally antiquated office chair that took up the near wall. A folding table for four sat in the middle of the room, and shelves of labelled boxes covered the longest wall.

Extending the folded t-shirt, Finn asked, "This fit okay?"

Setting down her purse on the office chair, Haley pulled off her blouse.

Finn's tongue rolled out of his mouth and his eyes bugged out of his head like a horny cartoon character as Haley slipped her top over her head. She wore a lacy silk tank top underneath that clung to every curve. Groaning to himself, he bit his tongue and looked at the ceiling.

Once her head was clear of the top, she snagged the shirt from his hands. Perfect fit, the Halseth's logo rested on one of her marvelously perky breasts. The vee of the top was not quite low enough to offer a cleavage window, but thanks to the silk-tank-top vision permanently imprinted in his brain, he could imagine well enough. Straightening the jersey cotton over her torso, she pulled her hair up in a messy bun, letting out a few rebellious tendrils that seemed designed to taunt him.

Clearing his throat, he untied his server's apron and handed it to her. She secured it around her waist and pulled out the notepad and a pen. "Ready."

Shit, she was fierce. Or foolish, not having a clue how much she was going to be hurting later. His first day behind the bar a few months back, he'd had to cover himself in icepacks the next day. Not to mention it had taken a solid week for his brain to recover. He ought to call his old coach and have them add waiting tables and tending bar to their training routine.

Her hip cocked out with arrogance, his gaze followed her legs down to her heeled boots. "You sure about this? It's not too late to change your mind."

She followed his gaze to her impractical shoes. "I've hosted parties for three hundred in stilettos. These are cross-trainers by comparison."

Shaking his head, he grinned. "Is there anything you don't tackle with attitude bigger than a quarterback's?"

Following her easy shrug, that wicked corner of her mouth quirked up. "Guess we'll find out. Break it down."

He ran her through the basics, the rhythm, the principles she may not have realized went on behind the scenes. "Because you don't have a food handler's card, I'll bring out all the food, but you can handle the rest?"

She mock saluted. "Absolutely."

Leading the way back into the restaurant, she headed out first. Exhaling as he watched those hips sway with each step, his name stamped on her back... maybe Tara was right. He needed a fling.

Haley had mentioned divorce. A nasty one at that. Sucked, but good chance she wasn't looking for anything serious either.

Halseth's was hopping, and Haley brightened the place with that fearless manner and wholehearted laugh. She made it look easy and, well, fun. Nothing seemed to get under that porcelain skin of hers. Stereotypes painted porcelain as flawless and easily shattered, but Haley proved that meant she was tough as steel.

By six o'clock, when families with kids under twenty-one could still come in, Haley handled picky eaters and messy tables with ease. As one toddler threw his milk at his mom, testing the mother's patience more than most would be able to handle, Haley appeared behind the little guy with a distracting peek-a-boo. Popping in front of him, then disappearing behind him again, she had his stuffed animal—and source of the outburst—playing a goofy game before returning it to his sticky arms. With her other hand, she delivered a fresh Halseth's shirt and a handful of wet napkins to the equally sticky, milk-soaked mom.

The dad immediately pulled out his wallet to pay for the shirt, but Haley shook her head. "That one's on me."

Breezing from table to table, Haley never ran out of energy. Or patience. If she did, she refused to let it show.

By eight o'clock, as she closed out a group of inebriated hikers, a sloppy brute grabbed her ass. A pissed-off growl rumbling deep in his chest, Finn tossed down his towel and headed their way. Before he reached them, he watched as she slipped out of the asshole's reach and growled a good one of her own, "Dude, really? Has that ever worked? Ever, in the history of come-ons?"

Blushing, the drunkard shook his head, the others at the table glaring at him, frowning in frank disappointment.

Haley finished her set-down. "Next time try to use your words and tell a woman you like her. Trust me, you'll fare much better." She waved at the rest of the table. "You guys have a great night. If it's not already on your agenda, check out Sundown Trailhead. The incline is steep but worth it."

Backing up, Finn tried to get back behind the bar before she realized he'd been coming to the rescue. Too late, she turned and ran right into him. Slamming into his chest, she caught herself, her hands pressed against his abdomen.

Inhaling sharply, he tried to say something, but exhaled with a laugh. "Sorry. Thought you might need some back-up, but you got it."

She looked up, those cobalt eyes locking onto his and that adorable lopsided grin about knocked him on his ass. "Thanks for the assist, but not my first foul." Biting her lip, she added, "What's the penalty for roughing the passer?"

Chuckling, he stood as still as possible, fearing she'd move her hands when she realized she was still touching him. "Really, I think you just have to know if you're offsides or not." He wanted to holler to the asshole that had grabbed her ass at the difference. Or knock him upside the head. Or make his knee bend the wrong direction.

Taunting him, her hands lingered on his waist as she brushed past.

The pace was steady right up until closing. Zoe had shut down the kitchen an hour before. Drying off her hands and tossing the towel at Finn before heading out, Zoe nodded. "Thanks again, Haley. Let me know if you need any help moving furniture; there are four of us Halseths and we know how to work. Like you. We owe you big-time."

When had they had time to talk? Zoe flashed him a wink as she escorted the last of the customers out the door, flipping the sign to closed and locking up on her way out.

While he wiped down the bar and sealed everything up for the night, Haley disappeared to the supply room and reappeared with the mop.

"I can get that," he said with a nod. "You've already done so much. Really. I can't thank you enough."

She grinned back. "If there's one thing I do know how to do after the last few weeks of my life, it's clean."

"Well, when you're done there, I have to share a bathroom with Zoe, and she leaves her crap everywhere..." Shit, he almost invited her to come over tonight. That would have been the world's worst pick-up line of all time. *Come on over and clean my bathroom, and I'll clean your...* Nope, there's nothing sexy about any of that.

Haley seemed to catch the terrible line and laughed, sweeping the mop side to side as she glided across the floor. "Sorry, bub. You're on your own there. I used to hire a cleaning service. Times have changed."

Ducking into the kitchen for a moment, he muttered on his way out. "Same here."

When he reappeared, she stood in the corner, wet floor all around. Looking around at her predicament, she threw her head back and laughed out loud. "Rookie mistake. Mopped myself into a corner."

"Need a rescue?" Not that she'd needed one before, and he suspected she preferred to claw her own way out of about any predicament.

"Nah, I got this." She shifted the bucket ahead and tiptoed out, mopping her way out of the corner and over to the edge of the bar. Pleased with herself, she leaned the mop handle against the wall and stood with her hands on her hips like a superhero.

Chuckling, he stepped closer. She grinned up at him as he approached. Damn, when was the last time a woman had looked at him like that? Like he was a juicy steak. Not in a creepy piece of meat way, but that he was done exactly right, exactly the way she wanted. Okay, he'd spent too much time helping his dad and Evan smoking meats lately.

He stopped inches away, needing her to make the next move.

Shifting from superhero pose, her hands moved to his waist, her fingers trailing along his abdomen. Inhaling sharply, he stilled. Through the jersey fabric, her touch left a blazing fire in their wake.

Looking up at him, the corner of her mouth quirked into a flirty smile.

Leaning in, he splayed his hand over her low back and hauled her against him. Her hand reached up and gripped the back of his neck, enticing him down until their lips met.

Detonating on impact, the supple spice of her lips, the velvet of her tongue melted away his hesitation. Angling his mouth with hers, he intensified the kiss. Hands encircling her waist, her hips, their mouths never parting, he scooped her up and set her on the bar.

She wrapped her legs around his waist and tugged him against her. Hands embedded in his short hair, she gasped as he kissed along the line of her jaw, nipping her ear before moving onto her neck. Tasting her skin, trailing his tongue down the pulse of her neck, he stalled when he met t-shirt.

Damn, he might have tugged it right off her if he hadn't remembered where they were. Hell, anyone walking by could see exactly what they were up to. And neither of them needed that kind of attention right now.

Both breathless, he scooped her down from the bar. She tossed her bangs out of her face and grinned up at him. The easiness, the lightness of her demeanor broke down the last of his barriers.

He laughed out loud. "Sorry, I, uh... you know."

"Yeah, wow," she laughed. "I'm sorry. As previously mentioned, I'm in the middle of a nasty divorce and apparently needed a little release, and not just of the rock-throwing variety."

"I know the feeling. Last six months of my life have been, well, weird as fuck. Not in a good way. And, not even close to the worst of it, my girlfriend just dumped me. So, yeah, I'm with you. Pent up."

"My friend says I need a rebound. Honestly, not something I'd considered, or would ever ask of someone as that's awfully pressuring—"

"Yes please," he blurted out. Stepping back, he leaned against the counter behind him. "That came out wrong. I mean, I'm not looking for anything either, but I really like it when you come in here and visit with me, distract me from everything else. So if you're asking me to be your rebound, I'm open. I mean, shit, this is why Zoe and Tara are telling me I need a fling; I don't even remember how to talk to a woman."

She grinned. "I like the way you talk to me. And kiss me."

"That too." He crossed his arms over his chest. "Nice work tonight. My head was about to explode when you appeared."

"You were right, it was hard, but exactly what I needed. I am officially in a good mood." As if startled, she reached into her back pocket and pulled out a stack of neatly folded bills. "I'm not sure how this is done, but I am aware splitting our tips is a thing."

"Keep it, you earned it."

"I'm not keeping it all. That would be weird."

"As you're not on the payroll, why don't we call it even? Whatever it is, it's not even half of what you deserve, saving my ass like that."

"Seriously, this is a huge wad of cash I wasn't looking for. Let me take you out to dinner sometime? Like a rebound thing, nothing serious, as I'm telling you up front, I'm still recovering from unsportsmanlike conduct."

"God yes. You let me know if I make any false starts." Damn, she was exactly what he needed. Hot, honest, and full of football references. He stepped forward and hooked his hand into her belt, tugging her closer.

Tracing his thumb along her jawline, he brushed his lips over hers.

Kissing him back, she trailed her hands over his shoulders, teasing her fingers along his skin under his sleeves. Pulling back, her eyes were as clouded as his. "'Night," she whispered, disappearing to the back to grab her purse.

He let her out the front door, watching her strut across the street and climb safely into her car.

7

Kickoff

Pounding on the bathroom door shook him from his daydreams. Fucking eh, he needed to get his own place. Taking his hand off his cock, he shut off the water and hollered at his sister on the other side of the door. "Wake your ass up earlier so I can take a damn shower in peace."

Wrapping the towel around his waist, he didn't hurry as he brushed his teeth, applied deodorant, flossed... taking his time to drive his sister nuts.

A few minutes later, the pounding started again. "Dammit, Finn. I've got a date tonight."

Fine. He swung open the door, nearly earning himself a punch in the face as she went to knock again. Catching her fist midair, he shook his head. "Not with the cyclist?"

"No. You were right, he was only looking for wham-bam-thank-you-ma'am."

Chuckling, he let go and stepped past her. "I believe I said he was a player, not interested in anything more than a night or two."

"Yeah, but I liked the way I said it better." She headed into the bathroom, holding the door open while she hammered him with twenty questions. "What about you? Did you make it clear to Haley that you're not looking for anything? You have to be up front about these things."

"She's in the middle of a divorce and has no interest in anything but my body. All good."

"Wow, I never thought I'd congratulate you on establishing a sex-only relationship, but I'd have to kick her ass if she tried to rope you into something you're not ready for."

He shifted his weight to his other foot. "You know, I'm not a complete idiot when it comes to women."

She rolled her eyes. "Sure about that?"

"Enjoy your date." He saluted and backed up before turning to hole up in his bedroom.

Snagging his phone, he glared at the screen. How did one ask a rebound on a date, without sounding like he was looking for a booty call? He genuinely wanted a friendly dinner. If more was on the menu, well, he'd play it by ear.

He dropped onto the foot of his childhood bed; full-sized and too damn small. He could hear his dad puttering around the kitchen. Zoe had started the shower. Evan should be getting back in tonight. Paper-thin walls, cramped quarters compared to his apartment in San Francisco, but it was good to be home.

After staring at the screen for longer than he cared to admit, he punched in Haley's number.

"Hey," she answered, panting and out of breath like she'd just had her way with him, slick and flushed atop him.

Shaking his head, he emptied the image so he could speak. Voice a bit hoarse despite his efforts, he responded, "Hey. You sound out of breath."

"I am." She laughed, still catching her breath but coming easier now. "I was putting my brand-new sheets on my new California king bed. This thing's gigantic, and I am not convinced the sheets I bought for it are accurately sized, but they were on sale so I can't complain. I've gotten a full workout getting the fitted sheet over the corners."

"Sounds like you're getting some furniture in."

"Well, I have a bed and a few lamps, but that's it. This starting from scratch business isn't easy. Plus, I want to get good stuff that I can link to whatever I highlight on my blog to make a commission if anyone uses my link to order one for themselves."

"Good plan. Seriously, call if you need help with anything. There's no gym in this town and I could use the workout."

"I'll be happy to help you with that." He could picture her lopsided grin on the other side, daring him to get closer. "Actually, this place has five bedrooms, so I was thinking of turning one into a home gym, but that's not going to happen for a while and will take a bit of research to get it right. And, as stated, fixing this place up is a hell of a workout."

"You don't need much equipment if you know what you're doing."

"You're hired. When I get to that room, I'm calling you."

"Sold." Before he lost his nerve, he blurted out, "Hey, so, uh, a buddy of mine owns a restaurant about an hour north of here. Nice place. Plus, less gossip."

"That is a plus. I don't need my ex finding any more excuses to drag me through the mud."

"Ouch."

"That's Nate. Anyway, yes, dinner away from the Foothills gossip mill sounds amazing."

"K. Can you make it tonight? Or I can swap with Pete, our other bartender, and we can do tomorrow? I'm open."

"I'm having dinner with my brother tonight. I can do any other night, so you don't have to switch your schedule around."

"No problem; Pete's flexible about that stuff, especially as it usually winds up with him getting extra hours." He laid back on his bed, his legs extended, feet hanging off the edge. "I guess I didn't know you had family in town."

"I'm from Foothills originally, but my parents divorced when I was in middle school and I moved to California with my dad." He could hear fabric moving on the other end of the line, like maybe Haley was lying on her bed too.

Too soon for phone sex? *Yes, definitely yes.* Real sex first. Damn, he needed to get that woman naked.

What was wrong with him? He and Trace had just broken up. In all the time they dated, he hadn't once considered phone sex. Hadn't once lost sleep imagining her naked, and she was attractive. But Haley... yeah, this rebound thing was a brilliant plan.

Shaking the phone sex idea from his head, he answered, "I didn't move to Foothills until freshman year of high school. Wait, who's your brother?"

"Brothers, but only one lives in town. Grady Mallory."

"Damn this is a small town. Grady was a few years ahead of me, but we were on a lot of the same teams, so we hung out a lot. He's been a good friend since I moved back. Wait, I think he said his sister just moved back to town. Married to some asshole that slept with everyone."

Snorting on the other end, she griped at her brother, "Thanks, Grady."

Finn winced. "That came out wrong. Really, your brother isn't gossiping about you. He knew I just got out of a heavy relationship. Grady and Asher and Zane and Lincoln dragged me out and got me trashed. You know, what guys do when there's a break-up. Honestly, I think Grady was trying to make me feel better by telling me about you, that it could be worse."

"That sounds so much better than ice cream and cookie binges women are stereotyped to enjoy. Lucky me, Nate had slept with all my friends, so I quit eating for a while and binged on STD testing instead."

"Damn, I'm so sorry."

"I'm over it. Well, not that you ever get over that sort of thing, but I've got a squeaky clean bill of health and am thrilled to be far, far away from it all. Anyway. You just listed half of my favorite people from Foothills. I had such a crush on Asher growing up."

Finn's abdomen vibrated as he shook with laughter. "You and all the other girls. Seriously, I was being wooed by half the Pac-12 coaches, made headlines on a regular basis, but all I ever heard, even from my girlfriend, was what a hottie Asher Sutherland was. If he wasn't my partner in advanced calc and my carpool buddy for running start classes, I would have kicked his ass. He didn't deserve half the shit he was blamed for anyway."

"Advanced calculus, and yet you made a career in football instead."

"Hell yeah. Doesn't take advanced calc to see I would have made a fraction as much money as an engineer or a professor." He rested his hand on his bare abdomen, holding the phone to his ear with his other hand. He really needed to message Pete that he didn't need him tonight, but he couldn't seem to tear himself away from the phone.

"Ahab's or Black Op?"

"What?"

"I can't picture you getting trashed in your own establishment."

"Oh, right. We hit Ahab's as Grady and Zane didn't want to risk me puking at their place. Why?"

"I'm just picturing the five of you raising hell. Two attorneys, two Navy SEALs, and a fricking hot wide receiver. Just saying, bet you guys turned some heads."

Realizing he was still wearing nothing more than a wet towel, he immediately pictured her doing the same. Didn't matter if she was or not, the image was too good to question. "Say wide receiver again."

"What? Why?" She giggled on the other end.

"Okay, I don't ever want to compare anyone, especially my rebound to my ex, but I like hearing that you know what position I play. She was completely ignorant of football, never quite understanding why I loved the game, maybe more than I cared for her."

"I'm sorry. I get that she would have wanted to be more important to you than a game, but you could tell just watching you play, that it meant the world to you. You weren't in it for the money or the fame. I remember the playoffs two years ago, when Green Bay intercepted, and you were knocked out of the playoffs; that was pure heart."

Damn he loved listening to her talk. She nailed it; that play had shattered him. "Send me the link to follow your blog. If we're going to talk shop on our date, I want to be well informed."

"I won't say I love it like you love football. It's more of a hobby. A marginally profitable one."

"Does it make you happy?"

"Yeah. Yeah it does. I like making things look fresh and new and homey and welcoming."

"Then I want to see it."

"Okay. I'll text you the link."

A fist pounding on his bedroom door scared the shit out of him. What had he been saying about getting his own place? Good to be home, but a shred of privacy would be nice.

Pops sounded confused, his rumbling voice asking, "Finn? Pete messaged me, wants to know if he's supposed to be working tonight or not?"

"Shit, sorry." He stood up and the towel unlatched, falling to the ground as he moved to find clean clothes. He covered the receiver and hollered, "No, I'm heading in to work in a few, thanks."

Haley yelped, "Oh, shit, me too. I said I'd be at Grady and Claire's at five. I'm not even dressed yet."

Insta-hard, he cleared his throat and couldn't help but ask, "Really? Is it too soon to ask what you're wearing?"

Enticingly lyrical, her laugh trilled as she answered, "If you must know, I had just put my clothes for tonight in the dryer when I got out my new sheets, so, well, I am in nothing but a bra and panties."

Exhaling slowly, he tried to find his voice. "I knew I shouldn't have asked. This hard-on's not going anywhere, anytime soon. I may as well call in sick."

"Aw, that's so sweet."

Chuckling, he snagged a t-shirt from his top drawer. "Hey, honesty is the best policy, right?"

"I think I'm liking this rebound thing. What time are you picking me up tomorrow?"

"Would it be pathetic if I said noon?"

"Noon would be fine, but we might beat the dinner rush by, you know, a few hours."

He chuckled. "Pick you up at six? It's about an hour away if we take the backroads. If we're early, there's a nice trail by the restaurant."

"Perfect. See you then."

8

Turnover

Hanging up the phone, Haley rushed to her stacks of clothes along the wall and grabbed a breezy tank top that made her feel pretty but required no effort. She was so late. And she really, really didn't want to explain why.

She had completely lost track of time; if his dad hadn't interrupted, they might have talked all night. Dashing to the laundry room, she snagged her jeans from the dryer. Shoes, shoes... where the hell were they? Before furniture, maybe she should pick up a shoe rack and shelves for the closet. Having her bedroom wall lined with stacks of clothes was getting annoying.

Her phone buzzed. Claire. *Left yet?*

Hopping in the car as we speak. Well, she was almost in the car.

Don't. Change in plans; we'll pick you up and go out to dinner.

Long pause.

Another message from Claire popped up. *Patricia invited herself. We thought eating out would be safer, as we've been busy with work and the house is a mess.*

Yikes. Good plan.

Tossing on a pair of heeled sandals from the overgrown shoe volcano in the corner of the closet, the pile collapsing behind her, she forced herself to stop moving and fasten her shoes, so she didn't sprain an ankle.

Decelerating when she reached the entry, she grabbed her moto-jacket from the hook and stepped outside. The evening breeze lifted the sunbaked cedar scent and whirled it around before whisking it away to make room for the evening chill. Breathing in the fresh evening, she exhaled the last-minute rush, her pulse slowing, shoulders relaxing... hmm, she really needed to power wash the entry and get some planters, maybe see how to make a fall wreath come October.

She locked the front door right as Grady's Forerunner pulled in. Hopping in the back, she noted the absence of Patricia. "So?"

Grady shifted into reverse and exhaled cautiously. "She doesn't ride in the backseat, and I made it clear that Claire doesn't ride in the backseat of *our* car, so she is meeting us there."

"Oh thank goodness." Haley laughed under her breath as she settled into the seat. "I mean, she's come a long way, but she's still Patricia."

"Don't I know it," Grady groaned. He pulled onto the main road toward downtown. "Since that intervention at the gala, she's been working on it. But that still doesn't mean she gets to see what happens to the house when we've both been working long hours."

"Nicely done." Haley nodded appreciatively. Within minutes, they parked downtown, right in front of Halseth's. Shit. Finn was working tonight.

And it would take a mountain of willpower that she didn't possess to keep her eyes off him. With the collection of fantasies she'd developed to stay sane the last few years, of which he was a regular, having seen him, kissed him, well, those imaginings were bit more vivid these days. No wonder she'd turned to a puddle of horny mush the moment she'd laid eyes on him; even before she recognized him, those arms had spent many fictional nights wrapped around her.

Town was pleasantly bustling without being crowded, clusters of groups moving in and out of shops and restaurants. As they stepped onto the sidewalk, her sandals clicking against the tidy concrete, Claire linked hands with Grady and asked Haley, "Have you been to Halseth's yet?"

"Yes, I have. Great food." And great service. She blushed just thinking about that kiss, ending the night flushed and thrilled and satisfied for the first time in... way too long. "Not going to Black Op?"

Grady shook his head. "Hell no. As much as Patricia is trying, she's still not thrilled I gave up the career she dreamed for me to go all in on a brewing company. I'm not risking bursting my safety bubble if she gets judgmental."

"Understandable. Let's go another night."

"Perfect. You'll love Halseth's. Finn, the bartender—his dad owns the place—he's a good buddy since he moved back a few months ago. He made varsity freshman year, of course, so we were on a lot of the same teams. He would have been in your grade though."

"Finn, oh yeah. Seems like a nice guy."

The window-framed door creaked as Grady opened the door for them. Breath catching with a shy thrill as she walked in, she immediately caught sight of Finn. Equally flummoxed, he stilled as he saw her, his chest rose and fell, and the customer talking with him rambled without noticing the bartender was on another planet.

Grady stepped up behind her and waved to Finn.

Lips turning up into an easy smile, he waved. "Hey guys."

Raising her finger to her lips without the others noticing, she silently told him their rebound plan was not something she wanted to share with anyone. He acknowledged with a subtle nod.

They settled in one of the four-tops in the corner. She hoped it didn't look obvious when she claimed the seat against the wall so she could easily see the bar. Not that it would make the evening any easier, but she couldn't help herself. It was either that or get a crick in her neck and be really obvious, knowing she wouldn't be able to resist watching him.

Finn plucked a stack of menus from the shelf and waved off a server she didn't recognize. He asked, nodding to the empty chair, "A fourth coming?"

Groaning, Grady answered, "Patricia."

Finn visibly winced. "Thanks so much for choosing my establishment."

Sitting closest, Claire nudged Finn with her elbow. "She's trying."

"I know, I know. I'll play nice if she does."

Nodding, Grady rolled his eyes. "But she does need occasional reminders to be a human." He glanced to Haley then up to Finn. "Not sure if you've met yet, but this is my sister, Haley. She just moved up from San Francisco."

Haley jumped in, "I've been in a few times. Finn tolerates me getting work done at the bar."

He bit the corner of his lip to stifle his grin. "What a coincidence, I just moved up from the bay area, too. Anyway, I gotta get back to the bar. Luce will grab your orders in a sec." As he backed away, his gaze lingered on Haley an extra moment, flashing her a wink before he turned. Backs to him, Grady and Claire didn't notice, but they might have noticed the blush that heated her cheeks.

Striding in, back ramrod straight, Patricia wore a stiff smile. Wow, she really was trying. Were those... jeans? She wore crisp white denim pants and a starched black blouse, as if trying to dress down as one ought when dining at a pub.

Grady and Claire caught the confused stare as Haley watched her mother attempting to fit in. Scanning the restaurant, Patricia almost, almost relaxed when she found them. Knowing Patricia wouldn't be rude in public, Haley rose from her chair and waved Patricia to the inside seat.

"Hello, Mother," she greeted as she sat down.

A moment later, their server appeared. "Drinks tonight?"

Patricia looked up at the bar and almost lost her composed expression. "If your bartender can manage, I'll have a Vieux Carré."

The server smiled. "I'm sure he can handle it."

Grady and Claire each ordered a beer. Haley asked for the bartender to recommend something on tap with bite.

Patricia began her elevated conversation when they were alone again. Haley ignored her family for a moment, watching the server deliver their orders to Finn. As she reported Patricia's snooty drink, and likely a snarky comment to accompany it, he rolled his eyes.

He glanced to Haley; she scrunched her forehead in apologetic wince over the disaster that was her mother. When the server got to Haley's order, Finn flashed her a wink and a heated grin that shot straight down her panties.

Before anyone noticed, hopefully, she straightened out her smile and tried to pay attention. Grady was clearly repeating a conversation he'd had more than a few times. "We're really, really not having a big wedding. If we have to go out of town to avoid offending anyone, we will."

Shoulders back, Patricia plowed on, "I have so few life moments to show off my children, and even fewer that you have been cooperative for. Give me this one special day. I will pay for the entire ceremony and reception, if I can create the guest list."

"I'm sure your friends will love the backyard barbeque we've been planning."

A look of horror radiated straight through Patricia's spine until Haley feared she might induce a compression fracture. "You wouldn't."

Haley intercepted, resting her hand on their mother's arm. "If you'll recall, I had five hundred guests at my wedding, my gown cost more than my car, and I spent the next decade of my life being belittled and cheated on. A small, backyard barbeque, something welcoming and cozy and casual, sounds like the perfect way for Grady and Claire to share their special day with friends, if that's what they would like to do."

Patting Haley's hand, Patricia shook her head delicately. "My poor dear. I know you struggled. It may be too late, but we should have had this talk back then. The best way to keep your husband in line, and his penis out of other women, is to be sure he knows you are smarter, faster, and hotter in the bedroom than any other woman he might run into."

Grateful she'd taken the outside seat in case she decided to bolt, Haley swallowed and closed her eyes before she said something truly nasty.

Grady jumped in before she could. "Patricia, I'm sure Haley is all of those things, but—"

Patricia waved her hand in the air to shush him. Haley took a drowning gulp of water. Not that she was thirsty, but it was either that or dump it over her mother's head.

Patricia began anew, "As a twice-divorced, thrice-married and once-happy woman, I understand the need to find an adequate partner. But it is also important to maintain a reputation for being able to keep your man's attention, so other women don't come sniffing around."

No. Not this conversation again. The number of sex tips Patricia had provided on the drive up from San Francisco still haunted Haley. Nate certainly hadn't made her feel adequate in the sack. They were both bored within six months of marriage. She should have listened to the nagging voice in her head that it wasn't supposed to be that way.

Yet, one mention of panties to Finn, and he claimed an untamable erection. No, Haley knew it wasn't *her* fault. And she was loving every minute of imagining all the good stuff she'd been missing out on.

Right as Patricia continued her detailed instructions on how to keep one's husband faithful, saying the words, "The woman should never expect an orgasm, but she can guide him along. And she must always be willing to take his penis—" Finn appeared, clearing his throat as he arrived.

Patricia glanced up at his untimely interruption.

His jaw clenched, flickering rapidly. "Dr. Mallory, your Vieux Carré. I don't get many requests for that one, but I'm sure you'll let me know if I didn't get it right." He slid the drink in front of her unceremoniously, refusing to take her bait.

Patricia's lips awkwardly contorted in what might be a smile.

He delivered the rest of the table's beers, asking Haley to let him know if the brew had enough bite to satisfy her.

Grady nodded to Finn. "We're thinking of seeing if anyone wants to go out to Ahab's tomorrow night. You in?"

Flipping the tray in his hand, Finn shrugged. "Love to, but uh, I've got some things to do up north."

"No worries. Next time," Grady offered. "Haley?"

Chewing her cheek, she tried to come up with an excuse. "I've got a deadline coming up. Next time?"

"Sounds good. Actually, while we're on the subject, Claire's birthday is coming up in a few weeks. I'll send you the info?"

Finn nodded. "Wouldn't miss it."

Patricia brought the fancy drink in clear glass to her lips, a near-smile teasing at her stiff cheeks. Satisfied, Patricia started on her next hot tip. Finn disappeared as she seemed to be heading into foreplay advice.

As she began what was likely to refer to male genitalia, again, Haley interrupted. "So, Claire, any interesting cases lately?" Haley really, really couldn't handle her mother saying the word penis again. Especially when she was still enjoying the image of Finn... well, of Finn enjoying their conversation this afternoon as much as she had.

Claire eagerly responded, "Always. I was rounding on a ranch a few miles downriver a few days ago. Most of the stalls were filled with the horses I had expected to attend to, but the last stall, typically empty, held a dog. An Australian shepherd in labor. The poor thing looked so exhausted. I jumped in and attended while she delivered seven healthy mutts. The family had no idea their dog was pregnant; they thought she'd been getting into the cat food again."

Grady reached under the table to link hands with his fiancée. His tone was dripping with sarcasm, but his smile genuine, as he said, "You are looking at the parents of a first-pick brown-and-blue-eyed mutt. In eight weeks."

"As if you could turn one down after helping with delivery." Claire gazed at her husband, grinning and utterly turning her fiancé to mush.

"As if I could turn down a free puppy. Not with that look in your eyes."

Patricia picked up her drink and took another sip. "I suppose your friend knows his drinks." Hey, a compliment. She really was trying. "We need to bump up that wedding so you can make me grandbabies. I will be a wonderful grandmother."

Silence. No one dared respond to that one. Patricia hadn't changed a poopy diaper or soothed a crying baby in her life.

Shutting her up, Grady grew a devious smile and said, "Why wait? We're practicing on a nightly basis."

"Really?" Patricia's eyes lit up.

"Well, there's an IUD in the way, but we keep trying anyway." He winked at Claire.

That shut up Patricia for at least five minutes. For all her talk of penises, she was flummoxed at the idea of her son using his.

Speaking of penises. Damn, not a good segue. Haley had been rather fixated on one in particular all evening. Didn't help she had a perfect view of him working the tap, tossing t-shirts and silverware bundles and whatever else back and forth with the server. She knew exactly how hard those arms were, how smooth and warm that skin was, and how those lips tasted like a guilty pleasure and kissed as skillfully as he caught a football.

And that cowlick. Who knew she was a sucker for rebellious hair?

Okay, shift those thoughts. No penises at dinner. "You know," she began, "It's so weird being back. I'm bummed Trace is gone for the summer; aside from you guys, I don't know many people in town anymore."

The server discreetly delivered their meals and disappeared. Haley inhaled the savory scent and dug into her sweet potato fries.

Claire released the lip she'd been gnawing on and lit up with a smile. "Sophie's been bugging everyone to make a hiking day happen. You would have been in Pippa's grade, right?"

Nodding her head, Haley swallowed her bite and said, "A year behind. Aside from Trace, Pippa was one of my besties in elementary school."

Grady looked up as if remembering. "I'd forgotten about that. If you don't mind sharing friends with your brother, we'll rope you into hanging out. Trace, well, she hangs out sometimes, but I'm not so sure... Anyway, we get together at least once a month with Pippa and Lincoln, Asher and Sophie, Zane and Freya. Finn and... well, Finn's a regular since he got back a few months ago."

"I don't remember Finn from when I lived here before." Was that too obvious of a lead-in to find out more about him?

"Oh yeah, you wouldn't. The Halseths moved to town after you left." Grady looked over at the bar, but Finn was busy taking orders. "He's had a rough time over the last few months, so we've been trying to drag him out."

"Oh, that's too bad. How so?"

Patricia chimed in, gesturing with her fork. "Football *player* is the least of it. His mother was diagnosed with breast cancer last year. He chose to finish off the football season, not even coming home until he was injured. When it got into her bones, he grieved by hooking up with an old flame. Now he's working as a bartender for his family's restaurant when he could be doing something meaningful, like getting on SportsCenter or something."

Grady shook his head. "Gee, Ma. Tell us how you really feel."

"I was just expressing my—"

Grady cut her off again. Good thing, as Haley wanted to kick her. "He's a good guy. Has had a shitty year. And he's my friend. Leave him alone. Whatever your gossip ring is spreading around, they ought to check their facts, and you can remember that you are a physician and would never treat one of your patients with such disrespect."

Spine straightening, Patricia took a delicate bite of lettuce. "My apologies."

Damn, Haley had missed a lot since her last visit. She'd never seen Grady stand up to their mother this way, or anyone, really. Nor Patricia back down so quickly.

Finn caught her eye, things finally stabilizing at the bar as he'd caught everyone up. Seeing Patricia's stubborn expression, the awkward pall that had fallen over their table, he smiled sympathetically. Looking around the restaurant first, he nodded his head toward the back. He caught the server, said something Haley couldn't hear, then disappeared to the back.

She cleared her throat and set down her napkin. "Excuse me a moment."

Claire scowled in a feisty jealous look.

Haley smiled. "I'll be five minutes." Maybe ten.

Strolling past the bar, she breezed right past the bathroom, only to find the hall empty. An arm reached from the door to the alley and yanked her outside.

Thrill rushed through her veins as she found herself enveloped in Finn's arms. Before she could catch her breath, he pulled her close and lowered his mouth to hers, savoring the stolen moment. Hand cradling her jaw, he pulled back just enough to gage her reaction.

Chocolate eyes laced with amusement and the same exhilaration that rocketed through her, he grinned. "Sorry if I startled you. Was going to be a rough enough night, thinking about you on the other end of the phone this afternoon, then having you walk in my door and not being able to talk, well, I couldn't resist." He nipped a quick kiss again.

"Thanks for the save earlier."

"Yeah, what the hell was that? Was your mother giving you blowjob tips?"

Haley nodded sadly, her cheek firmly parked in her teeth. "Apparently, if I want to keep a man around, I have to satisfy him in bed. Just asked twice-divorced Patricia, she is quite the expert."

"I hope your stepdad knows what a lucky guy he is." He rolled his eyes. "I really dislike your mother."

"It's mutual." She nodded grimly.

"Can I go let her know you're a hell of a kisser, and I have no doubt you'll blow my mind when we get to the rest of the good stuff?"

"Please no. It would only add more fuel."

"True. She's never really liked me."

"She doesn't like anyone."

"Fair point. Anyway, I really didn't steal you away to talk about your mother."

Trailing her hands along his abdomen, she looked up, the corner of her mouth quirking up. "What did you steal me away for?"

He nipped another kiss. "I was thinking of making some excuse, like nailing down plans for tomorrow, but I really just wanted to get my hands on you."

Rising to her tiptoes, she gripped the back of his neck and swept her tongue over his. Groaning, he spread his hand over the small of her back and held on, advancing the kiss deeper until she forgot where they were, spinning somewhere on a fluffy white cloud.

Pulling away, his pupils dilated until he blinked back to reality, he stepped toward the door. "We should get back."

Still blissfully shellshocked, she nodded.

He eased the door open and peeked inside. Coast clear, he beckoned her in first. She made a quick bathroom stop, then rejoined her family.

Patricia was returning the ticket to the server and smiled when she saw Haley approaching. "You know, there's a glow about you today. Are you sure you're not pregnant?"

"What? Mother. No." There was little doubt Patricia didn't know her at all, but her attempts to pay attention were painful.

She was tempted to say, *No, I'm glowing because the sexy bartender was kissing me. And enjoying it. Because I know what I'm about in that area. Don't need any tips. A bad marriage riddled with a terrible sex life does not mean a person isn't good in bed; it's all about the right partner.*

She was half tempted to call her old friends and ask if they found Nate as disappointing as she did, or if he managed to be an attentive lover when he was breaking the rules.

9

Rushing

After failing to take it easy on his daily run, Finn hobbled into the shower. Zoe was already leaving for work, so he snickered and cranked up the hot water. Within minutes, a fist pounded on the bathroom door. "Don't you have to work tonight?" His dad's voice thundered through the thin wooden door.

Groaning, he shut off the faucet and stepped out. "No. I worked it out with Pete, remember?"

Long pause. Scott continued, "Oh yeah. Okay." Another pause. "How come?" He'd totally remembered that Finn had switched shifts, he was just looking for an entry to ask for details without sounding nosy.

No privacy. No secrets in the Halseth family. Finn secured his towel around his waist and opened the door. "I just did, okay?" Damn, he felt like a teenager sneaking out to take his girlfriend parking.

"Huh. You usually like working Friday nights. Keeps you busy." Scott shrugged, but didn't leave the doorway. "I'll get another steak out to thaw then. Thought it was just me tonight."

"No, Pops, I'm, uh, I'm heading out tonight." He rubbed a hand through his sopping wet hair, wondering when he could close the door and get ready for his date. Haley didn't need the heartache of wondering if she was going to get stood up.

Scott backed up a step. "Great. That's great. Out with the gang again? I'm so glad you reconnected with some of your old friends."

"No. I, uh..." He didn't want any secrets with his family. "I've got a date."

Poor Scott looked like he was attempting the *New York Times* Sunday crossword. "I thought you and Trace broke up because you weren't ready to be involved. And she's out of town. Moving on a bit quick, aren't you?"

Shit. And this is why he was taking Haley far from Foothills. Trace didn't need the gossip mills wondering why he was dating someone else so quick. "Nothing serious. Really. Just a rebound."

"Rebound. Huh. She know she's a rebound?"

"Yeah Pops. Actually, I think I'm the rebound. She's wrapping up a divorce."

Scott visibly grimaced. "You sure about this? Getting in the middle of a divorce? Things can get messy when a married couple splits."

Oh man, this conversation was becoming so much more complicated than he had anticipated. And he was still wearing nothing more than a freaking towel. Scott wasn't about to let him off the hook now. "Yeah. It'll be final in a few weeks. The jerk cheated on her, leaving her with no friends. And she's new in town. Neither of us are looking for anything serious. Just some good company."

Scott backed up another step and scratched his head. "Well, I guess you know what you're doing. And if you hooking up with this girl will save on the hot water bill, I'm game."

Finn closed his eyes and exhaled slowly. Maybe his family was a little too honest. His dad headed down the hall and Finn was finally able to finish getting ready. A bit tighter of a timeline, he shoved Zoe's hair dryer and makeup and things he didn't know the name or purpose of into the drawer, then quickly smoothed down his hair, brushed, flossed, and dashed down the hall to his bedroom.

Tossing his towel on the chair that served more as a laundry receptacle than an actual seat, he opened his closet. Fuck, he should have donated all these suits. He hated the damn things, but it had gone with the territory.

He tossed on a pair of slacks and a charcoal gray button-up. Hated the cuffs, but he buttoned the stupid things anyway so he could skip the tie and jacket. Black leather belt, black athletic shoes, and he was ready. Yeah, he wanted to impress Haley, but he really, really couldn't bear to wear slippery, ass-wipe dress shoes.

He hopped in his Shelby and tore off toward Haley's. Easing off on the gas when he saw how efficiently he'd gotten ready, he slowed to half the speed limit. Such a fine line, too early versus too late, or looking suspiciously punctual.

He pulled in the driveway only seven minutes early. Checked his phone; no new messages or emails. Reviewed the traffic report; all clear. Triple checked his gas tank was full.

At five minutes 'til, he couldn't take it anymore. Stepping out of the car, he dashed up to the front door. He raised his hand to knock when the door swung open.

Like a fresh summer breeze blasting him back until he was high on giddiness, Haley stood in the doorway, that flirty lopsided smile knocking him on his ass. Hot as fuck, pretty as a picture, Haley stood in a silky pink dress that was playful and feminine. Her long legs reminded him of how she'd ensnared him against her that night on the bar. Her rich brown hair was down, a few inches past her shoulders with long curls. A simple teardrop necklace framed her neck.

And those lips. Damn, he could go on and on. He should wait. End of the date thing, remember?

Before his brain could complete the thought, he closed the narrow distance between them and slid his hand around her waist.

Leaning down, he tasted those lush lips.

Nibbled.

Grazed his tongue along her pouty bottom lip.

Gripping her hand around the back of his neck, she swept her tongue over his. As he eased in, she shifted, wrapping her lips around his tongue and tugging, sucking, releasing then delving back in, the heat of her mouth melding with his, erasing all coherent thought from his one-track mind.

His other hand reached down and palmed her hip, trailing down her dress in a desperate need to find skin. Score. He slid his hand up her thigh, cupping her very, very fine ass.

Sighing against his mouth, she pressed tighter against him, mouth plundering his with even more fervor.

Completely breathless, irreparably rumpled, they managed to pull away. Stepping back, he moved out of reach before he attacked her again. "Hey," he said on a heavy exhale.

"Hey." She blinked the haze from her vision.

He crossed his arms over his chest. "You look amazing."

"Thanks," she said, smoothing her dress. "So. Hungry?"

Biting his lip, he nodded. "Yes. But let's have dinner first."

Laughing, she turned and grabbed a jacket and her purse. He smoothed his hair as she locked up. Dashing around to the passenger door, he held it open for her. With a soft "Thanks." She swept her hand under her dress and slid in, her sexy heeled shoes moving in at the last moment like a movie star.

As he drove out of Foothills, she angled toward him and said, "I've never done this rebound thing. Please say we don't have to talk about our exes all night."

"Fuck no," he answered. "I mean, you can whenever you want to, but I'd much rather get to know you than some asshole that didn't deserve you."

She scrunched up her nose in a wholehearted grin. "Good. You can talk about yours all you want, but, agreed, I'd rather hear about you than her."

The restaurant looked familiar, but she didn't think she'd been there before. "Who's your friend that owns this?"

"What? Oh, old teammate and a good guy. It was in the beginning credits of that movie a few years back."

"Ah, that's it. I've heard it's amazing."

He shut off the engine and was around the car to open her door before she even reached for the handle. When Nate had pulled this chauvinistic crap, it felt like he was trying to put her in her place as the delicate flower he wanted her to be. When Finn did it, she knew he was trying to make her feel special.

As he held the door open, she stepped close to him and stood on her toes, brushing her lips over his. "You know you don't have to open doors for me."

"I know. I want to."

Pitter patter, she smiled and shook her head at him. "You are too cute for your own good, you know that?"

"Aw, thanks for thinking I'm cute. I think that's a first." He grinned at her, reaching his hand out to link with hers. "We've got half an hour before we're due inside, want to take a walk or see if they can squeeze us in early?"

She scanned the park that bordered the restaurant. "Let's walk another time. I'm starving."

"Me too."

At the maître d's desk, Finn started to speak, but was immediately recognized. "Mr. Halseth. You are expected. Please, your table is ready. Miss..."

"Please, Haley."

"Wonderful. Miss Haley. May I take your coat?"

They followed to a private dining room overlooking the valley beyond, the jagged peaks of the Cascades on the other side. Their drinks were served, a tapas plate moments later, then the server returned to take their orders. After the constant comings and goings, they finally had the room to themselves.

"This place is incredible. I don't think rebounds required impressing or wooing."

"How about we set our own rebound rules? I've been meaning to come here for years, but never got around to it. So, allow me to splurge."

"Good choice." Nate would hate it. What was the point of a fancy restaurant when you couldn't schmooze? Privacy with only your wife for company? No way, no how. "I wheedled information about you from my brother. He seems to think you're a decent guy."

"Oh man. How'd that go? Let me picture it." He leaned back in his chair and seemed to mentally paint the image. "'Grady, I was making out with one of your friends and am wondering if he's worth sleeping with.'" Grinning at his smartass creativity, he leaned forward and took a gulp of water.

A goofy laugh bubbled up in her chest. "Ouch, that sounds like a no-win conversation. I was much more subtle; really I should be a detective. Or, well, it was easy to bring you up in casual conversation at your pub. Despite my mother's disdain, Grady had nothing but good things to say."

Rubbing his hand through his hair, he unwittingly spiked up the cowlick that he must have worked hard to tame. "Oh man, Patricia is a real peach, isn't she? Grady was everyone's least favorite house for parties thanks to that witch. I mean... shit, sorry..."

"No, it's true. She seems like she's been trying. She flew down to drive home with me from San Francisco. Don't get me wrong, by day two, I was shoving cotton balls in my ears so I wouldn't have to listen to anymore of her bullshit, but it was a sweet gesture."

She leaned back in her chair, enjoying watching Finn relax as the sun set in the distance. His cowlick was officially wild now, his sleeves rolled up, his feet were crossed, and his ankles were leaned against hers under the table.

"Tell me about your family." She didn't want to push, remembering what Patricia had said about his mother, but she was hoping for a glimpse at what he had come home to.

Contemplating over a sip of his wine, Finn hesitated before speaking. "I've got a great family. You met Zoe; she's a middle child through and through, wedged between me and Evan, our little brother. Not so little, he's as tall as I am. Pops, Scott, is a great dad. He and Mom were practically kids themselves when they had me, but they never hesitated in their relationship. Pops says it was love at first sight through the last sight."

"I like that. Patricia said your mom passed away? I don't want to pry, so you don't have to talk about it." She bit her tongue. Not exactly date conversation. So she didn't want to talk about exes, but thought his deceased mother was fair game? She cringed, wishing she could take it back.

"No, it's okay. She was everything a mom should be. Kissed our booboos when we truly needed it, but when we didn't, made us get right back up and face things head-on. She got sick last fall, breast cancer. I tried to come home, take a break for the season to help out. She was too weak to work, and Pops went with her to every treatment; not that they asked for help, but they would have given up everything for any one of us. Evan got home first, dibs'd the apartment over the garage.

Zoe next. But Mom... Mom insisted I keep playing, otherwise what would she have to look forward to every Sunday?"

Smiling sadly, Haley linked her feet with his.

His jaw was flexed tight, but he kept going without prompting. "So, I kept playing. She and Pops flew down for my knee surgery. Mom looked like hell, skinny and pale and bald, but they wanted to be there when I woke up. A few days later, we flew back home together. That's when she broke the news. The chemo didn't do shit. Sometimes... sometimes it's not enough. She was gone a month later."

"I'm so sorry. That's why you and Zoe and Evan work at Halseth's?"

"Yeah. It was their dream, the pub. When the building opened up in Foothills, ideal location, they hauled us all the way up here."

"And now you're all back." She watched as he relived the memories, the emotion he tucked behind those melty brown eyes.

He sat up, taking another sip of wine. "That's an understatement. We're starting to make Mom a memory rather than a living, breathing part of the house. Not to mention, we're getting to that point where it's time to move out before we all kill each other. Sharing a bathroom with Zoe again..." He trailed off, shaking his head in silent helplessness.

Their food was served moments later. They ate in silence for the first few bites, enjoying simply existing in the beautiful place with the elegant meal and pleasant company. No pressure, no expectations.

When it was time to go, the five-course meal well settled, the night sky shined down on them like a blanket. She slipped her hand into Finn's as they walked to the car. The drive home was a charming end to a relaxing evening: clear skies, dry roads, and crisp summer air.

She enjoyed the view, watching as Finn's powerful forearms took the curves with ease, his eyes scanning the path ahead as he kept them safe on the mountain backroads. When the road would straighten out, he'd glance her way now and again, his expression thick with something he didn't say.

Pulling into her driveway, he had her door open, yet again, before she got to it. She stood and looped her jacket over her purse, toasty warm without needing the extra layer. He laced his fingers with hers to walk her in.

As she stepped to the front door, he pulled her back and had his hand buried in her hair, his mouth on hers before she could catch her breath. Up on her toes, she held on tight and kissed him back.

Plunging, the velvet of his tongue caressed hers, tasting, exploring, floating with her to the stars above. Shifting, she moved deeper, clinging tighter against him.

His hand splayed over her low back, pulling her against his groin. Breathless, she slipped her hands under his shirt, needing to feel his skin. Smooth and hard, feverish under her fingertips, his back was lean, his abdomen tight. Urgency building, she needed more.

Groaning, he slid his other hand up her thigh again, setting ablaze every nerve as he traced his fingers along the curve of her hip. Under her dress, his hand skimmed along her belly, his fingers teased along the rim of her panties.

Gasping against his mouth, she tugged his lower lip between her teeth and whispered his name.

Panting, as aroused as she was, he pulled away. "Wow, shit, sorry. I really, really hope no one drove by and saw... that."

Nodding, she fixed her dress, the corner of her mouth turning up in satisfaction at the bulge in his slacks. "Yeah," she said, unable to collect her thoughts. "I, uh, should, um, get inside before any of my neighbors..." She really needed to plant more trees to block her view of the road.

"Sure, yeah. I should get home. If you're hungry tomorrow, you can, uh, swing by the pub if you want; I'll be working."

"Yeah. Great."

He walked backwards, eyes hazy with lust like hers were. He watched as she unlocked the door and let herself inside.

Holy crap. If this was a rebound relationship, she really, really ought to have gotten a divorce years ago.

10

Naked Bootleg

The next few days creeped by at a damn snail's pace. Finn was waking up early to shower in peace, but even that wasn't enough. He even sent a preemptive payment to the water company before Pops saw the bill.

Haley came to the pub twice that week, but not every night, as it was probably already getting obvious that she was there for him and not the food. And equally obvious when she was there, he worked at half his normal pace, as when he wasn't visiting with Haley, he was watching her. Not in that creepy way, of course, he just, well, she was nice to look at.

Her eyebrows were about two shades darker brown than her hair; neatly shaped but a few strays caused a tweak at the edge that she smoothed when she thought no one was paying attention. When she couldn't think of what she wanted to type, she scowled and tapped her fingernails rapidly on the keys, not pressing hard enough to commit to a letter.

And he couldn't help but watch the door every sixty seconds when he knew she was coming in.

Thursday afternoon, she called him. Not that he'd been waiting for the call, but, yeah, he totally had been. Traipsing into the kitchen after a run, his knee already barking at him, he was heading for an icepack when she called.

"Hey," he answered on the first ring, grinning like an idiot.

"Hey," she answered with that flirty confidence. He could picture her wicked smile as she spoke.

Zoe and Evan sat at the kitchen island and went dead quiet the moment he picked up the phone so eagerly. Like a couple of Labradors waiting on their dinner, their heads didn't move, their unblinking eyes watched his every movement. He grabbed the icepack from the freezer, tossed it in the air before catching it again, then flashed a wink at his sibs as he backed out of the room. As he rounded the bend, their jaws dropped to the countertop.

Limping up the stairs, he closed himself in his room and hopped on the bed. He propped his knee up with a pillow and almost cried when the ice cooled his knee.

Haley paused her thought when he groaned. "You okay?"

"Yeah. Just got back from a run and my knee is fucking killing me. It's getting better, but I am still completely dependent on my daily icepack."

She giggled on the other end of the line, half his pain fading away at the delight in her tone. "There are worse addictions out there."

"Too true. I've seen guys get hurt so bad they can't function without their habits, and not just pain pills."

"But you can run on the knee okay? Didn't you have two surgeries?"

"Yeah, but the second was because I didn't do the physical therapy the first time and didn't heal right; didn't exactly seem as important as sticking with Mom. But... wait a sec, I knew you were a fan, but now I'm wondering if 'stalker' is more appropriate," he teased.

She laughed again, pure and hearty and always a glimmer in her eye. Damn, he loved that sound. "Hey, I worked from home and had a cheating bastard of a husband. Spending my lonely nights fantasizing about the NFL's hottest player? Hell yeah."

He laid back on the bed, his abdomen shaking as he laughed with her. "I should be creeped out, but I'm actually a little turned on right now."

"Please tell me you don't wear a shirt when you exercise. Just workout shorts that barely stay on your hips and running shoes?"

Glancing down, he chuckled again. "Okay, maybe you are a creepy stalker."

She sighed, "Just a healthy imagination."

"Then please tell me you're still wet from the shower again and aren't wearing anything but those lace panties I got a good feel of the other night."

"Nope, sorry. I am wearing paint-stained overalls and a ripped-up cotton t-shirt."

"Fuck, I want you so bad, that sounds even sexier."

"Really? I'll wear it when you come over for dinner."

"Overalls only. No t-shirt underneath. And skip the overalls."

She laughed again.

"Wait, did you invite me over for dinner?"

"I was working on it, but I hadn't gotten there yet. Finn? Would you like to come for dinner?"

"Hell yes. I'm off tonight."

"I know. I'm stalking you. Kidding. Sort of. I bumped into Zoe at the grocery store this morning. She said something about you stealing all the hot water?"

Clearing his throat, he sat up and ran a hand over his short hair. "Uh, yeah, about that. Have you considered investing in an on-demand hot water heater for your shower?"

"I am so confused, but I'm willing to try one so I can find out why you go through so much hot water."

"Oh, I think you'll find out."

"Really?" she chuckled. "Anyway, I'm not going to say I'm a great cook. I mean, I'm okay, but it's not restaurant worthy."

"Haley?"

"Yeah?"

"I would be happy to eat canned spaghetti if it meant an evening with you. Not that I'm passing judgment on your cooking, I'm sure I will actually enjoy whatever you're fixing."

"I'm not sure if I'm offended or flattered. I'll let you know."

He chuckled again. Damn, had he ever laughed as much as he did when he talked with Haley? "Need me to bring anything?"

"Nope, I got it. Just bring yourself."

"What about this bulk box of condoms I picked up a few days ago?"

"Oh, bring that. I got overwhelmed in the vagina aisle at the store and grabbed the box closest to the checkout instead. I'd never bought condoms before; it's very daunting."

"Vagina aisle?"

"Yeah, you know, the one with all the tampons, pads, vaginal medications, pregnancy tests, and, the item on today's list, condoms."

"Huh. Vagina aisle. Maybe you can show me your vagina aisle tonight."

"You are really horny, aren't you?"

"God yes. I don't think my dick has calmed down since that first kiss, and definitely not since I had my hands on your spectacular ass."

"You know, I'm sure I should be offended. Your dick and my vagina have entered many of our conversations. Yet, I am somehow unoffended."

"That's a relief, because those two particular parts of human anatomy, yours and mine specifically, have been on my mind pretty much nonstop since you walked into my pub."

She laughed out loud again. He completely forgot about his knee, the icepack having slid off a while ago. "Now don't take too long of a shower. I'm putting dinner in the oven in a few."

"Yes, ma'am."

He clicked off and took a record-fast shower. Tossing on whatever pair of jeans was on the top of the pile, an old USC t-shirt, mismatched socks, he grabbed the nearest pair of sneakers and dashed out of the bedroom. He was halfway down the stairs when he remembered the box of condoms.

His knee about collapsed at the one-eighty midway up the stairs, letting him know on the way back up that he still had a long way to go before he was fully recovered. Ignoring the twinge, he hobbled down the stairs and plopped onto the bottom step to put his shoes on.

Zoe and Evan walked into the entry, extra slow as if a ghost sat at the foot of the steps. Zoe's eyes looked from him to the massive box of condoms and back to him again. Evan raised an eyebrow at the mismatched socks and ripped up college shirt. Pops appeared behind them a moment later, his mouth opening and closing like a salmon gasping for its last breath.

"Uh," Pops said. "Going somewhere?"

Biting his tongue, he grinned sheepishly at the trio. "I've got a date."

Evan crossed his arms over his chest, nodding as he pretended to be okay with Finn's sudden change in demeanor. "Kinda gathered that bit. No offense, but are you sure you're ready for... that many condoms?"

"Well not *all* tonight. We'll save some for tomorrow morning." He picked up the box and juggled it in the air. Damn, wouldn't that be fun? Despite his nonstop hard-on since meeting Haley, especially since getting that first taste of her, he didn't think he could make it through all forty condoms so quickly. Too bad. "Guys. It's a fling. A rebound. Haley's not looking for anything, and neither am I. But she's fucking hot, and she wants me. So, you all have a lovely evening, but I'm outta here."

Pops nodded slowly. "Well, I guess, uh, have a good time."

Finn flashed a wink and backed out the front door.

aley realized she'd invited him over way too early. It wasn't even three in the afternoon. Dinner was most certainly *not* in the oven, and she was still covered in paint. She'd meant to say, come over in two hours, but she was greedy and wanted him *now*.

She was getting out of the shower when she heard his car. Wrapping her towel around her, she dashed to the door to the garage and clicked the automatic opener. Taking the hint, thankfully, so she didn't have to run out in a towel to let him know her plan, he pulled into the empty stall next to hers.

As he hopped out of his car, he caught sight of her standing in the doorway... in just her towel. "Uh..." he held his massive box of condoms in one hand, slowly closing the car door with his other.

Laughing out loud at her predicament, she waved him in. "I didn't mean to invite you over so early. But picturing you all sweaty and in nothing but your running shorts, well..."

Crossing the garage and leaping up the stairs to the house as if he had springs in his feet, he closed this distance between them in half a heartbeat. Leaning down, he took her mouth with his and pulled away again, running his tongue over his lip to taste her one more time. "I was a little impatient and didn't mess around in getting here."

She backed a few steps into the house. Finn closed the door behind him. He nodded down the hall past the stairs. "Your bedroom at the end of the hall?"

"Yeah."

Throwing the box of condoms straight down the hall in a perfect spiral, he had his mouth back on hers before the box slid to a stop in her bedroom. As he scooped her up, her legs wrapped around his hips. Her towel loosened, sliding down between them; her wet hair dripped onto her shoulders.

Groaning, his mouth left hers, drifting down, his tongue tasting each bead of water along her dampened shoulder, her collarbone. Flying weightless, she landed on the mattress. When had they made it this far?

He chucked his t-shirt and dove after her. Picking up where he'd left off, he kissed a trail between her breasts. Hands free now, he placed each around her breasts, tracing his thumbs along her curves. Taking a tight, pink bud in his mouth, he laved, sending electric shocks straight to her core.

Arching to meet him, she gasped, needing to feel his hands, his tongue, over every inch of her body.

Instead of the delicate touch she'd expected, he tightened his grip, kneading, gentle, intense. Shifting, he took the other breast in his mouth, sucking hard until she cried out, soaring halfway to orgasm on impact.

As she crested, feeling a thrill in places she'd never imagined, he trailed his tongue lower, nipping along her side, kissing again.

When he settled between her legs, pressing his lips to her, she nearly booked it out of there. Holy shit, she hadn't... No, no dwelling on the past. Rebound meant exploring what she'd been missing for too long.

Easing her thighs apart, she surrendered to sensation. Seeming to sense her hesitance, he kissed the inner curve of her thigh, and then asked, "This okay?"

She nodded her head against the pillow. "Yes."

"You sure? You hesitated. I promise, I won't bite. Unless you want me to." She couldn't see it, but she could feel him grinning against her skin.

She laughed again. "Really. Yes, I hesitated. Then I remembered we're rebounding, and I am open to trying... new things. I don't even want to think about it, but, well, I've never been with anyone but my ex, and... this wasn't his thing."

"Shit, I'm sorry. Well, stay open for me and I'll make it worth your while. I've been dreaming about how you might taste since the moment I laid eyes on you. Okay, so maybe not that moment. I am attracted to your brain too, but—"

She giggled and interrupted him, "Shut up and kiss me again."

"Yes ma'am."

And he did. With the lightest touch like she was a priceless artifact, he pressed his lips to her center. The zing shot straight to her head, her breath catching in her throat. Whispering, she bit her lip and smiled, "Do that again."

"Anytime you want," he murmured, his breath warm against her sensitized skin. "Tell me what you like."

He kissed again, a little more pressure this time.

Again, longer. He tasted, then he kissed her again.

"More," she breathed.

"I'm getting there," he laughed. "But boss me around all you want."

This time, his tongue ran the length of her, and again, pressing, lapping her up like she was the best delicacy he'd ever tasted, his groan proving it. He kept going, adding more with each pass.

Her breath came quicker, her soprano moan rhythmically cheering him on. As she was about to come out of her skin, floating above the bed, his tongue slipped down and plunged into her. More desperate, thrilled, she begged for more.

And more he gave. Again and again, harder, faster, softer, then he shifted and sucked hard like he had her breast. Crying out, she rocketed off the planet.

Coming up, dragging his thumb over the corner of his lip, he licked her off the tip of his thumb and grinned. "Never?"

She shook her head. "I'm glad I picked you for my rebound."

Still grinning, he snagged the box of condoms off the floor and tore it open. "We've got this whole box to go through. It may not all happen tonight, but let's see how far we get."

Giggling, she rose to her knees as he moved to roll on the first. "Wait a sec." She shook her head. Moving closer, she grasped his cock in her hands, trailing her fingers over the satin shaft. Solid in her grip, she explored, finding out what made him even harder.

"Okay, I can't take much more; that box will be rendered useless if I embarrass myself now."

Looking up at him, she held her hand out. Following her idea, he slapped the condom in her palm like a lucky high five. Rolling it over his shaft, she took her time.

"Dammit, Haley. I'm serious about things getting critical down there."

She backed up on the mattress and crooked her finger to beckon him closer.

Arm wrapping around her waist, he lowered her down to the bed. She looped one leg around his hips, pulling him tight against her. Hovering at the precipice, sweat already beading on his forehead, he kissed her sweetly, then plunged deep inside.

Already primed from his mouth on her, his delicious torment, she cried out as she swiftly rose with him.

He took the next few movements slow and steady, but she wrapped her other leg around him and gripped his hips, driving him with her. "Now," she whispered in his ear. She couldn't slow down, needing him to keep up with the frenzied rhythm.

Rocking with her, moving, thrusting, they came fast and hard together.

Pressing his forehead to hers, as spent as she, he whispered, "Thanks for picking *me* for your rebound."

"You are very welcome," she teased. He brushed his lips over hers, smacked her playfully on the ass, and stood up. Disappearing for a few moments, he returned from the bathroom spectacularly nude.

She leaned up on one elbow. "Gotta say, if I'd had any idea you looked like that under all that gear, I might have ditched that asshole I was married to sooner and have seduced you like all those other groupies."

He hopped back onto the bed next to her. Kissing her again, he grinned and pulled away. "There's no time like the present. You can seduce me anytime you want."

Running her hand along his deltoid, his bicep, along ridges she didn't know the names of, she probably should have felt silly saying out loud, "I had no idea muscles were so damn sexy."

He chuckled, running his hand along her thigh. "I like yours too."

"Ha, I don't have much on here."

"Yeah, you do. Some gorgeous ones." He went quiet for a moment, a darkness covering his vision. Shaking it off, he slipped his arm under her and rolled her on top of him. "Okay, I'm ready for you to seduce me again."

"Again?" She found herself giggling yet again, sitting atop him and feeling glorious.

"Did you see that box? This is going to take some training, stamina, and perseverance. And teamwork."

His hands trailed up her arms, then took her breasts again. Weighing, cupping, he bit his lip and groaned while he explored with his hands.

Sliding against him, she found he was as ready to go again as she was. Snatching another condom from the box, she held it up and grinned.

11

Pass Interference

They'd made a pretty decent dent in the box. Haley stood in the massaging spray of the shower, her body warm and pliant from a lively night. Living on bartender time, Finn was still tangled in the sheets on her bed, or so she thought.

As she rinsed out her conditioner, the shower door opened behind her. Hard body pressed against her back, Finn wrapped his arms around her waist. Without releasing her, he grabbed the soap from the shelf and started to glide the slippery bar over her skin.

"I already did that part," she murmured.

His cheek against her, lips at her ear, he smiled. "You never can be too sure. Some areas may need multiple washings to get it exactly right." Driving his point home, he returned the soap and grazed his hands over her, scrubbing further down.

Scorching already at the electric, intimate caress, she gasped.

He let go long enough to turn her toward him, prop her leg up on the step, and drove his fingers into her slick folds in a fluid plunge, massaging her inside and out.

Holy shit, he was unpredictable; in such a good way. Like he was always thinking of ways to surprise her, to find what new ways to make her soar. Wow, had she ever even realized a man would do that? Would be so... selfless? Attentive? Sexy?

Finn seemed to do it whether it brought him anything or not. Although he seemed to enjoy her reaction. Thoroughly.

His fingers moved inside her, stroking rhythmically, following her cues until a rip-roaring orgasm shattered through her and she melted into his arms, panting as if she'd run a hundred-yard sprint.

Picking the soap back up, he worked up a lather on his own skin. "That's why my showers take so long."

She looked up at him like he was nuts. "Because you're sneaking up on sex-coma'd women and transforming them to a state of permanent orgasm?"

He grinned, running the soap down his long limbs. "Because I'm brainstorming the many ways I want to elicit that steamy look in your eyes."

Rinsing out the last of the conditioner, she rolled her eyes and lived the perma-smile to go with the perma-orgasm that was going to follow her around all day.

Grabbing her towel from the ledge, as she had yet to invest in a towel rack, she wrapped it around her. She pulled another from the cupboard and set it out for Finn.

Heading out, she grabbed a favorite pair of jeans and an airy tank from her piles against the wall. She considered making the bed, but accepted it was going to get messed up again before he left. Instead, she headed for the kitchen and set the coffee pot to brew.

She pulled out two stoneware mugs that she'd picked up from one of the local shops; the beginnings of her eclectic dishware design. Opening the fridge, she pulled out a package of eggs, tomatoes, diced green chiles, and... Oo, she'd almost forgotten about the read-to-eat chorizo she'd bought at Halseth's.

As she set the pan on the stove, she heard a vigorous knock at the door. Freezing, she held her breath, hoping they would give up and go away. Then a key in the front door. Crap. She knew she should have changed the locks when she moved in.

Breezing in like she still owned the place, Patricia hummed as she carted in a paper bag that smelled of Hattie's breakfast sandwiches. Sharp Tillamook cheddar, sausage patties, fried egg, and sourdough bread. The scent almost made Haley happy to see her mother. Almost, but not quite.

"Oh, I'm so glad you're up. I thought we'd have breakfast together."

"Mother. Hi. I, uh, now's really not a good time. Maybe tomorrow?" She forced her eyes not to wander toward the main bedroom, willing Finn to stay away.

"Nonsense. You haven't even started to make your... concoction yet. You can put that all back in the refrigerator and make it tomorrow instead."

The coffee pot chimed its success. Patricia's eyes went to the pot and saw two mugs waiting. "Hattie must have let you know I was coming and had forgotten coffee. What would I do without that woman?" Haley bit her tongue before uttering, *starve to death?*

"Really. Mother. Patricia. Not a good time. I will call you later."

"I was hoping you could show me how your vlog is coming along. I haven't seen any videos posted yet, so I wasn't sure if you were still serious about that."

"That's because I'm making a series before I post them, so I know I have something worth watching." *Please don't come out here. Please at least have clothes on if you do*, she silently willed Finn.

Her phone was on the counter. She snatched it and went to send him a text. Ha. Telepathy had nothing on the modern era of technology.

Shit, too late. Finn limped down the hall, his knee still sore from last night's activities. At least he was wearing pants, if not a shirt or shoes...

He froze when he saw Patricia, then pasted on a smile and kept walking, playing down the limp as he came closer. "Dr. Mallory. Hi. It's nice to see you."

Her spine shot ramrod straight. "Mr. Halseth. Well. I was not expecting you to be here. With my daughter... in such a state."

"Mother," Haley chided. The woman didn't possess a tactful bone in her body.

Patricia powered on, "I guess I didn't realize that Haley and you were in a relationship."

No stranger to Patricia's rudeness, as he'd mentioned before from growing up as a good friend of Grady's, he powered on, equally unaffected. "Wow, Dr. Mallory, that smells great. How is Hattie?"

"She is doing very well, thank you. Now—"

He peeked in the bag, then moved to the coffee pot and filled the mugs Haley had set out. "Dr. Mallory? Care for a cup?"

Did he just invite her mother for coffee? Haley shook her head, tempted to stomp her feet and plug her ears at the crazy surrounding her. "Mother. As I said, now is not a good time. I have company. If you'd like to come for breakfast another time, that's wonderful. I'll call you later and arrange something. For now, please. You absolutely cannot stay, especially if you're going to be rude to my guest."

Huffing, Patricia adjusted her silk scarf and let Haley walk her to the door. She stopped with her hand on the knob, then rested a fist at her side again. Whispering in an I-know-he-can-hear-me voice, Patricia started on the real lecture. "Haley. This isn't like you, hooking up with some *playboy*. You don't know how many women he must have slept with, a hedonist showboat gallivanting across the country.

He's no more trustworthy than Nate, maybe worse. If you're looking to date again, I know some wonderful men your age."

Haley reached around and opened the door for her mother. So humiliating. "Later."

Turning, she found Finn munching one of the breakfast sandwiches, coffee at his side, sitting on the fireplace hearth, as there was no place else to sit.

She slumped down next to him. "Some people swear their parents are from another planet. Mine really is. I don't know where that woman is from, but it's certainly not Earth. I'm sorry she was so rude to you."

"Haley? I've met enough people like Patricia over the years. Including Patricia. Trust me, I've heard a lot worse criticism. On national television and right in my face." He nudged her with his shoulder, setting down his breakfast and rising to his feet. He returned with the paper bag and the coffee he'd poured for her.

"Thanks." She snorted, "At least I know she won't tell any-one."

"If it helps, she's never liked me. I'm sure she'd reconsider if she saw my bank account. Although I'm no longer the mid-dle-class kid that distracted her son from whatever shit she'd enrolled him in, but instead as a hedonist athlete, I'd rather not win her over with practical financial investments and a pristine background check, maybe a few personal references from old girlfriends."

"Oh god no, that would make it so much worse. She'd drive right over and demand you propose on the spot. After she convinced you to take some job on SportsCenter or some-thing glamorous." She took a testing sip of coffee, realizing it was already cold, she converted that to a huge gulp. "I don't think she realizes her stiff expectations and snobbery are part of what drove me right to the repressed adulthood I'd let myself settle for. What would *your* mother say, finding you half naked in some married woman's desolately unfurnished house?"

"First, it's not desolate at all; it's got promise. Second, it's not your fault you're still married. Third, she'd undoubtedly meddle a bit. Must be a mom thing. Not that Pops isn't known to meddle now and again."

Meddle. Sure. Pops was probably watching the driveway already, waiting for the report. He'd try really, really hard to not turn on his GPS locator Finn had actually appreciated, spending so many years on the road. It was nice to have someone know where he was.

Nah, he probably turned it on halfway through his coffee. Nosy man.

Finn probably should head home. He had to work tonight. Instead, he indulged.

Pushing to his feet, he crumpled up their breakfast wrappers and did a quick tidy of the kitchen. Last night, after they'd finally gotten around to dinner—actually, a pretty great meal of roasted veggies and walnuts with chicken—they'd cleaned up their mess and left the kitchen spotless. The countertop was still a hideous pink tile, and the cabinets were sturdy but outdated. She'd already done all the floors in the house, painted the main rooms.

"What's your plan next? Furniture soon or the kitchen?"

Haley joined him, topping off her coffee and scanning the great room. "I would love to do the kitchen, but I need a place to sit. I had no idea it was possible to live with so little. But, the limited distractions have helped with my productivity. I'm officially months ahead on my posts."

"Need help with anything?"

"Most of the living room furniture should arrive Monday, and I'll piece it together in a few arrangements for the blog."

"Don't forget the vlog."

She blushed, biting her cheek. "I don't know. I've been working on it, but I feel silly. The blog is so anonymous, but a vlog... that's all me."

"I'm sure it's great. It's damn hard to decorate a place. People will appreciate some sound advice and classy ideas."

"Maybe. I'm going to do some creative edits before I upload anything. For now, I'm keeping the bulk of my focus on the blog."

"Can I see what you're working on?"

"Now?"

"Yeah. The blog. You ended your last post with a cliffhanger. Will the bathroom paint stay dark or dry to a spa-like finish?" He grinned, loving watching her reaction. She'd doubted he'd actually follow, but it was actually entertaining, full of humor and creativity.

"Who's stalking who?" She grabbed her laptop from her purse and set it on the countertop. At his side, she pulled up her unfinished post and stepped back, holding the coffee cup in front of her mouth. Watching his reaction.

So put-together, positive... he was beginning to suspect she worked damn hard to either hide or overcome her insecurities. Maybe she got it from Patricia, that need to make things look composed on the outside, or maybe it was from being the perfect housewife for years... or maybe she was just plain tough and didn't let things get to her.

At the top of the page, she had a high-definition wooden banner with pink flowers scattered across, her blog name at the top. Scrolling down, he found links by category and a crisp, colorful lead-in to the latest post. He scrolled down and was brought to a fucking fantastic pic, a side view of her standing in front of ripped up flooring and a half-painted blue wall with a huge blue smudge on her cheek, her adorable lopsided that was laced with ornery.

He knew she loved her work, and it showed. Part of him wanted to rage and fly down to San Francisco and kick Nate's ass through the uprights. Haley was smart and bright and creative... yet she'd dropped out of college because it hadn't worked with Nate's schedule. Fucking asshole. It's not that she needed college to prove anything, but the fact that the asshole hadn't considered her future as important as his...

Jaw clenched tight, he heard that familiar squeak that told him to calm the fuck down before he cracked a damn molar. Air heavy in his chest, he stepped back. Haley watched his expression, his fury, holding the coffee mug to shield her expression.

Shit. Stepping closer, he hooked his hands into the waistband of her jeans and looked her in the brilliantly blue eyes. "I like your blog. I think your vlog will be fantastic."

Nodding, she bit her cheek and stiffened.

"Haley?"

"Yeah?"

"I looked pissed off, didn't I?"

"Yes."

"I was just..." Wow, he wasn't good at this stuff.

Wasn't that what Trace had been telling him? He didn't know how to *be* there for her?

Haley's uncertainty ate away at him; didn't matter how crappy he was at this. She needed it. "I am fucking pissed off." He didn't lighten the strain in his voice. "You're brilliant. Clever. Creative. Seeing how amazing you are at design, at writing, well, it got me thinking. Mostly about how Nate's a fucking asshole. For so many reasons."

Setting the coffee down on the counter, she leaned into him. "I think that's the sweetest thing anyone's ever said to me."

Laughing, he wrapped his hands around her waist and brushed his lips over hers. "We've got, like, thirty-six condoms left. I've got a whole repertoire of moves and positions I've been wanting to try..."

"I've got a few I've been considering doing myself. We may have to take turns."

Groaning, he tipped his head back. "Oh please god say you just implied you've been considering doing yourself."

"Not what I meant. I can do that anytime... without a rebound and a big box of condoms." Her head tilted as she challenged him with that lopsided grin.

"But *I* don't get to watch you do that anytime. Please?"

"We'll see. Right now, I was more thinking about right here." Her hands braced against the kitchen countertop, biting her lip in pure flirty taunt.

"How about this? Right here, right now. Then I snag your extra garage door opener and head to work. Then I'll sneak into your bed tonight. Tomorrow, you can make me breakfast, maybe I can help around here, clearing the patio, whatever. But as soon as that furniture arrives, you treat me to a show on your new couch."

Tipping her head back in laughter, she shook him to his core with her delight.

12

Looking into the Backfield

Damn, he'd never seen such a sluggish clock in his life. Well, not off of a scoreboard when they were ahead by a point, two minutes to go, and the other team was nearing field goal range. He liked tending bar almost as much as he loved the game; if he didn't, he'd have found some other way to be a part of the family business like doing the books or something.

Either way, he really, really liked sex with Haley and couldn't wait for the stroke of midnight. Didn't help the pub was dead tonight. Some days, they took in enough revenue for the whole month in one insanely busy night, like the night Haley had pitched in. Other times, like tonight, they were open only to maintain their reputation and to satisfy the downtown business tenets.

Foothills was a tourist hub, but they'd always had enough of a local following to stay afloat if times got tough. Scott and Brenda had always smoked a hell of a salmon, sausage, jerky, cheddar... Pops wasn't ready to diversify their sales and sell to retail, but Finn brought it up now and again.

Speak of the devil. Pops strolled in, noting the empty tables, scowled, then parked front and center at the bar. "Vodka. Neat. No ice or lime or any shit that'll weaken it."

Pouring the drink, Finn didn't take his eyes off his dad. Scott looked... haggard. Tired. Not the mountain he usually was.

Sliding the drink across the bar, Finn held onto the glass, demanding an answer first.

"Come on. I can go to another bar. Give me the damn drink."

"Pops? I'll let go, when you tell me what gives."

"Nothin'."

"Come on. You're always the one to find a reason to smile when the rest of us choke." Finn let go of the glass, recognizing it was Scott's first for the night. And a short one at that.

"Are you happy? Tending bar?"

"Yeah. I am."

"But you could be so much more. I've given you time. You've been home for months. It's time to consider all your options." What had he been saying about meddling? Pops may not pressure, but he definitely meddled.

"Don't tell me you want to take back all of your old responsibilities? How many years did you and mom work sunrise to set and then some? Maybe it's time for you to share the load a bit."

"I can handle it. Don't get me wrong, it'll be nice to set my own schedule and not run myself ragged through football season. Evan and Zoe have taken on a huge share of the load. They'd been planning on it for years, this was sooner than they had intended. But you... you never wanted this."

Finn gripped his hands on the bar, clenching his jaw. Trying to keep it light, he nodded. "I never planned on anything after football."

"You're a good lookin' guy with a hell of a career under his belt. You could do whatever you want. You have, what, two teams waiting on your call for assistant coaching positions? Have you even scheduled yet? Hell, with your history, your personality and knowledge of the game, you could work at any of the sports networks. But if you ostrich for too long, they'll lose interest and you'll lose the opportunity."

"Can't say I've ever thought about doing anything but playing. And, well, I like what I'm doing now."

"As the neighborhood bartender that listens to old men wail about the woes of the world?"

Finn recognized this conversation wasn't ending anytime soon, certainly not tonight. He moved to the other side of the bar and took a stool next to Pops. "I don't know that I want to be on TV or behind the sidelines. Hell, I only played in the NFL because that's how grown-ups get to play serious ball."

"And get paid."

He nudged his dad with his knee. "And bank a ridiculous wad of cash doing what I love."

"Was it worth it? I watch you walk on that knee, run on that knee, do squats and burpees and push-ups in the backyard until you go pale."

"Not my first injury. Just the worst."

"Did it break your heart?" Pops raised his glass, his eyebrows raising in question.

"What?"

Raising his eyebrows again like Finn needed to catch-up quick, he reiterated, "Realizing you'd never play competitively again?"

"Fuck yeah. But I've got this great family. A dad that cares about what I want. A brother and sister that rag on me for being... well, for being their jackass big brother, but I know they've got my back no matter what. And..." He debated not saying it, but did anyway. "And I had a hell of a mom that watched every game I ever played. Parents that made sure I always had a home to come home to. That refused to let me stew and regret."

A half smile, Scott nodded, the red puffiness around his eyes confirming what Finn had suspected. Pops coped amazingly well, but Finn knew he kept a lot of it to himself. "I miss her."

"Me too." Finn rested his elbows on the bar, rubbing his hands through his hair. "She knew we'd be a mess without her. Think that's why she gathered us all back home together. She'd been patient while we spread our wings, but she wasn't about to let us grow apart."

Appearing from the kitchen, no doubt having been listening in the whole time instead of finishing her closing routine, Zoe leaned against the doorway and folded her arms. She didn't say a word, just listened.

Scott took another pull on the vodka. "Occur to you that we're still living day to day? We packed up her stuff like we were supposed to. Cleaned out her closet, kept what we could, donated what we should. Despite all that, she's still in the house, and we're not moving on."

Finn nodded. "I'm not sure she's leaving anytime soon."

"Nah, she's got her work cut out for her, getting you kids settled."

"Hey. I'm doing fine."

Leaned against the doorway to the kitchen, Zoe snorted from her post. She had always been his nosy little sister, and he had no doubt she would continue that role until they were gray and confused in the nursing home together.

He shot her a glare. "No?"

"No," she snorted again, arms more wrapped around her middle than crossed now. "I'm not sure what to make of you these days. You go to work here five to seven nights a week, beat your knee to crap every day, then taking an embarrass-ingly long shower."

He flipped her off.

"No really." She crossed and uncrossed her feet. "You look like you're doing all peachy on the outside, but that's what you always do when things get tough. You put on your game face and won't let the rest of us see what's going on underneath. I'm worried."

"About what?"

Pops nudged his knee, then drained his drink by half. "What really happened with Trace this time around? You didn't seem to make much effort to take her out like you used to; I hardly even saw her once you got back."

Now would be a great time for a last-minute customer.

Brenda had brought them all together at the end for a damn good reason. She was the heart and soul of their little family, and wouldn't rest easy until she knew they were going to keep each other in line. Took them a while, they'd lived so far away for so long, but they were in it together.

"When I got home, I was hurting. Bad. I'd been counting on another few years in the pros. Of being able to go for a decent run without limping for the rest of the day. Losing Mom was fucking shitty; something none of us will ever be okay with." Moving on wasn't an option; he'd always be missing that part of himself, as would they all.

Zoe nodded. "And Trace? You two were joined at the hip back in the day. This time, it's like you weren't willing to let her back in."

"Getting back together with Trace was a mistake. I never should have crossed that line. Never should have strung her along like that. But it's over now, and I'm glad she realized it before it was too late, that I don't deserve her."

Zoe countered, "Do you deserve Haley?"

He grimaced; her comment stabbed straight into his gut. "Watch it. Haley and I are... no, you know what? You're the one that said I should have a fling. Haley doesn't want anything from me, and I don't have any expectations from this whole thing. I'm having fun with a beautiful woman who makes me laugh. Isn't that the point of a fling?"

After a long-ass pause, Scott drained the last sip of his drink. "Mom would have had your back. No matter what. Unless you were being a douchebag. I'm glad you're happy, but there's more to life than a good lay."

Finn and Zoe both raised eyebrows at him. Even for a cool dad, that was a whole conversation he'd never expected. What dad said douchebag? He didn't even say it himself.

"Oh, shut it. You kids know what I mean. We need to live our lives. I've been doing a little soul-searching, trying to figure out what your mom would think of all that's going on with us these days. Finn, be careful with Haley. For her and for you. Don't string her along, but don't you doubt for a moment that you deserve to be happy. We all like Trace, but if she doesn't light your fire, then it's a good thing it ended before you were in too deep." Scott rose from the stool and walked to the door. Hand on the bronze plate by the lock, he gazed out at the empty street before turning back. "I'm kicking you kids out of the house. Not today. Not tomorrow. But it's time for tough love before you kill each other. Or drive me bonkers. You've got four weeks." He nodded to Finn. "Clock's tickin'. Better schedule those interviews, or not, if that's not the direction you choose to go. But don't dick around or time will make the decision for you."

Well shit. Is this how Pops treated his players on the high school team? Move your ass or get it handed to you. Finn rose from the stool and walked to the door. "What about you?"

"Me?"

"Yeah. Going to move out or make the house *yours*? I'm not saying you need to forget her, but you need to be you. As much as you loved Mom's taste, it was hers. Do you enjoy silk flowers and embroidered armchairs? What's going to make you happy?"

Zoe laughed from her post in the kitchen doorway. "Oh my. He is sleeping with an interior decorator, isn't he?"

"Shut the hell up," he shot back, biting his lip to mask his grin.

Scott nodded, considering. "Think she's available for hire? That she wouldn't mind helping create my man cave?"

Chuckling, Finn shook his head and flipped the sign to *Closed*. Close enough to quitting time. "I'll ask."

⚘

Wrapping around her like a warm summer breeze, Finn's strength, his unassuming snuggle pulled her from a strange dream as he rested his hand on her abdomen. Cuddling in tighter, she rested her hand over his. His lips brushed over her bare shoulder, soft, sleepy, and then he laid his head on the pillow behind her, holding her close.

Flashing through her veins like lightning, her chest ached, her pulse pounded in her ears, and her breath came faster than she could handle. Lightheaded, she squeezed her eyes shut to block the memories.

She hadn't done this in months.

Sensing her go stiff, Finn whispered, "Hey, you okay?"

Unable to speak for fighting back the tears that threatened to flood out of her eyes, she nodded.

"No, you're not. What's up?" His voice crooned against the darkness.

Sliding out of the sheets, she stole away to the bathroom. After splashing her face with cold water, she leaned against the counter and let rage overtake the panic. Why did she let him do this to her?

Giving it a few minutes until she was sure she had a handle on it, even if she was still furious, she turned the knob and shut the light back off. She tiptoed back to bed.

In the blue glow of the moon, Finn sat up in the bed, watching. Waiting.

Unable to get closer, her skin prickling, sensitive, she sat on the edge of the bed and stared blankly into the darkness of the backyard.

"Anything I can do?"

She shook her head.

"Something I did?"

She shook her head again, still not trusting herself to speak.

"Want me to go?" He murmured, a crackle in his voice.

"No," she whispered. Breathing in the cool night air, exhaling away the emotion she refused to succumb to, she said, "I'm sorry. Nothing you did. Well, nothing you did wrong. I'd suspected Nate was doing more than working late. Odd things he'd say. Sometimes he'd smell different, like he'd just showered and it wasn't our soap. Occasionally he'd wake me up and try to start something, but usually he'd stay at the far end of the bed and claim he was too tired if I tried to start something."

Finn didn't move, didn't speak, but simply let her speak.

"So, when you came in and cuddled up, nothing you wanted or didn't want, if that makes any sense... And you smelled..." She paused, not wanting to sound needy, but knowing she needed to say it out loud. "You didn't smell like someone else. You've got this invigorating scent like the alpine air at the top of a mountain, but it's cozy at the same time."

He chuckled softly. "And here I thought I smelled like sweat and sausage and stale liquor."

Her breath coming easier, her pulse no calmer from thrill rather than fury, she laughed. "That too, but... in a good way."

"We could go take another shower. I've got lots of shower fantasies."

She couldn't help but laugh again. "Maybe in the morning. I'm sorry for unloading on you. I think that might be against the rebound rules. Aren't we supposed to keep things light?"

He moved close and sat behind her, wrapping his legs around either side of her, his arms linked around her middle. "I think that's the reason for a rebound. There's a lot of baggage that needs unloading, and the rebound is supposed to help you find yourself again."

"I like that." She leaned into him, drawing in his heat, his unaffected affection.

"Haley?"

"Yeah?"

"While you and I are doing what we're doing, until we've said we're done with this, I have no intention of being with anyone else. Besides, I don't know how anyone finds the time, or the deviousness it takes to string people along like that. Or why. I mean, I understand holding on when it should be over, I've been there. But if the sex isn't incredible, if the conversation isn't stimulating, or even something as basic as interests not aligning and it's not working, break the fuck up."

"Finn? I like you."

He laughed and kissed her shoulder.

"Busy night tonight?"

"Not at all, actually. Pops swung by to get hammered, but, instead, he and Zoe blitzed me."

"Ouch. How come?"

"Worrying that I'm going to ostrich my way through life. About not expressing how much life has sucked the last six months. Losing my career, then having that grieving process completely obliterated by losing Mom. Working long hours at the pub, getting together with my old girlfriend and then blowing it. Hell yeah, I miss football, but I knew it was going to end someday. I like the pub. I don't know that I want to move across the country to coach, but I guess I've never tried. I miss football. More than anything, I miss Mom like crazy, but I don't think there's anything I can or want to change about that; that's part of losing a loved one. Why would I want to let her go?"

His hands rested on her thighs, his thumb mindlessly tracing circles on her skin. He continued, "At first, we all were frozen, not wanting to touch anything of hers or even admit that she was gone. I didn't leave the house for a while, didn't call anyone. Then I gradually followed the path of least resistance, tending bar most nights, hanging out with my family, my ex. Your brother and the guys started dragging me out of the house. Things let up a bit. Still, I didn't have enough in me to balance a relationship, so I got dumped. Eventually, my family, we sort of cleaned everything of Mom's up in a frenzy; I packed all her books and crafts and other stuff no one else would use. Zoe cleaned out her closet. Most of it was donated, other stuff put up in the attic."

"You got dumped in the middle of all that? Awfully callous of her."

"No, it wasn't like that. I mean, yeah, it kind of was, but she dumped me rather palliatively, like she knew I wasn't up to giving her what she needed, so she let me off the hook. I was a shitty boyfriend. Honestly? She was ready to pick up right where we left off, like we hadn't grown into adulthood without each other. Lucky for us both, she recognized I wasn't capable of being there for her, that I was still working on finding myself again, so she ended it."

"You know what I like about you?"

"What's that?"

"You got dumped in the middle of huge life changes, and instead of being angry or resentful, you're complimenting the woman that did it. As long as you're not blaming yourself, I admire your lack of negativity."

"I could. But that wouldn't get me anywhere either."

"When my dad died, about a year or so after Nate and I got married, I fell apart. Depressed, angry, it took months before I felt like me again. I still miss him like crazy and have an occasional rough day thinking about how things should have gone. I think it's okay to grieve how and when you need to.

I think losing him and not letting myself accept it, that's part of why I let go of myself, why I became what Nate wanted. I was too busy missing Dad and isolating myself and eventually, Nate was all I had left, and he wasn't worth it. I could blame myself for not standing up for *me* sooner, but I completely, one hundred percent, no shadow of a doubt, blame Nate."

He chuckled, "Tell me how you really feel."

She leaned into him, his bristly cheek caught her hair as he kissed her temple. "Okay, so I wish I had confronted him sooner, that I had recognized that he was gradually knocking down the parts of me he didn't care for, manipulating me to be what he wanted. I can't say he did it intentionally. But, well, he was the asshole that didn't give a damn about my hopes or needs."

"I want to meet him."

"What? Why?"

"I'm curious what makes that asshole tick, to have not just cheated, but have blown it big-time. Emotionally abusive narcissistic asshole. Mostly though, I want to feel my fist breaking his face."

"You're so sweet."

"I'm a romantic, ask anyone."

She didn't say it out loud, but he was a romantic. She'd never felt so special as she did with him. "I'm tired."

"Me too."

He flipped back the covers, and they curled up together. Slider open to the cool air, listening to the resonant hum of a cleansing summer rain, she snuggled against him as sleep washed over her.

13

Special Teams

What kind of asshole texts a bartender at seven in the damn morning? Finn leaned over the side of the bed and snatched his phone from the pocket of his jeans.

Across the bed, Haley's phone chirped an incoming message.

Who in the hell would be texting them both? Grady. Typical. *Happy Saturday. Let's all go hiking. Riverside Trailhead at 0800.*

Haley groaned as she read the message. A text from her popped up on the group message, *Make it 0900.*

He chuckled as they were both dangling off the opposite sides of the mattress, texting with their phones still on the floor. He added another message, *Agreed, but if you make it 1000, I'll bring food.*

Asher's message came through next, *Zane's on beer.*

Another from Lincoln, *I'm not defending you if we get caught drinking on a very well trafficked federal trail.*

Grady texted again, *Nor are you living with me again if you get fired. Let's make it the old logging road off Tahoma instead.*

Pippa chimed in, *Beer is the priority? What are we, eighteen?*

And from Sophie, *Pip, we all know you didn't touch that stuff at 18.*

Finally, from Zane, *Not to worry, Pippa, I'll bring you an apricot lager.*

Before all the blood had completely pooled in the top of his brain, Finn sat up. Haley beat him to it by half a second. She tossed her phone to the end of the bed and nudged him with her foot. "They do this a lot?"

He nodded. "I've been back six months, and yes, yes they do."

"Grady and Claire had informed me I was going to have awesome friends that wouldn't have monthly girls' night in which we exchanged recipes and sex tips, only for me to later realize they were all using those tips on my husband."

Shuddering, Finn swallowed the nausea that threatened, imagining Haley surrounded by pretentious bitches that were fucking each other's spouses behind their backs. "What an asshole. No, most of this crew is happily relationshipped and not the sort to do that anyway."

At his side, Haley bit her cheek like she wanted to say something she hadn't quite worked out yet. "I'm not one to keep secrets, you know, the old 'secrets secrets are no fun?' But... wow, I really don't want to sound like a bitch or anything, but..."

"But you don't want to let on that we're rebounding together?"

"Exactly. I'm not interested in long-term plans or expectations, and you have indicated you are of the same opinion..."

"But the others will get all excited and start scheming?"

"Precisely."

"Then we are in complete agreement. Besides, while we're sounding like callous jackasses, I uh, I've only been officially single a very short time. If they knew I was hooking up with Grady's little sister without any intention of making an honest woman of her, while still fresh out of blowing a no-brainer relationship?" He visibly shivered. He threw his legs over the side of the bed and searched for his boxers.

"An honest woman? I'm considering being offended," she teased.

"Hey, I'm just anticipating potential older brother judgment. You can do whatever you'd like to my body, whenever and however, and I will be happy to do the same for you. That has no bearing of your status as an empowered, respectable woman."

She hopped off the bed and strutted gloriously naked, stopping inches in front of him, hands on her hips with snarky rebellion. Gazing up, he hooked his hands around her legs and trailed his fingertips up the backs of her thighs. She rolled her eyes. "Finn?"

He leaned forward and trailed his tongue along the line of her quad. She may not think she had muscle, but damn, she was so wrong. "Yeah?" he asked, nipping where he'd licked.

Chuckling, she said, "I don't have the slightest fear about you ever lying to me." Backing out of his reach, she headed into the bathroom.

He gave her a minute, waited for the shower to flip on, then snuck on in. And she was clearly expecting him. After a very, very long shower in which she did some very creative actions with her mouth and fulfilled another of his shower fantasies—yes, he had a list—they were running way behind schedule.

Her living room was packed with furniture, mostly in boxes waiting to be assembled, all stacked against one wall. Stopping in the middle, he turned around. "I'm sorry, I was going to help you with the furniture today."

Haley shrugged. "No worries. I'm ahead on my posts any-way, so it can wait."

"Yeah, but I keep distracting you."

"I haven't gone hiking in ages and would rather get outside. How about we'll hike today, then you can help me tomorrow before you head to work. Have you been to the old logging road off Tahoma?"

Strolling to the entry, he snagged his shoes from the boot tray she'd placed next to the door to the garage. "Of course. Foothills' equivalent of make-out point. Lost my virginity off that trail."

She giggled. "I guess I was too young for that last time I lived here."

"There are many great spots to sneak out of sight and see everything nature has to offer." Standing on one foot, he pulled on his shoe and pulled the laces tight.

She wandered to the kitchen and grabbed two mugs from the cupboard. "Perhaps not this time, but you'll have to show me the good spots one of these days."

He accepted a cup and looked over the massive open space where a living room should be. "I can crash here tonight, so I can give you a hand with this before I go to work tomorrow? If you want help."

She shook her head and grinned at him. "You are in quite the hurry to use up that box of condoms."

"I wouldn't say I'm in a hurry, but I'd hate for any to go unused. What a waste that would be." He pulled her in for a last taste, hating that he was going to have to behave himself for the rest of the day. "Meet you there?"

"Yeah. You sure you want to take your pretty car off-road-ing? From the sounds of things, that road isn't any more main-tained than it was when I was a kid."

"I'll snag a ride with Asher; he lives right down the road from me." He stole one more last kiss, then headed out.

Back home, his siblings were at the breakfast table, his dad scrolling on his phone. Probably on Facebook again. Guy was hooked on social media; his Instagram posts were hilarious.

Finn hiked upstairs and changed into athletic clothes, pulling on his knee brace, and popped a few ibuprofen in anticipation of a rough day. Asher had agreed to pick him up on the way out; a little too eagerly, actually.

In the kitchen, Finn packed a collection of soft-sided coolers with sandwiches with some of the new recipes Pops and Evan were trying out, added some chips, fruit.

Pops sauntered into the kitchen, watching him pack the ten-person meal. "Hungry?"

"Ha. No. Going hiking."

"With Haley? I know she's been to the pub a few times, but do you think she'll eat all that?"

"Smartass. Yes, she will be there, but Grady and Zane and the others will be there too. It's your fault for having all this good food around. Whenever I go out with the gang now, I'm volunteered to cater."

"Huh. You're with Haley a lot lately."

"Yep."

"Huh."

Ignoring whatever Pops was getting at, Finn threw in the icepacks and tossed the bags into a box, putting his lunch, plus a few water bottles, into his backpack. Asher's truck crunched over the gravel drive, saving him from having to dwell on his dad's implications. Nowhere in the rebound rules did it mention you had to limit the time you spent together. Wasn't that the point? A whole lotta sex with someone that made you feel... alive? Without any pressure or judgment?

Dashing outside, he found Asher's shiny truck in the drive, engine still running. Asher and Sophie sat in the cab, leaned into each other, visiting intimately over the center console while they waited. They were good together, no weirdness like so many relationships. He'd never once heard them argue about where or when or who, never criticizing or doubting. No puppy eyes wishing for a little affection that wasn't coming.

He hopped in the backseat. "Thanks for the lift."

Shifting into reverse, Asher grinned while he backed out of the drive. "It's entirely selfish. Let me drive that Shelby of yours, and I'll chauffeur you around anytime."

"No way, no how. How about I cover your tab next time you come to the pub instead?"

"I suppose that'll do. For now. You off today, or need to rush back?"

"Nah, I'm off. Pete's been wanting more hours. Baby on the way."

Asher shifted into gear and headed toward the mountains. Sophie turned in her seat, her wildly brown-blond hair pulled back into a ponytail. "You don't have to answer if you think I'm being nosy, but, all okay in your world these days?"

There were few that he would share with, but Sophie had been through more hurt than anyone else he knew, and Asher wasn't far behind. "Yeah. Actually, it's a really good day."

"Glad to hear it. Your dad doing okay?"

"Yeah. He's thinking of converting the family room into a man cave."

"Impressive." She smiled, settled comfortably as she visited. He could see Asher's hand reach across and rest on her knee. "I'm not prying, I promise. You can tell me to shove off, but have you heard from Trace at all?"

Only Sophie could get away with the personal questions, who knew why. Although, it may be because she was his accountant and knew a lot of personal information because of that. Aside from Haley; Haley was an open book with him and he couldn't help but be the same with her. Rebound thing. "Nope. You know we broke up, right?"

"I know. Pip was telling me how you guys were joined at the hip all through high school, so I wondered how things were going. Not that we were gossiping, but I think the consensus is that the break-up is temporary while she's out of town and you get your shit together. But, I have to say, you guys seemed... I don't know. Dull. No offense; I don't find either of you dull individually."

"None taken." Out the window, he took a long pull of fresh oxygen as they drove across a narrow bridge, the river raging underneath, particularly white-capped today, thanks to the heavy rains last night. "I didn't have the capacity to focus on the relationship."

Slowing as they approached the camouflaged road, Asher turned and hopped out, swinging open the unlocked metal gate.

Sophie glared, not at Finn, but in general. "I don't think that's how it works. A heart doesn't care if the timing is convenient. Especially if you're hurting. It sounds more like an excuse. I love you, and I love Trace, but do me a favor? If she doesn't set your hair on fire, don't get back together when she gets back in town."

Hopping back in, Asher didn't close the door all the way, but rolled past the gate, then hopped back out to close it again.

Finn nodded. "You're not wrong. It was a very polite excuse to avoid hurt feelings. Honestly? Whatever we had all those years ago? It's different now." She was right. It shouldn't take so much work. Hell, maybe it was because Haley was a fling, rebound, whatever, but he didn't feel like he had to work at it.

Asher and Sophie didn't look like they had to work at affection or the other critical pieces. Sure, they probably fought like everyone else. The Halseth home had shaken with some shouting matches over the years, but the love came easy.

Asher climbed back in. Sophie added, "If you want to talk, we've both been through a lot of loss. And dull relationships. Well, me anyway. I'm not sure Asher knew the meaning of the word before I hooked my claws in him."

Grabbing her knee again, Asher subtly squeezed a ticklish spot until she squealed.

"Anyway," she continued, shifting out of his reach. "It should be as easy as breathing. Not the relationship. Any relationship should have ups and downs and doubts. But the knowing that it's right."

Both hands back on the wheel as the truck bounced in every damn direction, Asher checked the rearview and caught his eye. "That sounded heavy. You seeing someone?"

Finn blushed. He actually blushed. That was a damn first. "No comment?"

Asher hooked a right as the path narrowed. "That may work on Grady or Lincoln, but cops require answers."

Flipping him off, Finn unsuccessfully masked a grin. "I don't kiss and tell."

Sophie laughed and turned around in her seat. "You'll be okay, Halseth."

B umping down the overgrown logging road, slipping and sliding over the muddy path, Haley drove the overpriced SUV through a huge puddle that was so deep it may technically be considered a pond, then her engine roared as she drove up the other side. Nate would be horrified as mud splattered all over the shiny black finish.

Grinning from ear to ear, squealing as her tires spun out, then caught a moment's traction on solid ground, she gripped the wheel and roared with satisfaction. What was the point in having such a badass vehicle, if she only drove it to and from the shops? Her grin grew to a lip-biting growl as she clawed her way out of the Nate-hole another inch.

The others were parked and gathering their gear as she joined them in the clearing. Her gaze landed right on Finn.

Something dynamic about him; or maybe it was the subtle grin as he stood with his backpack on, arms crossed, flashing her a secret wink as she hopped out of the car.

Tossing her backpack over her shoulder, she looked up at the crystal-clear sky, felt the breeze brush over her skin, still cool thanks to last night's welcome downpour. "Beautiful," she remarked to no one in particular.

Grady strolled over and reminded her who everyone was, as she'd met a few only the one time, at the awful gala her mother had thrown last January, when they had told Patricia that Haley was getting a divorce and that Claire had swapped brothers. Awkward was the theme of the night. It was tough to keep up, as so much had changed since she'd spent any calculable amount of time in Foothills. Freya had married Zane, the hunky ex-Navy SEAL that owned Black Op Brewing with Grady and the creativity behind the delicious brews she'd been sampling at Halseth's. Sophie, Asher's fiancée, was her new accountant, and they'd clicked immediately. Lincoln and Pippa were both friends from the old neighborhood. "And you met Finn at Halseth's."

Nodding, she swallowed the blush that threatened. Been there, done that. In many interesting ways. Hell, she'd even bought the t-shirt.

Finn stepped closer, but stayed far enough away to remain platonic. "Actually, we're old friends now. She's a huge Fire fan. Just saying. Think she was a little star-struck."

She rolled her eyes and was tempted to sock him. Shit like that was going to give it away and ruin the no-pressure aspect. "Ha. Maybe a little. But that was only after a few Black Op pints." She turned to Zane who was loading up a backpack that looked twice as heavy as hers. "The citrus brew was good, but the double hop was amazing."

Tilting his head with a subtle smile, he nodded. "The Olympic? A personal favorite of mine, too. I've got a few in the pack."

"Dibs." She quirked up the corner of her mouth as she staked her claim.

Finn pulled an insulated lunchbox out of his backpack and came around behind her. Without asking, telling, or saying a word, just his amused grin, he opened her pack and stuffed in the bag. Patting her backpack when he was done, he came around and stood next to her. The others headed into the trees beyond.

Finn hung back and walked next to her. She stayed away, her hand feeling oddly awkward, like a little magnet inside was reaching to link hands with him. "Subtle," she muttered out of the corner of her mouth.

He shrugged, looking downright pleased with himself. "I couldn't resist. Besides, they'll see right through us if we pretend we're not friends."

"Fair point." They followed after the others, the tall grass bristly against her bare legs. Inhaling every molecule she could fit in her lungs, she exhaled on a slow, satisfied breath. Damn, she'd missed the northwest. Stopping in the middle of the field, she looked up and closed her eyes, running her fingers through her hair, letting the sun wash over her skin like a hot shower.

At her side, Finn stopped in place, watching her savor the moment with his mouth hanging open.

She rolled her eyes. "Again. Subtle."

He bit his cheek and started walking again. "Your fault. I really like your hair. And your lips. And your breasts..."

She picked up the pace to catch up to the others. As she reached them, entering the canopied grove around the creek, Grady teased, "Such a city girl. Keep up."

"I'll have you know, I may have been one hundred percent out of shape a few weeks ago, but home renovation is hard work." She pulled up the short sleeve of her pink t-shirt and flexed her bicep. "Check that out. I almost have a muscle that you can see."

Claire released her lower lip from her teeth and smiled. "Nice. Maybe you won't need help getting all that furniture moved in."

Crap. Finn was going to help in the morning. "Thankfully, the delivery company brought everything inside, so it's more sliding." Phew. Close one.

They strolled along the creek until they came to a wide log that spanned the creek. Hopping onto it like he was part antelope, Asher started across. Following behind with equal grace, Sophie made it look like she did this all the time. Freya walked easily over in her barefoot-style walking shoes, Zane not hesitating either. Pippa squealed as she climbed on, both arms spread wide as she tried to steady herself. Lincoln laughed out loud and followed behind, but she made it okay.

No problem. Just like... nothing in her recent past. House-wives didn't cross raging rivers.

Growling at herself, she tightened her backpack straps and stepped up. Trophy wives didn't do a lot of things. If she couldn't cross a freaking log over a babbling brook, she may as well rejoin the phony sluts she used to call friends.

The log seemed pretty secure. Didn't wiggle as she stepped on. Hell, this thing was almost as wide as a sidewalk.

One foot in front of the other, she made it a quarter of the way across, before her legs started to tremble more violently than the log. Finn hopped on. The log shook like a blade of grass. This was no Golden Gate. Swallowing a squeal, she squatted and grabbed on with all fours.

She felt Finn easing closer, trying not to cause anymore shaking. She felt like such a wimp, but she couldn't budge, imagining one slight slip and crashing into the rocky creek. This sucked. Twenty years ago, she would have danced across the log.

Now... now the adventurous girl she'd been was as lively as a squashed bug. She wanted to sit down and cry that the stupid log scared the hell out of her. It wasn't even that far of a drop.

Panic bubbled up in her chest as the last decade of her life came crashing down. Despite the mask she wore, she was still struggling to fumble her way back to life.

Finn's rumbling voice crooned behind her. "You got this, Haley. Ease on up and stand with your feet turned out. Fourth position, right? Didn't you say you were in ballet?"

"Fourth. I can do fourth." She positioned her feet and rose to stand.

"Pick a focal point on the other side and keep your eyes on it like you're spotting a turn. Arms out, feet turned out, roll toe to heel, like you're walking across the stage." He held his ground, knowing any movement would have her right down on her hands again.

"Someday you'll have to explain how you know so much about ballet." She held steady, not breaking form as she crossed. It had been a long time, but the movement felt natural.

He chuckled from his post on the log. "How do you think I run on my toes so well?"

As she reached the other side, Grady held his hand out for her. She shook her head and released the breath she'd been withholding. "Thanks, but I got it."

He ran his fingers through his surfer blond hair and stepped back.

Leaping off, she landed almost gracefully, then put her hands on her hips and grinned.

Grady beamed, "There's that stubborn girl I used to know." He yanked her close and knocked the air out of her lungs with a bear hug. Voice hoarse, he said, "Not the time, I know. But I was afraid that bastard had beat her out of you."

Hot briny tears coated her eyes. She whispered, "He never hit me."

Still holding her close, her brother murmured, "Not with his fists. But I helplessly stood watch as he carved you into what he wanted. If I'd realized sooner..."

She pulled back to look at him, biting her lips together before she reached full quaver. "I hate that I let him. That *I* didn't realize sooner."

Grady's aquamarine eyes were heavy, his cheeks clenched tight. "You didn't *let* him. Shit, Haley. No one plans for anything like that. I remember when you guys got married. He practically kissed the ground you walked on. When I saw you the following Christmas, you were all smiles, but there was something missing. Then your dad died, and you were lost. Each time I saw you, less and less often, you'd slipped further from the girl you were."

"You tried to tell me." She offered a watery smile, hating that it had taken ten years and a rickety log. "But I wouldn't listen. I had everything I ever wanted. Wealth, a husband that put me on a pedestal, a social life." It hadn't been what she'd hoped. A trophy wife that knew how to schmooze, a yes-wife, an entitled hedonist.

Grady shook his head. "Don't you talk like that. You were making the most of a shitty situation. It just took him crossing that last line for you to wake up and remember who you are."

She took a deep breath and tried to let it go. To remember where she was and enjoy the day.

Crossing closer, Freya linked arms with her. "If you ever need anyone to kick his ass, give me a call."

Smiling, Haley nodded. "Happily, but I get first dibs at his smug face." She hated feeling helpless, but now, she felt a little less vulnerable.

She'd been furious, ready to crumble the day she'd walked in and found him with her best friend. He hadn't even cared that she was due home any minute.

Within days, once she'd declared it was over, she'd felt such a weight lifted. She hadn't even realized how oppressive the burden had become.

Turning, she saw Finn waiting perched on the log, listening. A soft smile on his face, a richness in his chocolaty eyes told her in one look that he had her back. With a few graceful steps worthy of a prima ballerina, he crossed the creek and hopped to the ground, most of his weight absorbed by his good leg.

Haley took a sharp breath, blowing out the knots that tangled in her gut. "I'm hungry. Let's go."

14

Fumble

Zigzagging up the gentle slope, they joked and let the past blow away in the breeze. Finn had missed Foothills even more than he had realized. He'd come back regularly over the years, but didn't see his friends much. A lot were still out of town or, like he and Trace, had grown apart. Asher had always been in San Diego, or all over the world when deployed as a SEAL. Grady and he had mostly been sports friends, as Grady had been a few years ahead in school, so they easily lost touch. With Trace, they'd tried the long-distance thing for a few months, but college football plus academics had overshadowed everything else.

Three or four shifts into tending bar, Grady and Claire had met up at Halseth's with Asher and Sophie. Like so many of the wounded animals she tended to, Claire had roped him into their little social circle.

Ahead on the trail, Haley walked next to Zane, laughing as he told her some comical spin on a war story. Damn, she had a nice ass, some great legs in those tiny shorts.

Behind them, Grady was telling him something about... wait, what was he talking about?

Haley tightly crossed her arms, rubbing her hands over her goose-bumped skin. Without thinking, Finn opened his backpack and snatched out a sweatshirt. Catching up, he reached around her and handed her the sweatshirt, then lagged back with Grady.

A soft, "Thanks," and she handed Zane her backpack while she pulled on the sweatshirt.

As they reached a clearing at the top of the hill, they reconnected with the terminus of the old logging road. A cluster of boulders marked the end of the trail, the view beyond was unparalleled. Jagged peaks lined the distance, the hill they stood upon felt miniscule by comparison.

Freya bounded ahead, picking out the tallest perch of the bunch for her picnic. Chuckling, Zane set his backpack on the ground and unzipped, revealing a can of beer for each of them.

Pippa rolled her eyes. "I still can't believe you packed that crap all this way for a picnic."

Offering her one, he asked, "Weighs a hell of a lot less than a ruck and body armor."

She accepted the apricot lager he'd carted up the hill for her and shook her head, smiling despite her feigned sarcasm. "I guess."

Finn didn't roll his eyes, but he was tempted. Pippa was such an odd addition to the crew. Sweet, bossy, often judgmental, yet was always game for adventure.

Haley claimed one of the smaller boulders with enough room for her and her alone. Yeah, probably a good idea. Her shorts were hidden under his sweatshirt that ended at her mid-thighs, plus she was flushed and sweaty like they'd just spent hours in her bedroom. Or the shower. Or the kitchen. Living room floor. They hadn't gone upstairs yet, but he was willing to check it out.

Asher dug into his lunch bag, loading up a slice of sour-dough with smoked salmon and cheddar. "Aw, Finn, you're so adorable. Did you leave me a little note wishing me a good day?"

Finn flipped him off and took a swig of his beer. "Hey, you want me to bring food, I'm doing it right. Be sure all those lunch bags and icepacks make it back to me or it's all over."

Licking a dribble of chipotle sauce off her finger, Haley said, "I never got notes from my mother in my lunch."

Grady sneered, "Yeah, that would have been a little too maternal. I wouldn't have wanted to open it anyway; it would have said something about 'don't forget to chew with your mouth closed.'"

Cracking open the IPA Haley had dibs'd, she rolled her eyes. "At least she would have cared enough to write something. Trace's mom included a note every Monday, including a little doodle to make her laugh."

Churning in Finn's gut annihilated his appetite. He held his beer in front of his mouth as a shield, terrified she'd see his reaction. Fighting the weird emotion that rocked him like a damn earthquake, he downed the rest of the beer in one gulp in a pathetic attempt to distance himself.

From his other side, Pippa laughed. "I'd forgotten about that. I miss her already. Did you catch her before she left? You two were thick as thieves."

Haley nodded. "It was great. Grady tipped her off that I was miserable and coming home and needed a friend. I'd been so nervous to come home after so long. Hearing her voice, remembering what goofballs we'd been was like a door opening, reminding me that I used to be fun."

The familiar rage, wanting to rip out that asshole Nate's spine roared in his chest as he imagined how that asshole had torn her down. Throwing off his equilibrium, in a nauseat-ing contrast, was the realization that they shared the same childhood friend, but from vastly different parts of childhood.

Shit, he remembered that first day at a new school, how he and Trace had instantly connected because she'd been lonely without her best friend and he was all alone in a new town.

Haley had brought Trace and him together. Now, Trace had brought Haley and him together. He hadn't even considered that they'd known each other. If he had, he wouldn't have dreamed that Haley was *that* friend of Trace's that he'd heard so many stories about.

He had no doubt that Haley didn't have a clue. If she did… no, she'd freak. Hadn't she caught Nate with her friend? And that he'd slept with most of her friends?

Yeah, she'd kill him. But she would absolutely never talk to him again if he lied to her. But what, was he going to say? *By the way, Haley, the woman I'm rebounding from is your oldest friend. But I'm sure she won't mind.*

Fuck, that sounded so crass. Didn't this whole twisted triangle break the rebound rules? But he wasn't ready to give Haley up. Not yet.

Forcing down the last few bites of his sandwich, he hopped down and tossed his lunch bag into his backpack, then brushed the lingering crumbs from his hands. He leaned against the boulder, blocking out the chipper chatter from the others, trying to figure a way out of the mess he'd made.

After repacking her backpack, Haley was all smiles, her expression relaxed, shoulders back. She strolled to the edge and breathed in the endless air like she had at the beginning of the hike. Sophie stood at her side, linking arms and whispering something. Who knows what. They'd only met a few weeks ago, and they seemed like they'd been friends for years. But that was Haley. Was there anyone that didn't instantly open up and feel completely at ease, absorbing her smile and warmth?

An ear-piercing snap, like a cluster of firecrackers downslope, echoed in his skull. Asher and Zane stilled, alert, one scanning the horizon and the other the forest behind them.

In a blink, Haley and Sophie disappeared. The edge of the hill collapsed so damn fast.

Pulse pounding so loud he couldn't hear himself think, Finn sprinted toward the edge.

Teetering as close as he dared, he held his breath and leaned out, desperate, swallowing the sheer panic that threatened to engulf him.

Scanning the debris, he caught sight of her. Maybe ten, fifteen feet below, Haley and Sophie lay sprawled in a pile of rubble where the slope evened out before declining again twenty yards out.

Heart lurching in his chest, he searched for a way to reach her without making it worse. Fuck, if he could dive straight over, he would in a heartbeat, but the flimsy bit of logic left in his brain held him back. Not risking going straight over, or else he send more rocks down on them, he dashed to the left.

Leaping over the ledge, he rode the steep slope foot after foot, sliding and hoping to hell he didn't cause another landslide. A knife-edged throb tore at his knee, but adrenaline numbed the pain.

Reaching the flat, he barreled over a boulder like a damn pile-on over a fumble, shoving off and launching toward Haley. Asher appeared from the other side.

"Haley, hey, you okay?" Finn dove to her side, assessing the slope carefully as he moved closer. All clear. Whatever was going to come loose had already toppled.

Sitting up, looking shell-shocked, Haley nodded. "Yeah. Yeah, I'm okay." Turning sharply as she began to take in what could have happened, her hands reached to steady herself as she turned to look for Sophie.

Sophie sat up, Asher already talking to her and assessing a gash on her thigh. She was as scraped and bruised as Haley. Asher looked calm on the surface, but Finn could see his eyes frantically scanning, terrified.

Haley turned back to Finn, eyes still wide as she took in the crazy pile of rubble that surrounded her. A trickle of blood streamed down from a half inch laceration on her forehead. Ripping off his sleeves, Finn used the scraps of fabric to wipe away the blood before it reached her eye.

As he held pressure over her wound, she looked up at him, her expression muddled with something dark, clashing with her natural humor.

He held up his hand. "How many fingers am I holding up?"

"Twelve," she mocked, the corner of her mouth quirking up.

"Sorry, looks like you've got a concussion. I'll have to call in a helicopter to get you out," he teased, the humor not quite calming the pounding in his temples.

"Smartass. I'm fine. I mean, I hurt everywhere and am not looking forward to finding what all is black and blue tomorrow." She groaned as she moved her legs. Pouting adorably pitifully, she added, "Or what isn't. Ow."

"Seriously though, you probably have a concussion. Did you lose consciousness?"

"No, just stunned."

"Think you can climb up and hike back down?"

"Really, I think I'm fine." Her own laugh jarred her, and she winced. "You might be right on the concussion bit, but I'm okay."

"Right. Okay. Try to stand up and let's see how you do." He released the fabric from her head, checking the blood had slowed enough for now.

She groaned as she stood, slower than usual, but she seemed okay. Taking a step toward the slope he'd come down, she did fine at first, but the moment her right foot hit the ground, she hissed. "Ouch. And an ankle sprain."

"How bad?" He laced his arm around her, blotted the blood that had trailed down again, then held steady for her.

Holding her own weight, she tried the foot again. Again, she hissed, but completed the step without wavering. "Not bad."

"Well, I've had a few dozen sprains over the years, trust me, don't push it. If you can get back to the cars on it, we'll ice it tonight and you can pop a few ibuprofen."

"Okay." She nodded, looking up at him. Her hair was a muddy mess. His sweatshirt was coming apart at the arm where she must have gotten caught on a rock on the way down. Nausea filled his stomach, threatening to pitch out his lunch as he pictured what could have happened, how that sleeve could have been her skull. Still, whatever she got caught on might have slowed the fall enough that she wasn't worse off.

Steadying her, even though he seemed to need it more than she did, he wrapped his arms around her waist. Running his thumb across her forehead, he brushed her hair out of her face and dabbed the trail of blood again.

Turning, she looked up the hill. Unable to let go, he followed her gaze.

The others stood staggered, far enough back from the ledge to avoid triggering another slide. Grady wore a puzzled expression, somewhere between *I'm going to kick your ass,* and something less antagonistic. Maybe appreciative, but it was too soon to tell, as he looked as stunned as the rest of them.

Haley took the scrap of sleeve from his trembling hand and wiped her own forehead this time, then stuffed it in her pocket. Asher and Sophie were climbing up the other side, Sophie a bit wobbly, limping a bit more than Haley, but good.

Finn stayed within arm's reach. As the adrenaline waned, his knee threatened to give out if he moved wrong.

Halting, Haley glared down at his knee. "Dammit, Finn. You didn't wreck your knee, did you?"

Shaking his head, he denied everything.

She raised her eyebrows, resting her hands on her hips. The dust coating her like Pigpen from Peanuts took the threat out of the admonishment, but she looked damn cute doing it. Maybe she'd let him help clean her up later in a long, hot shower.

"Okay, so it's a bit angry. We'll both sport icepacks and ibuprofen with our legs propped up tonight."

Smiling and shaking her head, wincing from the concussion that was undoubtedly going to hurt for the next few days, she turned and continued the climb back up to the others.

Sophie and Asher reached the top of the other side of the peak just before they did, looking equally shell-shocked. Sophie moved toward her backpack, but Asher wouldn't let her hand go, pulling her into his arms again.

As soon as they reached the top, Grady threw his arms around Haley and mumbled, "Don't do that again you scared the shit out of me."

She nodded and pulled away, walking with a slight hitch in her step toward her backpack. "Scared you? One minute I was admiring the view, the next I was ten feet lower and covered in dirt."

Nodding, Grady ran a hand through his hair again. "Yeah, there is that. You okay? Really? Good to hike back down? We can alternate piggy backs if you need it."

She laughed and said, "I'm fine. Thanks though."

So damn stubborn. After taking the supplies he needed, Asher tossed Finn the first aid kit someone had brilliantly thought to bring. Catching it, he caught up to Haley.

"I'm fine," she grumbled, still hobbling toward the trail.

"I know you are, but I'll feel better if I know that wound's clean."

She dropped her backpack and sat on the nearest boulder. Finn accepted a squirt of hand sanitizer from Pippa and scrubbed his hands, then rinsed again with the unopened water bottle from his backpack. He knelt down in front of Haley and swept her hair out of her face again.

Haley bit down on her cheek as he rinsed the gash on her forehead, silencing a whimper before it escaped.

"I know, I'm so sorry," he crooned. It would be easier if she'd cry out. Watching her blink away the tears, before they rolled down her cheeks, throttled him right in the Adam's apple. He opened a package of steri-strips from the kit and closed the wound as best he could, then bandaged her up with gauze and tape.

He wrapped the ace bandage around her ankle, wishing she'd accept the offer of piggybacks down the hill, but the jostling wouldn't help her concussion.

Sophie limped over and smiled. "You guys doing okay?"

Haley hoisted herself up from the boulder. She went to pick up her backpack, but Finn snatched it before she could. "I got it," he said.

She nodded and started down the trail. She tried to hide the sprain, but he could see her favoring it. Sophie limped alongside her, the pair getting a head start. The others followed behind, conversation gradually moving from stunned comments to a hum of friendly banter again.

Finn stood back, uncertain now that the fear of the unknown had faded. Heading back down the trail, the others started the trek back. What a fucking cluster of a day. Finn slung his backpack over his shoulder with Haley's and grimaced as he stepped down on a loose rock. Shrugging it off, he followed behind.

Grady hung back and hiked alongside him. "So," he said.

"So?" Finn shrugged, playing dumb. He didn't need the lecture right now. Deserved it, but didn't have the energy for it.

"So. You and my sister?"

"It's not like that."

"She falls down a damn cliff, and you go diving after her before the rest of us can even figure out what happened? What is it not like, exactly?"

"She's a friend. I... she's just out of an epically terrible marriage, not looking for anything. My life's been a damn cluster the last few months. We're, well... we're having a rebound thing." Wow, there is no way he could explain it without sounding like a complete ass.

"A rebound thing? Like... like you're sleeping with my sister with no intention of sticking around?" Grady's voice kept quiet so the others wouldn't hear, but he may as well have thrown things and shouted for the punch in the gut his words projected.

"No. I mean, yeah, but... You know what? Shove off." Finn felt pissed-off steam bringing his blood to a boil. His knee about shattered underneath him, but he refused to slow. "Haley's an intelligent adult. One that I like very much, and I would never do anything to hurt her. She wants nothing from me, especially promises, even if I were in any position to offer."

Grady stopped short, but Finn hurt too damn bad to pause, or his leg would lock up and he'd be the one needing a lift down the trail. After pacing and griping to himself, Grady jogged to catch up. "Sorry, man. It's entirely between the two of you. I've had enough lousy relationships in my life to recognize when sometimes you want to lie low and enjoy someone without any pressure. Of course Haley would want to feel normal and, well, maybe it's weird to say about my sister but I know what that asshole did to her; it must feel reassuring for her to know she's desirable."

Responding with nothing more than a nod, Finn kept moving forward. Somehow, despite it all, Haley was pure confidence, willing to dive into trying new things. Like crossing the log. She'd been terrified, but she did it anyway. Fell down a damn cliff and didn't even whimper. Taking that piece of shit old house and making it new and beautiful, making a business out of it. Made love with him like a goddess.

Hell, he was the one that needed to feel wanted. Haley was the rock. But he'd be damn sure she knew how amazing she was by the time she was done with him.

Grady paused to take a swig of water, hesitated, then caught up again. "You risked your life for her just moments ago. Are you sure *you* are okay with this no-promises thing? Being a rebound?"

"Of course." He shrugged. Why wouldn't he be? He would have leapt over that cliff for any of his friends. Admittedly, not as quickly.

Asher hung back from the others and flanked Finn's other side. "Okay, so I presume Grady's been back here grilling you on all the necessary big brother shit about you messing with his sister? I'm familiar with the talk. I got the friend version from him about this time last year."

"Yes. I have been properly admonished and apologized to. It's a rebound thing. Nothing more."

"Lucky. I didn't get the apology for a few weeks." Asher adjusted his and Sophie's backpacks on his shoulder, looking down the trail, ensuring they were far enough back that the others wouldn't hear. "Rebound, huh? Things almost got a little awkward for a few minutes back there, before the whole cliff collapse thing. You looked like you were about to pass out. I've got a question. Does she know you're rebounding from her oldest friend?"

Shit. He was so fucked. If these guys didn't kick his ass, he would later. Then find a way so she understood he would never have crossed that line if he'd had a clue it had existed. "I had no idea until she mentioned Trace at lunch."

Grady paused again, shaking his head and catching up. "You going to say anything?"

"There is no good way to tell someone something like that. Especially Haley. Not when her ex had been nailing her friends behind her back. But I can't lie to her."

Asher shrugged. "How about, 'What a coincidence? Your oldest friend happens to be my oldest friend and the reason I'm wanting commitment-free sex with you.'"

Growling, Finn was tempted to knock Asher off the damn trail. "Watch it."

Asher and Grady simultaneously hung back. Refusing to slow on principle, and so he didn't lose critical momentum, Finn kept going. He could hear them gossiping like a judgy sewing circle, but blissfully couldn't make out what they were saying.

Predictably, they caught up to begin their attack anew. Or maybe not. Grady sighed, "You know what? Why don't you and Haley figure this one out on your own terms. Trace will be gone another few weeks, and you can cross that bridge when you come to it."

"You working some kind of lawyer angle here? Trying to get me to confess something?"

Scoffing, Asher said, "Of course not. It's none of our business. You and Haley are just having fun. Casual sex. No promises, right? I'm sure it won't be a big deal at all. You'll have finished getting your play with Haley by the time Trace gets back anyway."

Grady nodded. "Haley will have probably moved on by then. After being stuck with that asshole since she was eighteen? She's going to want to play the field a while."

Adding with a flippancy that made Finn want to clock him, Asher said, "Damn, ten years with that piece of shit? Yeah, she's going to want to mix it up. Might keep you in mind for a hook-up now and again if you don't blow it."

Gnawing in Finn's gut digested the weird-ass day. Maybe beer on a hike was a bad idea after all.

15

Encroachment

"Ahhh, oh my god, ohhh," Haley hissed in blissful relief as Finn lowered the icepack onto her elevated ankle that was puffy and bruised. It had hurt like hell, but no way was she letting anyone carry her down that hill. She settled against the stack of pillows on her bed.

Finn laughed, then groaned with pleasure as he settled and set his icepack on his knee. "I know, right?"

He reached over and rested another icepack against her forehead. Taking over, she held it against the goose egg growing on her skull. Her head throbbed each time she even thought about moving.

Side by side, they leaned back against the mountain of pillows leaned against the wall, each with an elevated leg and icepack, her head boosted up on yet more pillows.

Both were still damp from the shower—not the sex-fest Finn had teased. By the time they'd reached the cars that afternoon, she couldn't hide the limp anymore as the sprain declared itself. Finn drove them home. They'd both hobbled into the shower, taking turns under the spray, rinsing off the thick layer of dirt from the fall. He'd cleaned her wounds again, massaged the mud from her hair, and then patted the towel over her skin. She'd snagged one of his shirts from the clean laundry pile and curled up in bed while he grabbed the icepacks.

Sitting up to see the clock, Finn dropped back down onto the pillows and sighed. "It's only six o'clock and I'm ready for sleep. You scared the hell out of me today."

"Thanks for coming to rescue me. All heroic and attentive. You even ruined your shirt for me." She grinned, only half teasing.

"I've got plenty of shirts. Not many women willing to tolerate me."

"You're such a chore."

"I know, right? I've been told, over the last year, that I've been broody and inattentive. They weren't wrong."

"Really?" She was genuinely surprised. "I know you said you weren't ready and your ex-girlfriend recognized that and ended things. But in the weeks that I have known you, you've been... well, not any of that."

He leaned over and kissed her cheek, groaning as he had to resettle the icepack that shifted off his leg in the subtle movement. "This rebound thing was a great idea. I do feel much better."

Yeah. She felt, well, great. Since leaving Nate, she'd felt pretty damn good. A complete mess, yeah, but an independent mess.

Lately, she'd felt like *her* again. She'd fallen off a cliff today and hadn't panicked. Okay, so the log had almost gotten to her, but she conquered it. Years ago, she'd thought herself a happy, adventurous person. And she was beginning to believe it again.

Even with sex. She'd always believed good sex was a thing. It couldn't be so popular if it was as anticlimactic as she'd experienced.

She rather liked what she had become and recognized she hadn't gotten here all on her own. Her family had banded around her, in their unique ways. Finn had a lot to do with it, letting her talk it out, pointing out her strengths, encouraging her to stretch her wings. This rebound thing was brilliant.

Finn scooted up and turned toward her again. He lifted her forehead icepack and scowled, inspecting her wound again. Hopping off the bed, he hobbled as he disappeared into the bathroom. He returned a few seconds later with the first aid kit she'd picked up after nearly driving a nail through her finger a few weeks ago.

He opened the plastic bin and shuffled through until he found what he was looking for. Opening a pack of antibiotic ointment, he dabbed a dollop over her wound. He redressed it, then closed up the kit and dropped it to the floor. "You probably should have gone in for stitches."

"I'm not going in for two stitches for a wound I hardly notice. Besides, I don't actually have any scars. I'll sound cool if I can tell people I got one falling off of a cliff."

He said with a goofy grin, "Puff up the story a bit, make it sound really good. Like it was a five-hundred-foot drop."

"And I'd been running from a bear."

"Because you'd been trying to protect its cub from a cougar."

"And I had to crawl up the sheer cliff face to get back up again."

"With the bear cub on your back."

She laughed out loud and curled into him. He wrapped his arm around her and held her close. He whispered, "Are you hungry for dinner? I can fix you something."

"Too tired. Unless you're hungry."

"Nope." He reached over and flipped off the lamp that still lived on the floor next to the bed.

She'd ordered a handmade matched set of beside tables she'd found online a few days ago. She preferred to have a vision in her mind when furnishing a room, but the iron-hardware over white pine had been irresistible. And they'd look great with the industrial lamps. Now to find a dresser. And a bedframe so she could put the mattress on something.

Finn relaxed at her side as he drifted off, and she melted into him. Snuggling without sex was surely allowed now and again with rebounds.

After falling off a cliff?

Definitely.

Bleary-eyed, Finn rubbed the fog from his vision. Gray light cast a shadowy glow in the bedroom. Still dim, he could see Haley starting to stir at his side. Her eyes fluttered open, a deep furrow in her brow as she woke.

Damn, he was never awake this early anymore. He turned toward the floor and tapped his phone to check the time. Four in the morning. When he'd first moved home, he'd often wake before dawn with a momentary panic that he was missing practice, only to remember that chapter of his life was over.

If his knee weren't throbbing so bad from running down that steep hillside yesterday, he'd get out and take a run before the rest of the world stirred. Like he used to.

Haley rolled toward him, propping up on her elbow. The corner of her mouth quirked up in a sleepy grin. "I'm starving."

He propped up to face her. "Me too. Why don't you hang out here, and I'll go make us some breakfast."

"I'm too hungry. How about a quick protein bar to tide us over, then a huge breakfast with eggs and bacon and cinnamon rolls and fruit and... okay, so all I have is eggs and toast, but you get the idea."

"Sure thing," he chuckled, then rolled off the bed.

His knee was talking to him this morning, but he managed to hobble for a quick pit stop in the bathroom, then headed for the kitchen. She'd already had the coffeepot ready to brew, so he hit start and dug around in the pantry closet for a pair of protein bars.

Haley wolfed down her protein bar in a few bites like he did. Maybe they should have had a quick dinner last night. Halfway through gulping down his coffee, he felt a few useful brainwaves starting to wake with the rest of him. Setting down his mug on the floor, he threw back the covers in search of Haley's ankle.

Sitting uncovered, wearing nothing but his t-shirt that wasn't covering much at the moment, Haley laughed. "What are you doing? I don't think I'm awake enough for that yet."

"Don't you think about anything but sex?" he teased, trailing his hand down her leg until he reached her ankle. He squeezed along the bones, reassuring himself again that nothing was broken. It was still pretty puffy, but no bruising. "How do you feel?" He asked, sitting up, facing her.

"Functional. Although I think I may be one big bruise."

"Damn, we got so lucky you weren't badly injured."

"Don't I know it. That would have ruined my day."

"How's the head?"

"I'll let you know in a bit. It's at a very dull roar right now, but it's teetering on the edge of pounding."

"Looks like I'm making breakfast."

"Mmm, you know what sounds good? I have a connection at Cascade Bakery."

"I'm not leaving you alone yet."

"She'd deliver if she knew I fell off a cliff. But she might go motherly on me."

Now that was a terrifying idea. Possibly worse than Trace walking in on them cozied up would be her mother. Sweet woman, but Ellen's heart would be more broken than Trace's. Ellen had Trace and his wedding half planned when they got back together. "Know what? I'll fix something decent, then maybe I'll pick some up tomorrow. For now, you get to chill right where you are all day."

"I'm fine."

"No, really. Don't mess around with a concussion."

She scowled but didn't argue. "How does it look?"

He scooted closer and scrutinized the bandaged wound. "Hell of a goose egg. Very cartoon-inspired."

She brushed her hair over the wound in a feeble attempt to cover it.

Chuckling, he hopped back out of bed. "I'll grab you some Tylenol and fresh icepacks."

Haley wasn't the worst patient, but she was vocal about her disinterest in lying around in bed all day. When her headache eased, they went out for a short stroll around the yard, then back in when her headache returned. He knew they'd over-done it when she was too nauseous for lunch, then didn't argue and actually took an afternoon nap.

While she slept, he snuck out and brought a box to sit on the patio off the great room. He texted Pete to call in sick, claiming his knee was acting up. It actually wasn't too bad compared to some of the dumb shit he'd done to anger it the last few months. He could tell it was slowly on the mend, even if it would never be normal again.

His phone buzzed a bit later. Staring at the screen, his jaw clenched tight, and he looked inside, not sure if it was safe to answer. Hating himself more than a little, he connected. "Hey," he said.

Lyrically soothing with her easy cadence, he could hear Trace smiling as she responded, "Hi. Did I catch you at an okay time?"

Rising to his feet, he strolled across the lawn in his bare feet. The grass was short and rough thanks to Haley's robot mower that currently hummed on the far side of the lawn. He grinned, remembering her hilarious blog post in which she'd named it, compared it to a faithful goat, added a pink bow, and informed her eager readers of its pros and cons, the alternatives she had considered, alongside her comical personification.

"Sure, I can talk."

Long pause. Then a chipper, "How has your summer been going? I'm homesick. Tell me something crazy about Foothills."

Shit. They hadn't chatted for fun in ages. Yeah, they agreed to stay friends, but he really, really didn't want to lead her on. Truth time. "Crazy, huh? Well, it's been interesting so far. Went hiking with Grady and everyone yesterday. Your old friend Haley came with us."

"Oh, I'm so glad. She's had a hell of a time of it lately. How is she? Does she seem like she's settling in okay?"

"Um, yeah, she's doing great—" Shit. How did one go about saying, *and I'm having completely commitment-free sex with her? Would you mind talking to her and personally telling her you don't mind?*

"I'm so glad. You should invite her to the pub to be sure she's getting out. Hey, you both lived in San Francisco. I'll bet she'd appreciate having someone to compare notes with."

"Yeah, that came up."

"Oh, and you know those cheesy croissants you love so much from the bakery? Those are her favorites, too.. Maybe you can drop one by for her on my behalf one of these days?"

Shit. Okay. Here goes. "Yeah, I'll do that. Trace—"

"But maybe she'll think that's weird, like you're flirting or something. Honestly, I encouraged her to go out and find a rebound, but now I think I pushed and what if she's not ready for that? I mean—"

"About that. Um, well—"

The sliding door to the bedroom opened and Haley raised her hand to shield the sun from her eyes. Barefoot on the flagstone, she still wore nothing but his t-shirt, her hair a little wild from the nap.

Bad fucking timing. As usual. He cleared his throat to interrupt Trace and said, "Hey, sorry, but I've got to run."

"Of course. Talk to you later." She remained chipper as she hung up.

He clicked off, stuffed the phone in his pocket and strolled across the lawn toward Haley.

She seemed to realize she looked a wreck and smoothed her hair, grinning shyly at him. "Hey."

"Hey," he said as he reached her. "Feeling better?"

"Getting there. I didn't mean to interrupt your call."

"We were just wrapping up."

"Okay. Don't you work tonight?"

"Nah."

She scowled. "Don't worry about me. I'll be lazing around anyway. Doctor Halseth's orders."

He winked. "Nice try. The second I leave, you're going to start working on the furniture."

Trailing her hand over his abdomen, she grinned. "Maybe." Skimming along the waistband of his jeans, she yanked him closer.

Gulping helplessly as she found skin, dipping lower, he stilled her hand. "Dammit, Haley. We're not having concussion sex."

She laughed, her voice still hoarse from the nap. "I need a shower. My head still hurts. I may need help."

The woman was relentless. "Don't make me look like the jackass that turns down a gorgeous woman, nor the guy that takes advantage of an invalid."

"Ouch," she teased. "Fine. I'll just go take my own shower and go back to sleep again."

She pulled off the shirt and flicked it on the bedroom floor as she walked inside.

Ignoring the image of her taunting curves strutting away, he headed for the kitchen to fix an early dinner. She went quiet after her shower. Didn't say it, but he could tell her head was throbbing and she was probably nauseous again.

Night came, and they fell asleep at sunset, rising at sunrise again. Her head was better, but still nagging. He texted Grady and had a hammock and pastries delivered within an hour.

Tearing open the bag, the contents still warm and gooey, Haley whimpered as she took a slow bite. "My favorite. Nothing like it anywhere else in the world."

Gnawing in his gut, Finn tried to work up the nerve to say something. Every time he opened his mouth to say it, he lost the words.

While Haley took a shower, he set up the hammock between two trees at the edge of the lawn. They spent most of the day rocking, dozing, reading, chatting, or simply watching the puffy white clouds passing overhead. He doubted either of them had indulged like this in ages, and he couldn't bring himself to ruin it.

By sunset, she was getting restless, which he took as a good sign that she was almost back to normal. Her ankle was looking much better already.

The following morning, she woke at dawn, showered, and appeared with coffees for them both as he rubbed the sleep from his eyes.

They snuggled up on the bed, sipping their coffee while the room brightened. "How do you feel?"

She inhaled slowly, draining the last of her coffee and setting it on the floor next to the bed. "No headache. No nausea. Ankle is still achy."

"Good." He grinned, setting his mug on his book that he'd dropped to the floor on his side of the bed as he fell asleep last night. He checked the wound on her head, clean and bandage free. He kissed her forehead next to the wound, moving his way down her cheek until he reached her lips. Holding back, he asked again, "What about now?"

"Better."

He took his lips with hers, drawing back again.

"Better," she said without prompting. "But not there yet."

Going slow and mellow, they made love as the sun rose, the night fading away.

Limping over to her neatly stacked clothing pile along the far wall, Haley grabbed a pair of jeans and her Halseth's t-shirt. He grinned, enjoying that she wore the shirt when she needed pick-me-up attire. Didn't hurt that the shirt hugged all the right places.

As she pulled the snug denim over her ankle, she let out a pitiful whimper. "Okay, I should have gone with sweats or at least boot cut jeans, but it's too late now. Ankles suck."

"Yeah, that ankle's going to be hurting another few days, maybe even a few weeks." He scanned the stacks, not seeing anything of the leisure variety aside from expensive yoga pants, which wouldn't be much kinder to the ankle. "Do you even own sweats?"

She rolled up the cuff of her jeans to take the pressure off her ankle. "No. Nate didn't like them."

"What business was it of his? Wait, don't answer that." What area of her life had he not micromanaged? Asshole. For Haley's sake, he didn't rant and bitch like he wanted to, for fear of making Haley feel even worse for staying with the dickwad for so long.

Setting her feet back on the ground, she shrugged. "I do like pretty things, so I dress for me, which luckily aligned with Nate's preferences. But I may have to invest in a few practical things. Like slippers and sweatpants."

She grabbed their empty coffee cups and limped out of the bedroom. He wanted to haul her back in here and not let her walk on the ankle until it had fully healed, but he could see the fierce independence set in her expression, her cheek parked between her teeth, her blue eyes boiling with stubbornness. At least her head was better.

Hopping in the shower, he took his time so she could have some time alone. He'd have to see if she was up for company another day, maybe start on that furniture, or if she wanted him to go. Drying off, he wrapped the towel around his waist and headed back into the bedroom. Dammit, he'd forgotten to move the laundry along last night. Probably smelled now, so he'd have to re-wash and stay at least until the dryer was done.

Heading down the hall, he froze, hearing some guy talking in the kitchen with her. Haley's voice was calm, but he could hear the monotone sneer in every clipped word. "Why are you here? I'm coming down in two weeks to sign all the final paperwork. The lawyers could have mailed this for me to review in advance."

"Come on, Haley, we were married for almost ten years. It's important that we go through this together. You deserve so much more than a share of our divided assets. Are you sure you don't want alimony?"

Did she still have that stubborn edge to her expression, or was she wearing the phony polite face? Finn stayed out of sight, unsure what she'd prefer. Having a near-naked man come out of her bedroom was not going to be helpful at this point.

This time, her voice raised a few decibels. "I don't want any permanent ties to you. Half of our assets should cover my inheritance from my father..." She trailed off for a moment, then continued, "And the fact that I gave up on my career goals to support *you*. I don't blame you. It's entirely my fault that I didn't ignore your insistence that you would make the money while I kept the house, but because of my stupid decision to drop out for *you*, I have no marketable skills. So I'm taking my share, and that's it. All ties severed."

"I miss you." Slimy bastard. "We were good together."

Haley's voice rose an octave. "No, we weren't. Our marriage should have ended long before you started sleeping with everyone."

"Haley. Sweet Haley. A man has certain needs, and if his wife isn't living up to his expectations—"

Okay, that's it. Finn shifted the towel so it rode extra low on his hips, barely hanging on, and mussed his hair, playing up the look. Strolling into the great room, he acted startled to see the stranger in the kitchen with Haley. "Sorry, Haley. I didn't realize you had company."

She bit her lips to mask her amusement. "Good morning, Finn. Coffee? Nate was just leaving."

"That'd be great. Why don't you sit down for a bit? My turn to fix breakfast." He rubbed a hand through his hair again, feigning exhaustion from a long night of sex.

Turning, she snagged a mug from the cupboard. Her weight all on the good ankle, she guarded her movements to conceal the injury.

Asshole Nate's jaw dropped open as he read the back of Haley's shirt, his head whipping back and forth from Haley to Finn. "Finn Halseth?"

Strolling closer, Finn accepted the coffee from Haley and leaned against the counter next to her. "That's me." He wrapped his arm around Haley's middle. "Impressive. You recognized me quicker than most, even faster than Haley." Playing it up, he teased his hands under the hem of her shirt, grazing his fingertips along her skin.

Calculating, struggling to figure out what was going on, Nate looked downright constipated. "How long has this been going on?"

Haley rolled her eyes and growled, "Oh my god. Nate, not everyone's like you. Vows mean something to some people. Namely, me. I met Finn a few weeks ago. He lives in Foothills."

"What a coincidence. He must have lived in San Francisco until a few months ago. You've been blaming me for my infidelity, and you've been hooking up with a professional football player all this time? No wonder you always had the game on." Nate paused, then turned to the door. "Look over the paperwork, Haley. See you in two weeks."

"Don't come back," she grumbled, letting him see himself out.

Finn held steady, listening to the engine start, then the sound of Nate peeling out of the driveway. "You okay?"

She stepped to the opposite cupboard, but hissed as she bore weight on her ankle. "Of course not. What a creep. I don't know what he wants from me. One minute he's begging me to come home, the next he's accusing *me* of cheating, then offering to support me for the rest of my life, then... I'm so done with his rollercoaster."

"I'm so sorry. You're almost free of him."

Nodding, she crossed her arms and stared blankly out the window.

Moving closer, Finn rested his hands on her hips, resisting the urge to yank her against him and hold on for dear life. Her head thudded forward and banged into his sternum.

She mumbled, "That was awesome, having his hero come out all naked and satisfied after clearly having had a good time with me."

"It was either that, or kick his ass, or let him know you're fucking amazing in bed and out, and he's the asshole with the problem. But that's none of his damn business. Hell, he probably had so many affairs to find a woman that didn't find him inadequate."

Haley looked up and grinned. "I like you, Finn."

He chuckled, "I like you, too." Moving to the fridge, he went digging for eggs and chiles.

Limping around the island, she pulled up one of her new stools and rested her elbows on the countertop. He refilled her coffee before setting a frying pan on the stovetop. She sipped her coffee and grinned. "I like the view."

Flicking off the towel without ceremony, her riotous laughter exactly the response he was going for, he cracked a few eggs in the pan, going about making breakfast.

16

Red Zone

"Ready for this?" Finn shifted into park, turning to Haley as she stared ahead at the house. Grady and Claire's house suited them. High ceilings, tall windows, but a cozy cabin vibe. An expansive field overlooked the valley beyond.

Haley sighed, then linked her hand with his over the center console. "A little weird, not having to hide anything. I guess there's no reason to pretend we're not having sex, now that they all know we're having a thing."

"I suppose I could have waited on top of that cliff for someone else to saunter down to you, maybe throw you a few bandaids and let you climb up on your own," he teased.

Haley rolled her eyes, landing her gaze on his. "Even if we weren't having a thing, I suspect you would have been down just as fast."

"Almost as fast. The others were moving that direction. I may have knocked some of them out of the way to get to you."

"Either way, with the gossip mill around here, I guess it was inevitable." She released his hand and climbed out. Grinning over the roof of his car, she asked, "Your family probably knew from day one, didn't they? From what I hear, it was Zoe's suggestion?"

"Pretty much. They're still ragging me about that bulk box of condoms."

"Aw, that's nice." She met him at the front of the car. "I guess I could say I wish my family was that honest, but I don't want to give Patricia any encouragement."

"No useful tips? I mean, it sounded like she was about to reveal the big secret to keeping a man happy."

Plugging her ears, Haley chanted *La, la la la la.*

Spinning her around, he gripped her hips. "Okay, I give. Actually, please don't share any of her tips. Bad enough she scarred *you* for life."

"I'm sure if you let her know you're out of a relationship, too, she'll be happy to impart some wisdom on you."

"Please no."

"Actually, I know things ended amicably, but, I just realized, Foothills is a small town. Who is your ex? It might get weird if, well, you know, if I bump into her sometime. We did jump in pretty quick."

Shit. Now's as good a time as any. Chest rising and falling with lead caked heavy over his ribs, he opened his mouth to answer.

Saved by the bell. Asher and Sophie pulled down the driveway. From the front door, Grady hollered, "Stop making out with my sister and get in here. Appetizers are ready."

Finn backed up a step and linked hands with Haley. "I've been wanting to talk to you about that, actually. Later." He cringed, hating putting it off again.

She was going to be pissed. Especially when she found out he'd been officially single for a matter of hours before hitting on his ex's oldest friend. Not that he'd known who she was. And things had been over with Trace, long before she ended it.

Haley dropped his hand and dashed toward the house. Hanging back, he watched as she headed up the front steps, her cotton slip dress clinging to her hips as she moved, the draped back tied together with a simple knot. Not once in his life would he have commented on a woman's style, or even noticed, but Haley wore clothes like a summer breeze brushing through a field of daisies.

A slap on his shoulder woke him from his daydream, well-timed before his imagination ran wild. Asher pushed him forward with his momentum. "Just picture it. A few weeks from now when you've moved on, she's moved on, and you don't get to gawk like that anymore."

What was that supposed to mean? He accepted the push toward the door and walked with him. "Hey. Rebound. Living in the moment here. And whatever happens, when I'm old and bald and can't get it up anymore, I will have plenty of memories to keep me entertained."

Sophie snuck up behind him and slapped his opposite shoulder. Leaning across to Asher, she said, "Give him a break. He's not about to risk ruining Claire's birthday."

Asher whined, "But I haven't gotten to mess with him since I kicked his ass in physics class. My hurricane totally crushed his bridge."

Swinging open the door before Grady could open it, Finn rolled his eyes. "You know, I thought I'd be bummed when you graduated early, and we couldn't carpool to our running start classes anymore, turns out, it wasn't so bad."

Sophie ran ahead to join the others, ignoring their infantile banter. Nearly matched in height, Asher rubbed his hand over Finn's hair like the obnoxious big brother he never had. "Aw, poor Finn. Didn't get to ride to school with his cool upperclassman friend anymore. Didn't know how to charm your way into straight A's all by yourself. All adorable with his steady girlfriend instead of playing the field like me."

Jamming his elbow into Asher's middle, Finn leaned back and whispered, "I haven't told her about Trace yet."

Unfazed by the elbow but not by the statement, Asher caught Finn by the elbow and pulled him back into the entry. "Why not? She's going to freak. Just get it over with."

Voice strained as he whispered back, Finn demanded, "What, was I going to tell her while her head was filled with firecrackers after that concussion? Or should I have waited until her ex-husband walked in on us? I was literally trying to tell her when you assholes drove up just now."

Wincing, Asher crossed his arms and looked out the front windows. Sophie and Haley were carrying picnic blankets to the clearing around the bonfire that Claire was adding firewood to. "Shit, man. You'd better hope she's about ready to move on, because if she finds out that you knew, and didn't say anything?"

"I know." Shoving his hands in his pockets, Finn clenched his jaw and tried to calm the brewing thunder in the pit of his stomach. Why should it matter so much? Why should he be so worried about what Haley thought of him, when they weren't beholden to each other? Wasn't that the point of the rebound, to get over something, not find new ways to feel guilty?

Asher nodded toward the kitchen. "Come on. You're not going to tell her tonight and ruin one of the few relaxed social outings she's had in years, and she's going to worry if you act weird and pissy. So forget about it for tonight and tell her in the morning."

Popping out from the kitchen, Grady carted a massive ice chest. "How's Haley feeling? Concussion better?"

Nodding, Finn popped open the lid of Grady's cooler and snagged a beer. Cracking it open, he had it downed by half before coming up for air. "She's good. Bit of a limp, so she was bummed to have to wear sneakers tonight instead of these fancy leather heels she had out."

Grady tossed a beer to Asher and closed the lid again. "You know, she's all about finding the old Haley again, but the Haley I knew wore nothing but Converse and Nikes."

Watching out the window as Haley and Sophie headed toward the house, Finn found the corner of his mouth turning up like Haley's fish-hook grin. "Yeah. Think she grew up and discovered she looks damn good."

Snickering, Asher smacked him on the shoulder and headed out the slider to the patio, Grady following behind. They were whispering something, probably the same gossipy shit they were on about before. Couple of fucking romantics, convinced he and Haley were following the same true-love path they were so hung up on. Finn hadn't born witness to their dives into the world of commitment... Hell, Finn had defined the word when they were still necking in the backs of their parents' cars with whatever women would have them.

Sauntering into the house, a bit less sway in her sneakers and a new hitch in her gait, Haley still managed to drive him absolutely wild with the way her dress moved over her thighs with each step she took. Whoever decided slits in skirts was a thing... fucking genius.

Running a hand through her slick waves, Haley stopped in front of him. Her hand slid down his forearm, slipping his beer out of his hand while he stood helplessly frozen at the sight. Guzzling the remaining half, she flicked her tongue over the corner of her mouth as she finished it off, setting the empty bottle back in his hand, then brushed past him.

Zane popped his head in the slider. "Dude, Finn, come on. I've been abandoned at the barbeque and don't have a clue how to tell when a burger's done."

Shaking away the vision that was going to occupy his dreams for the rest of eternity, Finn nodded. "Yeah. Coming."

He followed Zane to the outdoor kitchen and didn't hesitate to rag on his pathetic barbeque skills. Freya appeared with a mountain of veggie skewers, sneaking them onto the grill when Zane was distracted by her hand wrapping around his middle.

Okay, maybe it wasn't just Finn's imagination. He'd made friends with some diehard romantics. Haley walked down the slope to the natural landing where the firepit had been set up, the breeze playing with her hair as she moved.

Zane cussed and snatched the tongs from Finn's hands. Laughing, Zane flipped the variety of meats that were charred on the bottom. "What did I call you out here for? You're no better at this than I am."

Finn backed away, arms up. "Sorry. I pour the drinks, not cook the food."

"And I don't barbecue. Shut your ass up and don't ditch me. I am not taking the blame for a scorched dinner by myself."

Zane wasn't the chattiest of his friends, but he always had something interesting to say. They both enjoyed ragging on Asher as a mutual target. Freya was a mystery. Finn hadn't known her very well growing up, as she was a few years older and spent most of her time in the art rooms, but she was vibrant and he'd always noticed her.

They all sat at a tiled outdoor table, the umbrella overhead no longer providing much shade as the sun had dipped so low in the sky. After the easy dinner, he downed his last bite of charred burger and looked around. "Wait, where are Pippa and Lincoln?"

Sophie laughed out loud, covering her mouth as she swallowed her bite. "At a prenatal appointment then out for a quiet dinner."

"What?" Haley nearly choked on her own bite. "I thought that was planned for year three of marriage."

Biting her lip, Sophie shook her head, still trying to subdue her laughter. "Pippa called yesterday, completely freaked that her period was late. She was in such a state, I picked up a pregnancy test and drove it over. Which, by the way, I have no doubt the entire county will soon be convinced I'm the pregnant one after that very public purchase. Pippa will absolutely pay for that one."

"Oh no." Haley giggled maniacally, leaning up against Finn as she tried to maintain a shred of control. "When I was in third grade and she was in fourth, she made this comprehensive timeline of her life. From what it sounds, she hasn't strayed an inch... until now."

Grady nodded, his lips turned up in pure amusement. "I wondered why Lincoln was so irritable when he swung by Black Op yesterday. All he said was that Pippa had tossed and turned all night, grouching something about being late and saying that it was all his fault."

Freya looked to be equally lost in a giggle fit. "I'm so excited we get to throw her baby shower," she said, throwing her head back and slapping her knee. "After her wedding last year? Payback."

"What happened at her wedding?" Finn knew Pippa was intense, but what was so funny about an accidental pregnancy? Shit, had Haley had a period? Oh shit. Was it hot out here? Finn tugged at the neck of his shirt and grimaced as he couldn't slow his rapid breathing.

Asher groaned, "Bridezilla doesn't even begin to explain it. Pippa likes to plan. When her plan is, well, strained, she sort of freaks."

Rising from his seat at the table, Grady stacked plates. "That's putting it mildly. I thought she was never speaking to either of you again when you hooked up and threw off her plans."

Sophie air-toasted. "We tried to keep it secret, she just needs to learn how to knock."

"On the front door of her parents' house at eight in the morning?" Asher nudged his shoulder into Sophie's.

Pushing the pile of plates in front of Asher rather than taking them himself, Grady started collecting silverware. "At least Sophie was in on it. Claire came on to me before I even knew she'd dumped my brother."

Cringing, Claire stole the handful of silverware from him. "I thought you knew. Can you imagine how much fun we could have had if you had known? I've been thinking about that pool table ever since."

Finn tried to focus, but his wires weren't just crossed, they'd turned into a pile up. Was this what a stroke felt like? Everyone else at the table seemed to be having a hell of a time. He'd been with Haley, what, most every night for two, almost three weeks? And had gotten close enough to know another week before that. Was it good luck that she hadn't had her period, or were those condoms faulty? His skin drew pale, and spiders crawled all over his skin as sweat beaded from his pores.

Grady grinned. "That's it, I'm buying a pool table."

Asher popped up from the table and carted the massive stack of plates, Grady snagged the napkins and other debris, opening the door for Asher and Claire. The trio disappeared into the house. Clearing her throat, Sophie rose from her chair to join them.

Slipping his hand in Freya's, Zane leaned back in his chair and settled in with his wife. Freya smiled. "You don't think we should go in and help?"

"Nah," he joked, "Finn and I are off the hook. We cooked."

Snorting, Freya jabbed at him. "Nice excuse. I think Grady and Claire did most of the cooking, while you two stood all manly by the grill and burned our food."

"Well if I messed that up, I really shouldn't risk ruining anything else."

Haley kicked Finn subtly under the table, eying him suspiciously. She mouthed, *You okay?*

Nodding, he rose from the table and led her down toward the bonfire. Not ready to sit back down, he paced for a minute. His pulse thundered in his veins, ice cold and anxious and terrified and... well, a little thrilled.

"Finn? What is up with you? You look like you're on crack or something. Not that I've ever seen anyone on crack, but you look ill and won't sit still."

May as well rip off at least one band aid tonight. He glanced up the hill to make sure they were alone. Zane and Freya were far enough they wouldn't hear.

"All that talk about Pippa got me thinking. You, uh, we're, um... I mean, it's been a few weeks and you haven't..."

Haley's sweet laughter trilled in the air. Or laughed her ass off, anyway. She grabbed his hand and yanked him close. "I'm on the pill and I take it obsessively on time. I only have a period when I feel like it. Trust me, nothing's getting past the condoms *and* the pill."

His breath whooshed out in a cluster of relief and, well, something else he wasn't willing to acknowledge. His swimmers were admittedly a little disappointed at the near miss. "Wow, okay, wow, that's so good to hear."

She released him long enough to snag another round of beers and sat on the blanket she'd laid out by the fire. It was roaring, a toasty orange glow of embers at the base.

He sat behind her, their backs to the others, and encased her in his arms and legs. Resting his cheek against her, he wanted to say something, but anything about to come out of his mouth was downright sappy.

Setting his beer on the grass behind them, he took advantage of their solitude. Grazing his fingertips along the smooth skin of her thighs, he scooted up the hem of her dress. Leaning into him, she closed her eyes and absorbed the moment. Trailing his lips across her shoulder, he was drowning in thoughts that were boiling over, begging for release. He stayed silent, swallowing the words that he couldn't say out loud.

He didn't want any lies between them. His history with Trace was already hanging over his head like a damn time-bomb, waiting to explode and ruin everything. And that wasn't half as dangerous as the thoughts in his head.

Haley melted into Finn, the scruff of his jaw massaging against her temple, the strength of his arms enveloping her. A novel sensation, overwhelmed with red hot arousal mixed with trust, exhilarated as she fell from the sky, already buoyed by the safety net that was Finn, steady and strong. One of those few moments in life where she wished she could hit pause and savor.

Claire cleared her throat, speaking loudly as she and Grady approached. "Beautiful night."

Haley sat up a little straighter and fixed her dress.

Dancing from behind her, Freya caught up to Claire. "You picked a good birthday."

"I totally planned it, too. Kicked my mother's cervix and insisted this would be a good day to be born."

Claire passed a blanket to Haley, then curled up by the fire with Grady's and her blanket. Finn reached around and spread the plaid cotton blanket over them. Haley hadn't even noticed the chill in the night air.

The rest settled around the fire, joking and teasing and, well, being normal. These people all liked each other. Not one hint of phony. Even in their teasing of Pippa, they cared.

"Haley?" Claire asked.

Haley blinked and looked over, wondering how long she'd been trying to get her attention. "Yeah? Sorry, I was enjoying the moment."

"I'm glad you're relaxing. When is your birthday?" Claire was leaned against Grady like he was a comfy armchair.

"December 8th."

Grady frowned. "The last few years, it seems you always had other plans, so I haven't gotten to celebrate with you in forever. We are definitely doing something this year."

Sitting up a bit, Haley bit her cheek as she remembered. "Last year actually wasn't so bad. The year before, Nate threw a party for me. All of our friends, his coworkers, a few clients he was courting. I entertained seventy-five people I either didn't know or didn't care for, ate three bites of perfume-flavored white cake—which I hate... okay, I'm not dwelling. But I had too many of those."

Sophie asked, "Then what made last year different?"

"Nate was going to take me out to this swanky club, undoubtedly so he could schmooze and mingle. But there was a blizzard in DC, and he got stuck there overnight. So, for the first time in my adult life, I sent the staff home, ordered pizza, and curled up in my pajamas on the couch in the living room and watched football."

Chuckling at her back, Finn's scruffy chin rubbed over the top of her head. "I remember that day."

"It was the beginning of the end for Nate and me, or at least, when I started to realize I had forgotten who I was. Foolishly, I should have grabbed a firmer hold of that epiphany and done something with it. It wasn't for another month that I caught him with Mariella. Bitch. And she'd given me perfume that birthday. Should have known then; it was the same stuff she wore." Scowling, Haley took a deep breath. "Sorry about that. Someone, anyone, please talk about something else. Sophie, what did you do for your birthday last year?"

Sophie leaned back and nuzzled into Asher. Raising his eyebrows, Asher grinned. "Me."

From across the fire, Zane chucked a hunk of grass at him. Whacking it before it hit him in the face, Asher didn't lose the grin.

The crew joked and chatted, thankfully moving on from Haley's sad history. She needed more good stories. It would take time, but she was building more and more each day.

Finn nuzzled against her. "If we're still doing what we're doing by the time your birthday rolls around, let's do something fun. No stress, no weirdness. Whatever you want."

His hands still rested on her thighs under the blanket. She moved her hand over his and slid his hand higher.

Groaning silently, he gently caressed, whispering, "Let's head home."

Chuckling, she shifted her backside against him and whispered back, "May want to tame that first."

Stilling his hand, he fixed her skirt and swallowed audibly. "Talk about anything else."

"I can't believe I didn't recognize you when I first saw you. Last year on my birthday, they stopped you on the field and interviewed you."

"My hair was longer then. And I had a beard. Zoe says I looked like I was going for that broody movie star look."

"I liked it. A lot. Actually, I dreamed about you all night that night. Woke up that sex drive I'd lost."

"That is a good birthday. Was dream me as good as reality?"

She shrugged. "Meh."

Pinching her side, he growled, "Okay, let's get going. I want to hear everything dream me did."

Laughing, she sat up and turned. "Might take a while. You helped me get through my divorce."

Groaning, he folded the blanket and held it in front of him while Haley picked up the rest of their stuff. He waved with his free hand. "Happy birthday, Claire. Night guys."

17

Gauntlet

Why was she so nervous? Haley smoothed her denim skirt and ensured that her top was wrinkle-free. She checked the mirror and reassured herself that her hair didn't look as frazzled as she felt. Accepting that she was what she was, she hopped out of the car.

The house was pure adorable. Cheerful blue siding, bright as the summer sky, and was accented by charcoal gray trim and white window frames. No annuals this year, but the established perennials declared the curb appeal was timeless. Fine gravel was lined by solar powered lights that accented a welcoming path; the concrete steppingstones guided her to the front porch.

Reaching the front door, she took a steadying breath before ringing the bell. Zoe appeared seconds later, swinging open the door. "Haley, I'm so glad you came. Come on in."

"You have a beautiful home." She stepped into the eight-foot square entry. A wide opening ahead led to the kitchen and what she suspected was a connecting family room. To the left, a short hallway led to a formal living room that looked untouched, with another hallway that looked to connect a main bedroom. Also to the left, a narrow stairwell with steep steps told the true age of the structure. A coat closet was on her right, concealed with louvered doors. Noting the recently vacuumed floors and Zoe's fluffy green socks, she kicked off her ankle boots and set them in the basket.

"Oh, you don't have to take off those cute shoes. We're casual around here."

"No worries. The floors look so nice, I'd hate to be the one to mess them up."

Zoe laughed, "Pops insisted we prepare for our guest. We haven't really had anyone over since Mom passed, so we've all had to remind ourselves what manners look like."

From the kitchen, she heard Finn's rumbling voice holler, "Haley?" Appearing seconds later, Finn was wiping his hands on a pink tea towel, looking adorably flustered. "Sorry, kitchen emergency."

Glancing behind him, she asked, "I'm good, do you need to take care of it?"

"Nah." He grinned, tossing the towel back with an easy lateral into the kitchen, not looking to see that it had landed on the corner of the island as intended.

A voice remarkably similar to Finn's griped from the kitchen, "Don't worry about me. I've got eight arms."

Zoe rolled her eyes. "That's our little brother. He's helpless. I'll fix it." As she wandered into the kitchen, Haley watched as she shrugged before disappearing around the corner. "Don't get your panties in a twist, I'm here."

Finally alone, Finn leaned against the doorway and grinned at Haley. Her cheeks heated as she suddenly felt completely on the spot, toes curling inward on the worn linoleum floor of his entry as he stood so at home, grinning like a fool, barefoot in old jeans and a faded black t-shirt, gauging her impression of his family.

An exasperated voice bellowed from the family room, "Finn? What channel is the game on?"

"NBC," Finn hollered over his shoulder, then looked back at Haley and grinned again. "Want to risk the chaos, or head straight upstairs so I can show you my bedroom?"

Rolling her eyes, she set her hands on her hips. "And miss the Seahawks?"

Tsking, he stepped closer and wrapped his hands around her waist. "I'm only letting that slide since the Fire don't play until tomorrow. First game of the season, first game without me. We'll see how they fare." Leaning down, he brushed his lips over hers. "But I'd better still be your favorite player."

Nipping at his lip, she teased, "You've always been on my fantasy league."

"MVP?"

"Hall of Fame."

Groaning, he pulled her hips tight against his, kissing her again.

From the family room, she heard another holler, "Finn? Stop making out with your rebound and help me figure this thing out."

Without releasing her, he shut his eyes and cringed under the closed lids. "As part of his man cave, he switched to satellite so he can watch any game at any time." He slid his hand into hers and led the way into the fray.

The kitchen was bigger than she had expected, bright and open with high ceilings overlooking the family room. Lighting up as they approached, Scott tossed down the remote and hopped up the four steps from the family room to the kitchen where she stood next to Finn. Like his son, he moved like a gazelle. Strikingly handsome, he looked remarkably like Finn, plus twenty years, if that. "You must be Haley. It's nice to finally meet you."

Accepting the friendly handshake, Haley was so disarmed by the casual ease of the home, the family, she felt the tension drain from her shoulders. "It's great to meet you Mr. Halseth."

"Scott, please." He winked, then released her hand. "Can I get you something to drink? Beer? Lemonade? Water?"

"I'd love a beer."

Finn squeezed her hand. "I can grab some."

Scott shook his head. "No, you figure out that damn TV. I'll bring you a beer if you can get me Seahawks." He turned to Haley. "We've got the latest from Zane. Why don't you come pick out what you'd like."

How many parties had she been the one offering drinks? Not serving them, of course. She'd snag an occasion-specific signature apéritif from a caterer's tray and toast with her guests.

"Great." She smiled, following him toward the fridge.

From the oven, another handsome Halseth turned and waved. "Hi Haley. I'm Evan. Hope you like halibut. If Finn didn't butcher it beyond salvaging."

Finn griped from the family room, "Next time, buy it de-boned, dipshit."

Haley flipped her hair to its usual part, forgetting about her wound she'd been hiding. Chopping a bunch of spinach at the island, Zoe caught sight of the scar. "Oo, is that from the fall? That's a doozy."

Of course he'd told his family. Haley was realizing that the Halseths told each other everything. No wonder they were so relaxed around each other. No secrets, no sneaking around, no worrying about silent judgment. "Yes. I probably should have gotten stitches."

Scott pulled out a handful of beers. "Just make up a good story. Like you were diving off the Great Barrier Reef."

"As if falling off a cliff isn't daring enough?" She jabbed back, laughing at the charming quirkiness that was the Halseth family.

Displaying the variety for her to choose from on the island, Scott nodded appreciatively. "That is impressive all on its own. Pick your poison."

She grinned again, her cheeks almost growing sore from smiling so much around genuinely enjoyable people. "I'll take the Hound of Hell. I haven't tried that one yet."

"Good choice." He poured a few into glasses for those ready for football. "Evan? Zoe? Want a beer or not yet?"

Jumping back as oil from the pan splattered as he set a battered strip of fish in for homemade fish and chips, Evan winced. "Now would be good. This may cause severe burns. May as well start numbing the pain."

Snorting, Zoe glanced back at his progress. "Join the club. You need to spend more time at the restaurant rather than lazing about while your meats cook themselves in the smoker, turning them every so often so you look like you have something to contribute."

He flipped her off, grabbed a beer gratefully from Scott, and stood back as he used some long-handled tongs to flip another fish.

Scott motioned down the few steps to the family room. "We'll leave them to it. Now, down to the important stuff. Can you make this place into a man cave?"

Nodding, she scoped out the mid-sized family room. "I can't say that I've ever made a man cave, but I've got some ideas. I'd like to see what you have already so I know what we're starting with."

Finn leaned forward from his spot on the couch and took her hand, pulling her back to sit next to him. "Don't do it. You'll get trapped in there forever."

"What?"

Scott snorted, plopped on the floral armchair, and aimed toward the game. "I've got a few boxes in the garage of sports memorabilia. From games I've been to, pretty much everything ever printed with Finn's name on it, some stuff from my stint at Arizona State. And, of course, some from the high school team."

Haley winked conspiratorially. "I'll come over sometime when Finn's at work so we won't be interrupted."

Tracing his thumb over their joined hands, Finn squeezed a subtle affirmation, while saying out loud, "If you're still sorting all that crap out after I close up the bar that night, I'm not rescuing you. And don't say I didn't warn you."

Assessing the room, Haley asked, "What's your budget and what specifics are you looking for?" Not that she'd ever even considered a man cave, but she enjoyed a challenge. Nor had she ever walked into a room she didn't have mentally redecorated within twenty minutes, but sharing her ideas out loud was generally not considered socially acceptable.

Scott ran through some numbers, some ideas he'd been bouncing around. "Nothing too cave-like. I mean, we have the formal living room that I'd eventually like to update into a place people actually want to sit, or for grandkids to play in if these goofballs ever get around to it. But I want this room to say, 'come on in, put your feet up, and watch the game.'"

Considering, Haley chewed her cheek for a moment, then cleared her throat. "The layout is perfect for that. They've got some great couches for sale at Mountaintop Furniture that have loungers and cupholders. We'll see what you have that might look good on the walls. With all the natural light in here, this wall would look great in a deep blue tone, but we'll need to add more lights on the inside wall to take the 'cave' out of 'man-cave.'" She continued to float on-the-fly ideas, hoping she wasn't missing the mark. It had been tough designing her own home, finding the line between classy and cozy and disallowing anything that wasn't inviting.

All ears, Scott nodded as she spoke. "You're hired," he said. "I have no idea what to pay an interior decorator, but I'll more than happily pay at least the going rate."

"What?" she asked. "No way would I charge you. This is fun, not work."

Scott shook his head. "But there's a lot of work to it, even for something fun."

"Yes, but I'm still not accepting anything."

Before Scott could insist again, Finn cleared his throat. "Wait a sec, I have an idea. Why doesn't Haley take some before and after shots and do a feature series for her blog. Then, Haley, let me know if this is crazy, but maybe someday if you're interested, you could offer e-consults for a reasonable fee. For people like Pops that wouldn't dream of hiring someone normally, but would appreciate a natural eye and a few mock-ups for less than a formal consultation would cost?"

Her heart flipped in her chest as she thought about what he'd said. "Wow. I could do that. Add a whole series of unique styles to build a portfolio. Maybe some kind of tele-consults. Even just ads on the portfolio pages could generate more income." It would be slow going to start, but if she advertised well... she picked up her beer and drained it by half, too flummoxed to say anymore.

Evan announced that dinner was ready. Zoe was plating the baked sweet potato fries, spinach salad, and fried halibut while Evan set out silverware at the farm-style wooden table off the kitchen. Overlooking the backyard, the expansive windows made it feel like they were sitting out in the windy summer evening.

Dinner was surprisingly... fun. The Halseths laughed heartily, genuinely enjoying each other. Stories bounced around the table, supportive yet ripe with teasing. While Brenda was clearly missed, her life was laced through their conversation, and, she suspected, their mannerisms, as Finn and his brother and sister were a lot like Scott, but all seemed to share a left cheek dimple, rebellious cowlicks, and quirky jokes that were unique to only those three. However she helped create this man cave, traces of Brenda would be necessary, or something would be missing. Just not the pastel fabrics.

Until the meddling Finn had mentioned. Not near Patricia-severity, but classic.

"Finn? Did you schedule those interviews yet? Pete's got that baby coming soon, and I'll be busy with football season starting back up. I need to know if I should be planning on hiring another bartender." Scott scooped a dollop of barbeque sauce on his fries and chewed nonchalantly.

Finn set down his beer, his jaw clenching tight. "Not yet."

"Season's started. Hiring's pretty much wrapping up for the year. The longer you wait, the better chance they'll find somebody else."

Roaring cheers erupted on the TV, a heavy metal rift rocked the tinny speakers as the Seahawks made another touchdown. Finn hopped up from his chair, bringing his plate to the sink. "I'll make some calls in the morning."

"Keep your options open. Just let me know as soon as you decide."

"'K." Finn rinsed the plate, grabbing the nearest dirty dishes to load the dishwasher.

Silence.

Evan cleared his throat and said, "So, Haley. You grew up around here, right?"

Nodding, she was grateful for the subject change. Finn still hadn't turned around. "I did. Sounds like I moved away right as you guys were moving in."

"I wonder if we had some of the same friends." He grinned, chattier than she'd seen him all night. Helping steer the conversation from Finn, she suspected. They were a unit in so many ways. As she and Grady and Ryder had tried to be for each other, until their lives had drifted apart, but she felt they were slowly coming back together.

Turning on his heel, Finn appeared before she could answer and snagged empty plates from the table. "Of course she did. She's Grady and Ryder Mallory's little sister."

Zoe lit up, flipping her hair back and adjusting her posture. "I had such a crush on Ryder. What's he up to these days?"

Laughing, Haley hadn't heard that one in a while. Where Grady had the blond hair and blue eyes like he'd grown up surfing in Honolulu, Ryder was pure slick style.

Each had coped with a rough start to life very differently. Patricia wasn't exactly the world's best role model. Grady and Ryder's dad had died young, but the divorce had already been finalized. Haley's dad was good to his stepsons, but it had been tough on Grady and Ryder to lose him to a brutal divorce as they were on the cusp of adulthood. Husband number three was reasonable, but not very involved. Too little, too late. Grady had fought Patricia's superior influence, eventually levelling out into the guy he inherently was. Ryder was... working on it.

"He's busy. He's living in Arizona and working his way up the ladder at a marketing firm."

Evan rose from the table, taking his plate to Finn at the sink. "Sounds about right. I heard he and Claire were engaged until she met Grady."

Haley hadn't been around for it, but she'd suspected the gossip had run rampant. "Not exactly. Yes, she had been with Ryder, but they'd broken up."

Biting the edge of her tongue, Zoe nodded. "Still, must have been awkward. Swapping brothers like that. Could have been worse, like if they'd been best friends or something. I mean, brothers will fight it out and move on, but that would have destroyed—"

Finn snatched Zoe's plate and grabbed her half-consumed beer right from her hand. "I'm sure Grady, Claire, and Ryder would prefer to stay out of gossip circles."

Haley rose from her chair and brought her plate to Finn. "Grady felt awful, falling for what he thought was his brother's fiancée."

Taking her plate, Finn rinsed and added it to the dishwasher. "I would imagine Claire felt terrible, moving on so fast, and not with just anyone, but her nearly-brother-in-law."

Dishes nearly done thanks to Finn's efficiency, Zoe and Evan filtered out of the room, and Scott returned to the game.

Grabbing a rag, Haley dampened and rang it out, wiping down the countertops while Finn worked at the sink. "Sore subject for all involved. Which is why you and I have chosen to rebound; no fuss, no muss. Just fun." She stood on her tiptoes and planted a teasing kiss on Finn's jaw.

"Yeah," he said with a half-smile, his jaw muscle ticking from the effort. He'd been off since Scott brought up the interviews. Haley wanted to pick his brain about it, but he shut off so severely, she'd have to find the right moment.

When they were down to the last plate, Zoe popped back in via the slider to the backyard and flagged her down.

Haley set down her rag and crossed the kitchen. "Hey," she answered.

A mischievous twinkle in her eye, Zoe gestured outside. "Come see if you want starts of these shrubs."

Following Zoe to the park-like backyard, a veritable maze of fruit trees, winding paths, and eventually opening to a native forest, she mentally took notes on ideas for her own yard.

As they neared a rose garden, Zoe crossed her arms over her chest. Rather than talking gardening as expected, Zoe didn't beat around the bush, so to speak. "Finn is really happy." Zoe scowled, her foot tapping against the gravel path.

"That's great." Haley nodded, unsure what Zoe was getting at. With how her jaw was clenched tight like Finn's when he was upset, she didn't mean that in a good way. The wind was still fierce, blowing her hair across her face. Haley ran her hands through her hair and held her hand on her head to pin her hair in place.

"I like you, Haley. You're really good for him."

And this is why this rebound thing was so tricky and so filled with rules. Why they should have kept it a secret. Not that she'd want him to lie to his family. "He's been really good for me, too."

"He wasn't happy with… her. When he came home, we were so caught up in managing the pub for Mom and Pops, then… then letting Mom go. He'd worked damn long hours to get things caught up like the rest of us, as things had been stretched thin without our parents running the business first-hand. He was in and out of surgery, physical therapy, dealing with the end of his career. I mean, football was his life. In the middle of all this, he reconnected with his old girlfriend and that was a disaster. Nobody's fault, but you can't go back."

Haley didn't dare respond, but goosebumps spreading over her bare legs in the menacing wind.

Crossing her arms again, Zoe looked back at Haley. "Then he met you. Admittedly, I encouraged him, thinking a fling was just the thing to get his mind off everything."

She shoved her fingers back in her wild hair as another gust threatened to blind her. "Is this why you brought me here? Not for dinner or my professional opinion, but to blitz me?"

Zoe bit her lip, her eyes red and puffy. "Can you see why I have a problem? Dammit, you even speak football. I know your divorce isn't even finalized yet and you two both needed something easy. But whatever he wants to call this, a fling, rebound, whatever… he cares about you."

Heat pounded in her cheeks, her veins, behind her eyes as she was bombarded by emotion she couldn't acknowledge. Haley backed a few steps toward the house. "Whatever you think, I care about Finn. If leaving him will spare him from further heartache, then I'll go."

"No, that's not what I meant."

Haley shook her head, refusing to stomp her feet and demand the easy way out. "I've spent the last ten years of my life under someone's boot. Ignorantly following the path of least resistance while *I* slipped away. While I let some asshole destroy my confidence. I'm done answering to anyone else." She turned back toward the house.

Zoe caught up and grabbed her arm. Haley shook her off and kept walking. Running ahead, Zoe blocked the path. "I like you, too, dammit. You're so good for him. I don't want you to leave him. I just... I shouldn't have said anything. What I really wanted to say is... First, will you *not* leave my brother?"

Blinking away the tears that threatened, the hollow pit in her stomach eroding from the inside out, she shoved her hands in her pockets and stood frozen in the path. "I lost myself. I'm still trying to figure out who I am. To rebuild the strength I gave up for someone else."

"I understand. You should always come first. If you need to walk away, then walk away. But talk to him. Watch his actions. If you're not standing on your own two feet with Finn, then he's not worth it. Whatever you two decide... please don't walk away because you think you should, make sure you're walking away in the end because he's not the one." With a watery smile, Zoe added, "Second, we have a bunch of forget-me-nots and rose campion and daffodils that need dividing. Would you like some for your yard?" She grinned pathetically.

Breathing in the gust of wind, Haley smiled. "I would love some."

18

Blindside

Haley and his sister came back in the house as he was pouring a rare second beer, about to settle in with Pops to watch the rest of the game. Walking arm in arm, eyes a little red, they looked to have duked something out and come out the other side friends. Whatever the argument had been about, they were clearly better because of it.

He poured half of the beer into another glass and held it out for Haley. Without a word, she smiled softly and accepted the glass. He extended his hand and she joined him. Walking up the narrow stairs, he led her to his bedroom.

Not that it was even half as messy as it had been as a kid, but he'd tidied when he knew she was coming over. And vacuumed. And put on clean sheets. Just in case she decided to stay over.

She stepped into the room and closed the door behind her. Smiling, she leaned against the door and surveyed the room.

Looking at the small space, he tried to imagine it with her eyes. A simple navy blue and gray quilt was tucked neatly over the full-sized bed that was centered on the main wall. A massive poster of an empty football field under the lights at night took up most of the wall over the oak headboard, a matching desk in the opposite corner, with a small faux-leather club chair in front of the sliding closet doors.

Without a word, Haley grabbed his beer and set both of their drinks on the stack of books on the desk. Stepping closer, she looked up at him with a familiar, yet quiet heat. Her hands trailed down his abdomen until she reached the hem of his shirt. With a light touch, she traced the line of his hip, of each muscle he'd hard-earned from hours at practice, and then hooked her hands on the waist of his jeans.

Immobile as she continued her exploration, he held still as she unlatched his top button and slid the zipper down. Grazing her hands back up, she slid his shirt out of her way. He tugged the shirt over his head and tossed it aside. Her fingers tormenting him with her delicate touch, she lowered his jeans, his raging erection springing free.

She ran the back of her fingers tenderly along his shaft, then shocked the hell out of him, gripping him tight and tugged. Lost in sensation, he was utterly hers. Her jaw was set, her concentration fierce, she was taking what she wanted.

Before he knew what she was about, she dropped to her knees and her hot mouth was over his cock. Gliding, sucking, she was on a damn rampage, and he was wholeheartedly on board.

Nearing the tipping point, he groaned and pulled away; still without a word, she rose to her feet and locked eyes with him. Those sapphire blues were on fire.

Yanking her top over her head, she tossed it aside.

"Hang on," he whispered.

In his bedroom in her bra and the ridiculously sexy skirt that clung to her hips, she was like nothing he'd ever seen. Daring. Lithe. Training his hands over her sternum, he leaned down and pressed his mouth to her breasts, tracing his tongue along the edge of her bra.

She slipped her hands to the front of her bra and unhooked the brilliant front-closure contraption, her spectacular breasts suddenly free of the thing. Breath catching in his chest with pure appreciation, he took her breast in his mouth, sucking and pulling until she gasped, then suckled harder.

She leaned into him, her breath coming quicker. Shifting, he slid her skirt over her hips, surprised by the fucking perfect sight that greeted him. "No panties?" he asked.

She bit her lower lip as she grinned. "I wanted to see your face when you noticed. Better than I'd hoped."

Lowering to his knees, he pressed his lips to her core. "You utterly, completely astonish me." Licking, tasting, he nearly came as she leaned into him, biting her cheek to silence her sweet moans as he laved.

Rising to his feet, he carried her to the bed. He pulled a condom from the bedside drawer, the last of the box, and rolled it on.

Before sliding inside her, he paused at the precipice. Wrapping her legs around his hips, she gripped his waist, pulling him closer. Running his hand along her side, her abdomen, he savored.

"Now," she whispered.

Meeting her gaze, he locked on, unable to pull away. That heaviness she'd worn since after dinner had only intensified as they'd pleasured each other. Refusing to look away, loving that she held his gaze, he slipped inside her.

Connected, her eyes never leaving his, he kept his movement slow, feeling everything as she tightened around him, then released as he thrust again. Faster, intense, she moved with him.

Her eyes fluttered shut as she squeezed him, her breath coming fast, her soft whimpers tipping him over the edge. As he neared his climax, he whispered, "Haley?"

Still in the grips of sensation, her eyes flashed open and met his. Refusing to release each other, they finished together, rhythmically, powerfully.

As he rolled to his back, she came with him, resting her head on his shoulder. Neither moved for hours, until the cool of the night brought a chill to the room, and he pulled the blankets over them. Glued to his side, she slept wrapped around him... and he couldn't have let go if the house burned down around them.

Thunder boomed over the house as morning closed in around them. Haley breathed in one last taste of Finn. Zoe was right; they were crossing lines they hadn't intended. Last night, they'd broken all the rebound rules.

Sitting up, Haley quietly slipped on her clothes and tiptoed down the stairs. She made it all the way to the door before she ran into anyone.

Scott was waiting at the entry, leaned up against the doorway to the kitchen like Finn had. He held out a spare cup of coffee, as if he'd been waiting for her. Nodding to the kitchen, he beckoned her in.

"I really ought to get home," she futilely argued.

"Five minutes. Finn doesn't wake early, but you'd know that better than me these days."

At Scott's instruction, she sat on one of the bar stools while he pulled up the one next to her. Accepting the impending lecture, meddling, or whatever it may turn out to be, she took a testing sip of her coffee.

"When Finn was a baby, we were so terrified. Brenda was only eighteen at the time, a senior in high school." He stared blankly across the kitchen. Haley couldn't help but listen. "Quite the scandal, as I played for ASU at the time. We lived in an apartment off campus when Finn came along, getting by on her wages as a server while I worked the kitchen between homework and games. But she never let me quit. Gave up everything for me."

Burning in her gut nagged at her, knowing this wasn't going to make things any easier. That she would regret it if she didn't stay to hear it.

"When Finn was thirteen, she came to me one day and said, 'Scott? There's this adorable town up in Washington. And a perfect little building with a lot for sale downtown.' Not having a clue what she was getting at, I said, 'And?' That's when I realized how much she'd given up for me. At the time, I was coaching Finn's team, working at the local butcher's smoking meats and cheeses. Brenda, she stomped her foot and took both of my cheeks in her hands and said, 'I love you. You're a great father and a hard worker. But it's my turn. We're opening our own a restaurant.'"

Smiling, Haley realized the conversation wasn't going quite where she had expected.

"So, we made an offer and uprooted the family. Finn was pissed, not wanting to leave his friends, his team. But Brenda was right. It was her turn. We took out a hefty loan from the bank and bought the property. Poured our hearts and souls into creating a unique menu, building a restaurant that would stand the test of time.

"When she went through that last PET scan, and it was clear the cancer had beat an unbeatable woman, I was devastated. Not Brenda. She grabbed my cheeks again and claimed, 'It's not my turn anymore. I would have liked more time, but sometimes life's stupid that way. Let's bring the kids home. It's their turn now.' She knew they were floundering."

"She must have been an amazing woman." Haley thought of the family photos that lined the stairwell, the smiles and love between them.

"She was. Will always be with me." He drained the last of his coffee, staring into the bottom of the cup. "Know what did it for me?"

"What?"

"I can't say we had planned anything. We'd been having fun, two stupid kids that figured we were just fooling around. Well, we all know how that story ends." He toasted his coffee. "But we stuck together. She wouldn't marry me right off, told me she didn't want a pity proposal."

"What made her change her mind?"

"That day in the delivery room. Holding Finn in our arms. I brought her the biggest bunch of flowers I could afford and said I'd put up with her hemming and hawing for nine damn months. That she was the strongest woman I'd ever met. That no one else set me on fire like she did. And that baby was so perfect. That it didn't matter what tomorrow brought, as long as she was with me."

"Did she say yes?"

He chuckled, "She stared at Finn for a minute, his fierce scowl that she said looked just like mine. Said this wasn't her plan. About the time I was starting to panic, thinking she was about to dump me, she said things don't work out the way you think they will, but sometimes life drops something better in your lap."

"You have an amazing family. I'm truly envious."

Scott hopped off his stool and brought over the coffee pot, topping them both off. "Finn probably told you I like to meddle."

She grinned, taking another sip. "He implied as much."

"Well, consider this a proud father standing up for his son. He's an incredible player, and I don't want him to miss out on anything life has to offer. Whatever he decides, he needs to know it was his choice, not mine or anyone else's. That he didn't get stuck with the burden of taking on what Brenda and I created."

"I get the feeling he easily follows the path of least resistance."

Scott winked over his mug. "You got that right. If that ex of his hadn't ended things, it might have taken him a few years to figure out she wasn't the one."

Uh-oh. Not another ambush. "I should get going."

"I know. I figure Zoe already gave you the run-down last night, but I wanted to make sure you knew why. Finn has come alive the last few months, more so since you came around. He's happy, more than I've seen in years. But it's up to him to fight for what he wants. I know you're not ready, like Finn wasn't ready not too long ago. But... don't let him off the hook yet. I suspect it'll do you both some good."

She drained the last of her coffee and rose from the stool, placing the empty mug in the sink. Did they want her to let Finn go so he could decide on his own, or tie him down for a lifelong relationship? More confused than ever, Haley promised to route back with him in a week or two with the ideas for his man cave.

That erosive pit in her gut followed her home. Hung around as she took an efficiently short shower. Didn't let up when she looked in the fridge but couldn't find anything worth eating.

Stomping her foot, she hopped in the car and drove to Sutherland's Hardware and bought a few gallons of paint. No better time than the present to tackle the upstairs rooms.

19

Turnover

When her phone rang a few days later, distracting her from the unrelenting pit in her stomach, Haley juggled the phone in a desperate rush to answer. Swallowing a threatening teary lump, she blinked away the disappointment. Not that it was Trace, but that it wasn't...

Nope. Not going there. Answering, she sported her chipperest voice, "Trace? Are you back?"

"Yes, I am home, jet-lagged, and already lonely, and I want you to invite me over to do projects."

She laughed, but feared it came across as a donkey's bray as she hadn't felt the sensation in days. A good friend might wash away her own loneliness. "Lonely? Who did you hang out with before I stumbled back into town?"

"I've only been back a year or so, and, well, I've been busy. I spend time with the other teachers but not socially, I've got my folks, and, well, the ex and his friends that were sort of my friends but with how things ended, well, I'm letting the dust settle and plan to call him when the jetlag wears off to work things out, one way or another, before we see each other socially. Hence, my clinginess to my old bestie." The end of her monologue lilted with unabashed optimism.

"Do you enjoy painting?"

"Like for artistic purposes or walls?"

"Walls. Lots of them."

"I'm in."

"Fantastic. You can fill me in on your summer while we make this place beautiful. I'll snap a few befores for the blog while you pick up breakfast."

"Better yet, I'm walking over and will arrive with breakfast in twenty minutes or less."

"Are you at your folks' house?"

"Yes. The lease was up on my rental and my landlord was a butt. So, I'm crashing here until I find something better. If I don't commit patricide."

"Ouch, I'm sorry. He's not building another playhouse, is he? I still have visions of him sitting in the middle of the lawn with pages of instructions floating in the air like maple leaves, the 'foundation' a bungled mass of two-by-fours."

"No, he's not allowed to attempt carpentry anymore. I'll fill you in when I get there."

"Hurry over. I'm starving."

Haley snapped a few shots of empty rooms, paint cans, and patched up walls where she'd taken down outdated curtain rods. After getting home from Finn's last week, she'd taken advantage of the solitude. Sort of. More, she'd ripped all the old crap off the walls, then patched up her carelessness. Every time she picked up the phone, she'd put it back down and found something else that needing demolishing or scrubbing or caulking.

The doorbell snapped her out of another pity party she wasn't willing to acknowledge. Ditching the camera on the entry table, she swung open the front door.

A paper bag filled with savory goodness filled her nose and stirred her tummy. Grabbing the bag, she tore into it, then paused. "Hey." She threw her arms around her friend and then pulled the cheddar pastry from the bag. "I'll fully acknowledge you in a moment. I missed your mother's cooking. And the lovely woman, but..." She sunk her teeth into the gooey goodness and groaned as the flaky pastry melted in her mouth.

"How do you think I feel? I'm living with that smell every morning now."

"I'm so sorry." She wasn't sorry at all. Not emotionally anyway, but this stuff would be hard to burn off.

"Okay, finish up and let's get painting." Trace gestured to her cute paint-friendly attire. Yoga pants, what must be her father's t-shirt tied in a side knot, and a bandana over her strawberry blond wildness.

Haley gestured down to her own paint-stained overalls and Finn's t-shirt with the ripped off sleeves that he'd used for her makeshift field bandage. She'd only slept in his shirts the first few nights without him for something cozy; she'd taken all her old nightgowns to the dump after filing for divorce. Today's choice was entirely due to the fact that she didn't have another old shirt available. "Ready."

After giving Trace the tour of what she'd accomplished so far, they got to work. Haley had forgotten how easy it could be to chat with a good girlfriend that wanted nothing in return, just friendship. No phony compliments or hiding your real thoughts to avoid looking foolish. They spent the first hour talking about parents and Paris and the transition of moving from the chaos of big cities to laid-back Foothills.

The nautical gray she'd selected for her office upstairs was already looking better than she had anticipated; a bit dark until the paint dried, but was already bringing the crisp warmth she'd craved. Good thing she liked it, as her overalls were stained beyond repair, and she sported a tattoo-like stripe on her arm.

Not quite as messy of a painter, Trace had little more than a smudge on her yoga pants. Trace filled her in on the events of her busy summer as they tackled the sunny room.

When Haley could no longer avoid the topic anymore, Trace reloaded the roller and asked, "Okay, I'm done unloading. And you're done hiding. Tell me, did you have your summer fling? With the sexy arms from your chandelier-holding model? Your foot snuggler in the hammock with you?"

Snorting, Haley wiped away the smudge she'd bumped onto the white window trim. Were they done, or giving each other space? How did one end a rebound? Wasn't it supposed to be easier than the reason for the rebound? "Yes. I completed a successful summer rebound."

"Aha," Trace giggled. "And can you say your sex life has taken a positive turn?"

Tugging at the corner of her mouth, Haley couldn't fight the smile. "That, I can absolutely say."

Rolling on the seaside gray, casually allowing Haley the freedom from visual scrutiny of her expressions, Trace pushed a little further. "Yet you have a broody attitude. Can't have been that great."

Setting down her brush before she completely messed up the edges around the window trim, Haley answered, "The sex part was amazing. Mind-blowingly, epically spectacular. Honestly, I can't figure out how Nate managed to sleep with so many people, yet didn't seem to care about a single one. Not even his wife."

Trace set down her roller and her face fell with guilt. "You fell for your rebound. My fault; I shouldn't have assigned such a tough project."

Haley scowled and shook her head. "No, it's my own fault. I wouldn't have rebounded if I wasn't ready. I sort of fell into it, no effort required. Things were so incredible. Easy as breathing."

"That sounds nice. But you're speaking in the past tense. What's the problem?"

"What's the problem?" Haley repeated, jamming her hands on her hips, not caring that she now had gray handprints on her overalls. "I fly down to San Francisco to finalize my divorce *tomorrow*. I'm still married. Ten years of living under someone's thumb. Sure, I had a hell of a lot of fun with my rebound. But I was getting attached, and he was getting attached and... I'm still trying to navigate *me*, and I don't have room to figure out an *us*."

Looking out the window at the forest beyond, Trace sighed, "I'm sorry you lived through hell with Nate. When we were kids, you were this unstoppable force, always diving into the next adventure. I was a little jealous of your fearlessness. Sure, you never dared say no to whatever club and sport your mother pushed you into, but you did it all vibrantly. I know you say you lost all of that with Nate. But seeing you now, and it's not just because we've been apart for so long, but I can see that fierce girl that wasn't afraid of anything, and she's found her way to the bright light of day. If falling for this guy truly scares you, I'm sorry. But is it a future with him that scares you, or something else?"

Haley couldn't even answer that. She wanted to shout that she wasn't afraid. Nothing about Finn was scary. He built her up unlike anyone she'd ever known. But she needed to stand on her own two feet. Without any support. "Not yet. That's all."

"I get that. You need time to recover. This is going to sound weird, but when I saw you six weeks ago, you were bright and happy and bouncy. Today, well, you seem blue. And not from the paint all over you. Getting over your rebound looks like it's hitting you way harder than getting over Nate. Just saying."

Shit. She was right. "Puh-hoo."

"Okay. Let's talk it through. Keep painting before your brush dries."

"Okay," she said, nodding. She didn't really want to talk about it, but she couldn't run away from it either.

Long pause. Trace picked up her roller. Following suit, Haley picked her brush back up and coated the tip with paint, gliding it along the edge.

Clearing her throat, Trace said, "I guess I'll start. Sex was good?"

Haley chuckled, keeping her hand steady. "You keep landing on that. Yes. It was amazing. I got to try out all the fantasies I've been bottling up over the years."

"Aw, I'm so jealous." She cleared her throat again. "I mean, sorry, I ended things with someone right before you got back. Things were a bit vanilla, like going through the motions of the relationship. He had a lot on his mind, and I guess I wasn't any more engaged in *us* either."

"Maybe you should try a rebound." The corner of Haley's mouth tugged up as she thought about the difference.

"You may be right." Trace nodded. "He and I used to be so good together. I don't know, maybe in a few months when our lives are more settled, we can try again."

"Did you love him?"

"We'll get to that later. We're not done with you, so stop trying to get out of it." She raised her eyebrows in a wicked taunt. "Tell me why you're not still having this epic mind-blowing sex."

"The last night we were together..." Her heart skipped a few beats, sinking into her gut as she relived the moment she'd been refusing to think about since it happened. The stupid L-word had nearly passed her lips so many times that night.

His wicked grin as she'd walked into his house that night. Curled up together watching the game, his hand resting easy on her bare legs; a mindless gesture for him no doubt, but the effortless affection had shaken her. Then when they'd gotten to his bedroom...

She wasn't even going there. She still couldn't handle the volcano of unspoken emotions that had erupted between them, even during the quiet of the night, snuggled up on the cramped bed.

Dipping her brush back in the paint, she continued, "Anyway. He made me laugh. Taught me how to throw with power. Reminded me that I'm strong, not because he wanted me to be, but because I had it in me. Okay, I sound crazy now. Probably reading way too much into things."

"Let's pretend for a minute that you weren't married to a jerk for the last decade. That the timing was perfect. You feel like you, confident and vivacious. Would things have worked out?"

"Probably not. He might be moving anyway. Honestly, I'm not sure that he wants to, he seems to really love tending bar at his family's pub. But he's got a few interviews for coaching positions all over the country. And he's been through so much, still so heartbroken, I don't think he's any more ready than I am."

Trace bumped her roller against the ceiling, then cussed. "Sorry." She grabbed the ladder and a damp rag to wipe up the mess. "Did he, I mean... tell me this. Do you think he loves you?"

Haley shrugged, holding the paintbrush still for fear of hitting the trim. Heavy conversation might have been a bad idea while painting. "I don't know. But I know we meant more to each other than either of us intended." She sighed, setting her brush on the tray, then plopped her butt down on the drop cloth. "He's nicer than I deserve. All the while I'm ragging on Nate, Finn has nothing but good things to say about his ex; blames himself for messing up with her."

Pausing, Trace pulled her roller from the wall. Lowering it, she stepped back and cleared her throat. "I'm sure it's not entirely his fault." She pushed her roller in the tray and loaded up more paint, inhaling as she methodically applied the layer.

"I guess sometimes it comes down to the details. How could you tell you meant something to him? I'm curious. I could never tell with... well, with my last relationship."

Heaviness churned in Haley's chest. She hugged her knees and looked out the window at the trees whipping with the wind outside. "Little things. Everything. I guess it's hard to say. He was just so easy to be with. Affection was natural and unforced. We could talk for hours about nothing and everything. And I've never had anyone look at me like he looked at me." A chime at the doorbell startled her. "Sorry, it's probably Patricia again. She has notoriously the worst timing. Even narrowly missed walking in on us once."

Checking her feet were clear of paint, Haley dashed down the stairs and swung open the door.

On her front porch, markedly haggard with his hair in a spiraled mess around his cowlick, his brown eyes were weary, and his ancient USC t-shirt had a new rip in the hem. "Hey," he said. His Mustang was parked in the middle of the driveway, not hidden in her garage like usual.

"Hey."

"Can I come in?" He shoved his hands in his pockets as she desperately wished he'd reach for her, pulling her in for an urgent kiss like he had so many other times in her doorway.

"Sure. I'm, uh, painting, so I can't visit long."

He nodded. "I won't stay. I just wanted to see if you were all set to head down to finalize the divorce, and to let you know I'll be out of town for a few weeks."

"Okay." She nodded, her head bobbing like an idiot.

"I, uh, scheduled a few interviews. Got a call from USC too."

"Wow, that's great," she said, heartily meaning it. "What is that, three teams now?"

"Yeah," he said as he shifted his weight on his feet. "I've also got an interview with ESPN."

"That's so great." She was turning into a bobble-headed agreeable moron. "Scott must be thrilled."

He shrugged, his hands still wedged in his pockets. "He's on cloud nine. Anyway, I'm trying to line them all up and get it over with. Lund, hell, he'd asked if he could put my name out there, and I suspect he actively advertised."

Resisting the urge to hook her arms around his middle and not let go, she jammed her hands in her own pockets. "I'm glad you're exploring all of your options. Will it make you happy, being in the football world however you can?"

"Honestly? I don't know. I'm happy where I'm at, but Pops seems to think I can't truly decide that until I see what all is out there, so I promised him I'd check it out." His jaw ticked rapidly, clenching tight again.

Haley hated whatever weirdness was between them, but didn't doubt they both realized they'd better pull back or they'd irretrievably fall in. "Aside from playing, if you could pick anything in the world, starting all over again, what would you do?"

"Hell, I don't know." His smile softened, his eyes rested on hers. "I genuinely don't know. The last ten years have been a whirlwind. Great, but intense. The last few weeks, I feel like... I don't know. Settled."

Haley swallowed the thrill at his words, that she was what he wanted, also swallowing the bile, regretting that he wasn't what she needed. And vice versa. She was so far off from being settled.

He exhaled, then looked around before speaking again. "Haley, there's something else I've been needing to tell you before... About my—"

As he spoke, Trace came down the stairs. Finn froze solid like he saw a ghost. "Trace?"

"Hi, Finn." She paused on the last step, leaned against the rail, biting her lips together.

Haley looked to Finn and back to Trace, making the obvious connection. Her face fell as she took in just how much deeper into shits-ville this rebound thing had descended.

Awkward was a drop in the damn bucket of the epic cluster her life was becoming. Trace's brow furrowed as she studied Haley and Finn, standing inches apart, longing sparks zapping between them. She whispered, "Haley, I had no idea until a few minutes ago. I'm not... Please don't think this changes anything between you and me or you and Finn."

Finn ran his hand through his hair, guilt radiating off his blushing cheeks.

The metallic taste of blood seeped over her tongue as Haley bit down on her cheek. "You knew?" She seethed as she watched Finn's reaction.

His jaw clenched so tight she could hear his teeth grinding together, he exhaled cautiously and said, "I found out that day at the hike, you mentioned Trace over lunch. I wanted to tell you... shit, this sounds like a lame excuse, but I hadn't found a good time to tell you. Just now I was trying to... I mean, you fell down that cliff, and then the concussion, and then Nate, and well... after the other night at my place... it didn't seem as critical anymore."

"What?" She hollered, shocked at the glass-breaking rage in her voice. "That it wouldn't matter that I was sleeping with my friend's boyfriend?"

"Whoa." He put his arms out to calm things down. "Ex. Ex-boyfriend."

"Friends don't do that, ex or not. I wouldn't have imagined you were rebounding from someone I even *knew*, but my oldest friend? That happens to be a positive part of my life now that I'm free of that asshole? One of the few girlfriends I've had in my life that *wasn't* screwing my husband?" Adrenaline pumping through every inch of her body, she paced like a gorilla at the zoo, then stood and glared out the great room window out at the forest beyond.

Finn ran to catch up. "Haley, it's not... you know what? It doesn't matter. I fucked up. I should have said something the moment I realized."

Standing back, Trace walked halfway to them, then stopped, her arms wrapped around her middle. "Guys? I'm sorry if I'm butting in on something. I've been gone and clearly a lot's happened. Haley, yeah, Finn and I have a history, but we broke up before I left town. No hard feelings. Clean break."

Finn reached a hand for her, his brow scrunched, jaw clenched, but Haley stepped back, muttering, "I can't."

Her stupid phone rang again. Not giving a damn at this point, as her day couldn't get much worse, she answered.

"Haley?" Her lawyer sounded apologetic already. Icing on the damn cake. She was flying down tomorrow for what should be their last mediation. He'd better not have any last-minute changes. Nate would know she'd be done with this whole charade and accept about anything. "I wanted to give you a heads up before you arrive. Nate is countering. He's claiming you were having an affair with some football player and says he's got documentation of a significant amount of funds you spent on this guy."

"What? That's not true, and if it were, have I asked him for one red cent that he spent on his *many* affairs?" Her vision turned red.

"I'm preparing a response, detailing the funds he's spent on his own infidelities. He won't get away with it. California's a no-fault divorce state, so the worst he can do is reduce your share, but he will need to present adequate proof, and this might turn into nickel and diming, which could add on another six to twelve weeks. Don't sweat this, Haley, I'm on it. I didn't want you to come in blindsided. We're going to stop this. Nate doesn't want to go to trial any more than you do."

She flashed back to the weeks following their wedding. *Let's put all the accounts in both our names. I'm better with numbers, so it makes sense.*

"Okay. Thanks." She ended the call. Trace was still in the middle of the room, her feet mobile as she decided whether to go or stay.

Legs drooping like a leaky faucet, Haley wanted to collapse.

Strong arms wrapped around her before she could. Finn pulled her against him and whispered in her ear. "I'm so sorry. I shouldn't have come out that day and let him see me with you, but that son of a bitch was so damn smug, I wanted to piss him off." He pulled back and cradled her jaw in his hands. "You are so much stronger than he is. Than anyone I know. Even if he gets away with this, you're not alone. We'll make it work. Do you want me to fly down? As a witness? As a friend? I can pull my financial records, alibis, whatever you need."

She wanted to hide in bed and not wake up until it was over. "No, thanks. I'm going to call Sophie and see if she can help compile everything, and maybe I'll be able to find where he's getting his numbers."

He pressed his lips to her forehead and wrapped his arms around her again. For a moment, she let herself sink in. Standing in the sun-soaked great room, she let herself pretend she could hold on forever.

She caught Trace heading out the front door in of the corner of her eye.

Finn backed up, releasing her hand only when he was too far away to hold on. He opened his mouth like he was going to say something, but didn't. Instead, his chest rose and fell, then he turned and walked out.

20

Delay of Game

She was going to kill him. She'd think he didn't listen, or that he didn't believe that she could do this alone.

She was so wrong. He needed her to know she didn't have to do this alone. Hadn't she spent the last decade battling that shit-show of a marriage alone?

Waiting in her attorney's office, he forced himself to sit in one of the lobby chairs, his jaw clenching and releasing at breakneck speed. As his teeth squealed together, he bit down on his cheek to save his tooth.

Resting a hand on his shoulder, Sophie whispered, "She'll be okay."

As Haley had said, it wasn't about the damn money. Even if Nate took it all, Haley had friends and family that would support her, plus a promising business that was stable enough, and he had no doubt it would be a huge hit once she worked up the courage to post her vlog and maybe even start taking clients. If she refused the help from her family, or his offer to invest, she'd easily secure a loan from the bank and could ramp up her business.

"Chill," Lincoln whispered from across the lobby, looking cool as a cat, clearly comfortable in the setting.

Finn hated the damn suit. Had even worn a stupid tie; felt like a monkey on display in the thing. Even for Haley, he'd drawn the line at dress shoes. One advantage of being a professional athlete was that he could wear sneakers for every occasion.

Now if he could wear cleats, that would be ideal, so he could deliver Nate a studded kick in the balls.

An assistant in cuffed slacks and a trim sports jacket popped into the lobby, his hair long on top and shaved on the sides. "Mr. Halseth?"

Popping out of the chair, he followed the guy into a huge meeting room with a long glass table in the center. The massive wall of windows should make the place feel open, but he felt closed-in with vertigo, the city sprawled out in the distance.

Fuckhead Nate was dressed sharply in a shiny silver suit, his attorney equally snooty. Across the table, Haley's attorney wore a more subdued charcoal suit. He may not like the things, but he had enough of his own, he knew the look. Another guy sat at the head of the table, must be the moderator. His crisp black suit with a pink tie said he didn't answer to anyone.

A cool breeze in the suffocating room, Haley sat front and center in a tailored navy-blue cap-sleeved dress that accented her sapphire eyes. She must have been surprised to see him, but she was smart enough to hide her reaction.

Clearing his throat, the assistant directed Finn to the seat at the end opposite the moderator.

Nate looked fantastically surprised to see him. Lips pursed tight, his eyes darted anywhere and everywhere like a terrified bunny. Haley's attorney began to speak, and all eyes turned to listen.

Except for Nate, who took the opportunity to fire a glower at Finn. Finn flashed him a wink, smirking in satisfaction as Nate's eyes grew wide, quickly shifting to the conversation.

"In light of the significant accusations and previously unseen evidence presented by Mr. Salsborough today, I have been in contact with Mr. Halseth, who was gracious enough to fly down to help clarify his involvement with Mrs. Salsborough prior to the last six weeks. Lack of involvement, I should say. If his truth is not enough to help settle this without advancing to more in-depth legal action, I have several other witnesses prepared to support Mrs. Salsborough's story, which has not changed once in these proceedings. At the end of this meeting, I expect Mr. and Mrs. Salsborough to sign the previously agreed upon divorce decree, without the last-minute changes presented by Mr. Salsborough."

Finn bit his tongue to hide his grin, enjoying Nate shifting in his seat. When questioned, he accurately and precisely described his relationship with Haley, sparing the intimate details that were no one's damn business.

Nate's attorney tried to trip him up, but he'd been grilled by enough smartasses over the years, convinced they would have done the play better, would have juked right rather than left. "You expect us to believe that, while living for the last six years within five miles of Mrs. Salsborough, who was a tremendous fan of yours, coincidentally heralding from the same miniscule town hundreds of miles away, you never once communicated with each other, and only assumed a relationship with this married woman within days of her returning to your mutual hometown?"

"Yes," he answered simply. He restrained himself from firing back, that if he'd met Haley before, they would have been having this conversation a hell of a lot sooner.

His very favorite was the end of his interview. Realizing he was drowning, Nate blurted out, "Come on. I don't believe it for a second. Haley hasn't shown the slightest interest in sex in ages. She must have been getting her play somewhere else. You two looked pretty comfortable when I saw you in Foothills."

Finn opened his mouth to respond, but he held his tongue to let Haley take this one. "Oh, Nate, I'm so sorry you think I wasn't interested in sex. It's just you that turns me off."

Clearing his throat, the moderator masked a smile and nodded. "Thank you Mr. Halseth. Would you step out while we determine our next steps?"

H aley's heart pounded in her chest, leaping into her throat when Finn walked in. Comfortable, casual, he didn't hesitate. She should be furious at his presumptuousness.

But the moment he walked in, she realized just how long it had been since someone had stood up for her; so long since she'd let anyone.

Unable to talk privately, she had no idea if they'd have a chance to talk before he left. His interview with Minneapolis would be this afternoon. For that, she hoped he was already heading back to the airport.

Every muscle in her body ached, tired and sore and needy as she wanted to tell him to wait for her, that she'd go with him like he came for her, but she wasn't sure what that would change. He deserved so much more than she was able to give right now. He needed to find his own path as much as she did.

Her attorney continued. "Mr. Salsborough, the changes were your suggestion, so I leave the decision to you. Would you next like to hear from her accountant, who has brought detailed documentation from the last five years of financial records that will show absolutely no evidence of transactions supporting your claims? Although there are a number that ran through your card, hotels and flowers and dinner that most certainly were not spent on Mrs. Salsborough. Or perhaps Mrs. Salsborough's mother, the neurosurgeon who has rescheduled her patients to come give testimony as to her knowledge of Haley's relationships; honestly, this may be an interesting one, as she clearly disapproves of Mr. Halseth, which makes her testimony that much more relevant."

Haley almost burst out laughing, imagining Patricia waiting outside to rake Finn over the coals, for Haley's sake. Were they both here? She imagined Patricia glaring at Finn across the lobby, in his suit and sneakers.

"The folks from Foothills are a tenacious bunch. I have more witnesses than I know what to do with. I can also call on the police officer that ticketed Mr. Salsborough for double parking in an alley while harassing my client in her hometown? Perhaps Mr. Halseth's last significant other that can attest to his whereabouts for the months prior to Mrs. Salsborough's arrival in Foothills? I also have a handful of character witnesses. I couldn't say no to the plethora of offers of support for my client."

Nate tugged at his tie, mouth wide in a false smile. "I don't think that will be necessary."

Her attorney raised his lips in a devious smile. "How about one more? For fun? Your own attorney?"

Haley blushed, not liking where this was going. Nate's lawyer's wife had been one of Nate's lovers and had pretended to be a good friend of Haley's. She'd never liked her anyway.

The lawyer gulped, his face paling. "I cannot imagine how that would be helpful. We accept your evidence that she has no significant transactions or investments that would alter our prior plan. As she was willing to divide their shared assets equally without spousal support, I think we can comfortably return to that plan."

She flashed back to about two years ago to their annual Fourth of July party, stepping out onto the darkened balcony with the crowd to watch the fireworks, and jackass lawyer's hand rested on the small of her back, whispering something in her ear about him knowing she was against swapping, but offering they could sneak away and no one would ever know.

Her stomach turned as she realized this was bigger than she had imagined. Not that she'd even been able to eat anything yet today, the furious butterflies threatening to throw back anything she may ingest. The image settling in her brain was so much ickier.

Had Nate and their "friends" been swapping regularly? He would have known she'd have bailed at the suggestion of something so revolting.

She pushed the image to the back of her mind. "If it's all the same to you, I'd like to sign the agreed upon paperwork and go home."

Her attorney shoved the original paperwork toward Nate, holding out a pen. "Any attempt to contact my client again will not go your way. You have jerked her around in so many directions, I would advise her to take you for everything you're worth and ruin your name, but, and correct me if I'm wrong, Haley, you'd rather leave this all behind?"

The moderator cleared his throat. "If we could wrap this up, I'd appreciate it."

Haley nodded. "Please. I want to go home. I have no doubt that Nate's activities will catch up to him without any interference from me."

After thanking her attorney, she held steady as she strode out of the room. The sight that greeted her knocked the wind from her lungs, filling her with something better.

A mass of friends greeted her in the lobby. She was pulled into hug after hug from all of her friends from Foothills, and even her mother. Nate and his creepy lawyer slunk out the door behind them, completely ignored.

"Did you twist his balls until he signed over everything?" Patricia raised a devious eyebrow Haley didn't think she'd ever seen before, her voice loud enough so Nate could hear as he stepped into the elevator.

"Um, no. Just my half. But, thanks for your support."

"Well, I will let you go celebrate with your friends. I don't want to miss my flight." Patricia offered a stiff, shoulder-blade-pat hug, then marched out.

Jumping up and down, Pippa cheered, "Let's go celebrate. I've planned a whole night on the town for us. Dinner on the wharf; I made reservations, then there's this great club—"

Sophie linked elbows with her and motioned her hand for Pippa to take it down a notch. Sophie restrained her friend and said, "But we are flexible and will do whatever *you* want. We'll leave you alone and head home, or we'll eat ice cream and get trashed in your hotel room, everyone but Pippa anyway, or we can all go out for a night on the town per Pippa's itinerary."

Grady, Claire, Asher, Zane, Freya, Lincoln, and Trace stood waiting for her answer. She swallowed her disappointment that Finn was gone, but she'd have booted him on the plane to Minnesota anyway. "Dinner out with you guys sounds amazing. Just please, please tell me you're not all swapping behind my back."

Horrified, they all looked each other over. Asher scowled. "That's disgusting. And not just because I'm related to a third of the women here."

Haley felt the waterworks threatening, the pressure in her eyes almost matching the thrill beating in her chest. "Good. Just... yeah. Good. Let's go have dinner on the wharf."

Seventy-five degrees, clear skies, a bustling crowd, the wharf welcomed her back. Pippa gave her name to the host and they were led through the crowded dockside restaurant and out onto the deck. A salty breeze fanned over her from the bay, seagulls coasted on the updrafts, and hundreds of boats bumped over the waves as they came in and out of the harbor.

Inhaling the savory scents of the restaurant, Haley's stomach rumbled at earthquake levels as the butterflies faded away. A large table awaited their crowd, and she selfishly nabbed a seat overlooking the water. Her friends filled in around her, Grady whispering as he sat next to her, "Doing okay?"

She nodded. "Yeah. All good."

"You're officially done with that bastard. I get it if you're still shell-shocked, but you're withdrawn. Just say the word if I can do anything."

"I'm worn out."

"I'll bet. I am, and I didn't even have to talk to that asshole."

They put in their orders, and Haley absorbed the moment, the setting, her friends.

Last year at this time, she was a few restaurants down, in the upstairs room with swanky lights at a schmoozy party Nate had dragged her to. She remembered staring out the window, alone, wondering if this was it. Reliving the same day over and over; wake up, check in with the staff, a light breakfast, see Nate off to work, hide away in her office and work on her blog, then spend an hour getting ready for another event, bored out of her mind with people she either didn't know or didn't respect. Or had it been *Groundhog Day*, and she couldn't get out of it until she found herself?

While the others laughed and visited over chowder and a beer, Trace leaned back and whispered to Haley, "If I didn't make it clear enough, I will forever be your bestie. Whatever you and Finn decide, I support you both."

"But weren't you thinking of getting back together with him?"

"Honestly?"

Haley interrupted, "Of course honestly. I don't ever, ever want another shred of dishonesty in my life."

Trace bit her lip in a sweet smile. "I promise you will only ever hear the truth from me. Have I ever lied to you? Remember when you cut your hair short in seventh grade and you asked what I thought, and I said you looked like a dork?"

"Yes. And then you made your mom teach me how to apply make-up and hair product so I looked like a rock star." She smiled at the memory. How long had she gone without genuine honesty and support?

"Exactly. Which is why I am now going to deliver another hard truth that, if handled carefully, should end up even better than having all the girls in Foothills follow the trend you set with your spunky haircut." She paused, continuing as the breeze kicked up off the bay. "I did want to get back together with Finn. We were really good together in high school. He's the best friend I've ever had, second only to you."

Nausea washed over Haley; she really, really didn't want to hear it. She was still creeped out that they'd shared him.

"No, hear me out. I can see you putting on the mental earmuffs." Trace raised an eyebrow and applied her stern face. "This time around, he was lost and broken when we got back together. Our relationship was a burden on him. It broke my heart, but I couldn't watch him try to juggle one more thing. I'd hoped he'd be in a better place to try again when I got home, and that we could make it work when he had a better handle on things. Third time's a charm, right?"

The others joked and chatted and watched the boats coming and going, dodging the seagulls that dive bombed for scraps.

Trace continued, "I have to admit, it threw me, seeing you two together. But I think it was a good wake-up call." She stared out at the water, leaned shoulder to shoulder with Haley. "Finn and I were nice together. We never fought. I'd thought it was because we were easygoing. I never lost sleep over him. I thought it was because we'd had a good rhythm."

Haley watched as a party boat motored by, the happy crowd laughing and celebrating so loud, their voices echoed off the restaurant windows behind her. She bit her lips together, letting a self-pitying wallow brew in her throat and sap the last of her energy.

"In the five minutes I saw you two together... he was so different, and in such a good way. He has never fought for me like that. When you rejected him, he went so pale, so helpless. And then when your phone rang, and you were so angry you could hardly stand, he broke down that barrier and held you... it was an awful moment, yet you two were so in tune with each other.

"Then he was on the phone with your attorney so fast, seeing what he could do to clear things up. Rallied all of us to come down and show our support, even if we wouldn't be useful for your divorce, you would know we had your back. Trust me when I say, I know him very well, and I've never seen him so livid. So desperate. Not even when it came to football."

Biting her cheek, only to remember she'd chewed it raw and it still burned, Haley felt the sting of a salty tear trailing down her cheek.

At her other side, Grady leaned back in his chair and whispered, "I could pretend I wasn't listening, but, you know me, I'm nosy." He made sure Trace could hear. "I can attest that Trace and Finn were nice together, but boring. I could go on and on about how he dove off a cliff to get to you, but you know that was extraordinary. Instead, how about that night at Halseth's, when you and he were making eyes at each other all night? I didn't even know you two were a thing, but even I was blushing with all the steam in the air, and I'm pretty comfortable with that sort of thing. Or when he called to ask if I'd drop off your favorite breakfast and a hammock to give you some place else to chill while you recovered from that concussion?"

Freya leaned closer from Trace's other side. "I know you're scared, but you can't argue with pheromones."

Asher nudged his cousin and nodded. "Or lust, whatever."

Pippa rolled her eyes at her brother.

"No really." He shrugged, sporting a wicked grin. "I was surprised that campfire didn't turn into a wildfire at the heat in the air at Claire's birthday party."

Oh boy. She could claim she didn't come out to be ambushed, but getting hit with example after example of how much the man loved her was... intense. In a good way.

Sophie raised her glass. "To Haley. Instantly one of my heroes, and I have a lot of those in my life." She squeezed Asher's hand. "Hit rock bottom, and instead of floundering like others would, she held her head high and drove across the country—showing the ultimate bravery in traveling with Patricia at her side." The table chuckled with eyes wide, reaching for their drinks to toast that part alone. "And with pure muscle, is building something beautiful out of a tired old home. Crossed a raging river to show her bravery, climbed up the cliff that tried to knock her down. Fought for what she deserved, not giving in to pretentious assholes. And with pure passion, found love where there was hopelessness."

With a round of whoops and cheers, the table toasted. Licking her lips, she tasted the gush of tears that cleansed the last decade from her soul. Raising her glass, she whooped right back, "Love you guys. Thanks for coming to stand up for me."

21

Touchdown

Watching oneself on camera was... odd. What was with her eyebrows? Was her voice really that high pitched? Sitting in her nautical gray office with its crisp white trim, navy blue curtains, and whitewashed antique desk, she rechecked the video for the umpteenth time. The footage seemed to have been taken forever ago, but it hadn't even been two months. Eventually, she would be posting the creation of her home office, highlighting how she chose both light and dark blues to accent the gray, with a splash of salmon to jazz it up. She would include how to choose exactly the right desk considering style and purpose and ergonomics, then adding a closet organization system to keep it neat, and a plush white couch with coordinating patchwork quilt from the local farmer's market for brainstorming.

She closed her eyes and let the wave of anxious thrill buzzing in her skull tease down and out through her fingertips. Stomping it out, she took a deep breath and hovered over the submit button. Three, two... oh just fricking click.

Done.

Running her hands through her hair, she stepped back and watched as her video went public on YouTube. Vlog episode number one: *A New Day.*

She wanted to walk away and call it good. Wasn't that enough? Her limbs were heavy from the emotional exhaustion of putting herself out there, but she wasn't really out there until others knew about it.

Routing back to her website, she completed the post, the link, and sent the announcement over the big bad internet. And then her newsletter. And then social media. All of them.

Her phone buzzed in her pocket. A text from Patricia? That was a first. *I'm watching my new favorite YouTube star.*

Way to go Patricia. That was actually thoughtful and rather maternal. Maybe she wouldn't be such a terrible grandma. Not that Haley was planning on helping her with that anytime soon.

Scary, thrilling, but freaking awesome. She was officially expanding her business, taking steps to maintain a respectable income. Haley strolled down the stairs, refusing to stare at the screen all day for follows and likes. They would come. Or they wouldn't. Either way, she was out there.

Reaching the bottom step, she turned and faced the great room. Buttery tan leather sofa, natural wool fiber rug, wood-stump glass coffee table, iron and reclaimed wood accents. Next, throw blankets and wall hangings and candles to warm it up. Not bad. Hopefully her viewers would appreciate it.

Her phone buzzed again. Like a fool, she juggled it out of her pocket, nearly dropping it. Not Finn. Why wouldn't he call?

Dumbass. Of course he wouldn't. Ball was in her possession.

She knew she couldn't call him yet. For them both, she needed to stand on her own two feet first. For him, he had to believe he was on his own. He had a tough career decision, and she wanted him to make the choice for him, not stay here because of her.

Gnawing on her cheek, she opened the text from Claire. *Girls night?*

A flutter of panic pounded at her ribs.

Nope. Done. She closed her eyes and pushed away the fear. The past was exactly that, behind her.

Yes. Please. I have this beautiful new room and haven't gotten to show it off. Want to have it here? She held her breath, hoping.

I'm in!

Within the hour, Haley's home was overrun with carefree laughter. Trace brought wine, Pippa brought pizza, Freya brought a massive salad, and Sophie brought Trivial Pursuit.

When had she ever gotten to play board games? And no one exchanged sex tips. Not that they weren't open and goofy about that sort of thing, but they were very possessive, lovingly so.

Except Trace. While the others moved to the next square in the game, Trace grabbed the next bottle of wine for refills. Something was up with her. Her smile was genuine, but subdued.

"Hey, you okay?"

Nodding, Trace smiled. "I'm great. Really."

"Great might be an overstatement. You're fine, not great."

Trace nudged her in the side, then leaned back against the kitchen counter. "And this is why I haven't had a good girlfriend since you. And why I'm never giving you up again. I have a great phony smile; everyone falls for it."

"I've worn it myself too many times to count. What gives?"

Trace wrapped her hands around her middle, but her expression was strong, her lips twitching at the corners as she considered giving in to a genuine smile. "I confess, I am a little lonely in this crowd. Love these women, but, well you've all fallen head over heels for guys that adore you. I'd hoped for that with Finn, but it wasn't meant to be. Now don't start again. As I said before, what he and I had was fine, but I want more than *fine*. I want to be all fluttery, sap-happy, emotionally tied and miserable like you people."

Snorting, Haley felt a tug pulling at the corner of her mouth. "I think that sums it up."

"What if Finn takes one of these coaching jobs? Or even ends up some sportscaster?"

Haley snagged the bottle from Trace and topped off her glass. "You know I'm never giving everything up for someone else again. Been there, done that. But I've also never fought for anyone, nor had anyone fight so hard for me. I have a plan."

"Oh my. She has a plan. Scary thing when Haley has a plan."

"Oh shove off. What about you? You going to be okay?"

"Of course. I love you and fully support you. But let me be a little self-pitying as I find my way."

Haley set down her glass and hugged her friend. Not that phony air kiss or pat on the back or condescending crap, but a real hug that set off the waterworks.

Freya hollered from across the great room, sitting cross-legged on the floor as she landed their piece on a square. "Haley, get your ass back in here. It's a sports question for a piece of the pie, and Pippa and I are utter failures at these."

Pulling away, Haley grabbed the bottle and set it on the coffee table while Trace leaned against the counter and watched.

Sophie cleared her throat and read the card. She watched the room as faces contorted at the detailed factoid it would take a serious fan to know.

Haley grinned. "Nobody knows this one? Come on guys. It was Finn's rookie year? He gave Jerry Rice a run for his money."

Nodding with a comically serious face, Sophie added, "And your answer is?"

"My boyfriend." She grinned and snagged the green wedge before the answer was even confirmed. From her perch in the kitchen, Trace shook her head and smiled.

The evening was a first for Haley. Laughing, joking, a hint of serious, and utterly relaxed. With no staff to take care of the clean-up, Haley started clearing as things were wrapping up. The others pitched in, and within a few minutes time, the house looked as pristine as it had a few hours prior.

She slept sprawled across the massive bed, listening to the wind rustle the branches outside her window. The sun took its time rising in the distance, its subtle glow brightening her bedroom as her eyes fluttered open.

Hopping out of bed, she took an extra-long shower, then tossed on a favorite pair of jeans, a simple t-shirt, and low boots, looking forward to fall so she could wear her knee-highs again. Dashing upstairs, she grabbed her notebook and set up at the kitchen island for coffee and a light breakfast.

Within the hour, she had finalized her ideas and drove to the Halseth's home. Scott greeted her as she arrived, still working on his coffee, as he'd been working overtime at the pub in Finn's absence. "You're awfully chipper this morning," he said, smiling over his mug.

"I am." She nodded, unsure what he was getting at.

"You know Finn's not home yet, right?"

"I didn't think so, but I haven't talked to him. I'm here for you, actually." She held up her notebook. "I thought I'd drop off a few ideas, unless you have time to go over it together?"

"That was fast. Come on in."

He poured her another cup of coffee and she laid out her ideas at the dining table. Together, they rearranged a few things, adding a few framed jerseys on the walls, adjusting colors and furniture placement. Knowing his stash of memorabilia was impressive, she added a wall of shelves with baskets to store his favorites that didn't make the cut to display, but could easily be brought out to show off or reminisce.

Wrapping it up, she closed her notebook. "I'll put in some orders and be back in a few days to snap some befores and start bringing things over?"

"Absolutely. I... Finn gets back tonight. You, uh, haven't talked to him at all, huh?"

"No, I wanted to give him the space to decide what he wants."

Scott chuckled, rising to his feet. "We've got something in common there. He's been so complacent since he got back, I'm not sure even he knows what he wants."

"That's why you encouraged him to go to all the interviews?"

"Yeah. Don't want him to have any regrets. I didn't make the cut to go pro like he did, but I don't think I could function without football in my life." Scott refilled his coffee, bringing the mug up to his lips, the steam spiraling around his face as he took a steady sip.

"And you don't think he'd be happy tending bar for the rest of his life?"

"Halseth's was Brenda's dream. I liked it well enough, but I needed more. Coaching Finn's teams when he was a kid, then staying on with the high school, that's been the light of my life. Aside from my family, of course." He paused, leaning up against the counter. "Finn would make a hell of a coach, commentator, whatever he wants to do. But I know he'd be happier playing than anything. His knee has been pretty good lately. I've seen him sneak onto the high school field to run drills when no one's around. I was good. Finn is gifted. Shame he'll never play competitively again."

Haley stood from the chair and loaded the notebook back into her purse, hooking the bag over her shoulder. "Not competitively, but what about recreationally?"

"No rec teams around here for adults."

F inn swung his garment bag over his shoulder, watching the other passengers depart way too damn slow. From the air, he'd fired off a few emails with all the appropriate thank yous, responding to the offers that had already come in.

He crossed out of the secure area, strode across the gleaming off-white tile floors with shiny metallic flecks. Past the lines of folks tapping their feet, checking their watches as they stood waiting to go through security, he hopped on the escalator. Crossing the sky bridge toward the dark garage, he breathed in the crisp Washington air wafting around. Nothing like it; every time they landed in a new state for away games, he'd breathed in the air, comparing it to home.

He tossed his bags in the trunk and took off. Dammit, he was ready to be home. It had about killed him, not calling Haley. He'd picked up his phone dozens of times, then reminded himself she needed the space to decide what she wanted. To find her footing without him.

Not that he had a clue what he was going to do if she decided that footing didn't include him. Or what if she was disappointed in his decision? A dull ache festered under his sternum, like just seeing Haley's fishhook grin could relieve the crushing pressure.

His phone buzzed as he hopped onto southbound I-5, the digital voice reading out a text from Pops, *Meet me at the football field. I've got something to show you.*

Shit, he should have told him his decision already. Pops was probably dragging him out to the field for a serious talk about his future. Wouldn't be the first time.

The afternoon sun held strong as he drove into Foothills. He was wiped out and just wanted to drive straight to Haley's, lay it all out, and get started on the rest of his life.

As he pulled into the high school parking lot, he saw a familiar Land Rover near the field. Erratically pounding in his chest, his heart launched straight into his throat and about choked him.

Rejection was acceptable. Haley didn't need anyone to make her whole. She was strong and independent and her own person. She could fall down a cliff and come out okay. Could fall in love and get her heart broken, and come out stronger for it. She had her own life, a future she was looking forward to, and a past she'd never be okay with, but knew even that hadn't defeated her.

But damn, she really wanted Finn. Who else would dive off that cliff with her?

She wouldn't blame him for saying no. That night, their last night together, something inside her broke. Not in a bad way. It was the crunchy shell she'd coated herself in, swearing to never let a man get to her again. What remained was stronger, yet more sensitive as yearning had flooded in.

The thing was, Nate had never gotten to her like that. No one had. Finn burrowed right in, as if he'd always belonged there. Only weeks away from meeting as teenagers, befriending the same gentle soul, then living within a few five miles for much of their adult lives, the dream of him already stirring something inside her.

The afternoon sun was toasty, but the breeze brought in a welcome relief from the August heatwave that had settled over Foothills the last few days. Standing in the middle of the field, Haley had nothing to do but wait. And hope.

The sun at his back, his walk powerful, purposeful, Finn strode across the field, meeting her at the fifty-yard line. His cowlick had completely taken over from the long trip across the country, his t-shirt wrinkled, his shorts rumpled. But his smile, all hesitant and sweet and curious, fired right at her like Cupid's arrow.

Stopping a few yards away, he ran his fingers through his hair before settling his hands on his hips. "I'm really, really sorry for stepping on your toes and calling your lawyer without your permission."

"Are you?" She put her hands on her hips, cocking one out and raising her eyebrows.

Grinning, he shook his head. "Okay, I'm not sorry for making that asshole sweat, but I am sorry for not asking your permission. I knew you'd say no, and I wanted you to know your people had your back, whether you needed anyone or not."

"I would be mad, but I was so angry with Nate that I was taking it out on myself. By the way, my lawyer is hoping you'll send an autographed photo. And he was pretty impressed with your grace under pressure."

Finn's feet held firm to the ground, but his shoulders relaxed. "Grady says you guys went out and raised hell in San Francisco after."

"Yes. Pippa knows how to plan quite the night out."

"Did she take you to that club she'd found? She was practically bouncing on the plane, convincing everyone to go once she found out it served virgin cocktails."

"I was sorry to disappoint her, but I really didn't want to go to a club without a decent dance partner."

Finn stepped closer, his hands reached out and traced along her bare arms. Fluidly, she completed the connection, resting her palms against his abdomen. "I'm not one for club life, but I'd love to take you dancing."

She grinned. "How about we try out a few moves at home instead?"

Chuckling, he nodded. "I can go with that. If it doesn't break any rebound rules."

"I had a good talk with Trace."

"Okay." He said, freezing in place.

"I'm going to get scared now and again. Of us. After ten years of not knowing what it felt like, not realizing how things could and should be, it's going to take me a while to get used to it, and I'm going to mess up sometimes."

He hesitated, as if he'd heard her wrong. "Haley, I know we promised to not make any promises. But I made a mistake. I promise to never, ever take you for granted, or make you feel anything less than remarkable. And if you ever feel like that's not happening, please kick my ass." He slipped his arms around her waist. "And I know you didn't want more than a summer fling. I'm sorry, but I accidentally fell in love with you and don't want to give you up. Not now, not ever."

The corner of her mouth quirked up, irretrievably snatched on a fisherman's hook.

Leaning down, he brushed his lips over hers in a possessive kiss. Resting his forehead against hers, he whispered. "Tell me you love me."

She shook her head. "Not yet." Adrenaline pumped through her veins, warming her from the inside out.

"What?" he yanked her hips against his, grinning.

"Whatever you decide, I'm with you. If you want to live in Minneapolis and coach, I'll be there. If you decide to be on TV, I'm there for you. Not because you need it, or because I am sacrificing my happiness for yours, but because I can work anywhere, and because you empower me to be *me*. And I want to be with you."

Kissing her again, he said, "But what do *you* want?"

"I want you. I want to keep posting my stupid vlog and take the risk. I want to finish your dad's man cave because it will be fun and I like your family."

"It's not an exciting place, but would you be okay with living in Foothills for the rest of your life? With marrying a washed-up, football-player-turned-bartender?" The insecurity in his gaze could break her heart all on its own.

"Only if he sneaks into our bedroom every night and snuggles until dawn."

"Now tell me you love me?"

She grinned, melting with his chocolate eyes. "I love you, Finn Halseth."

"Is it too soon to propose? I mean, I know you want to be one hundred percent independent. Haley, you are. And I'll do everything in my power to give you space when you need it, and be there for you when you want support, but, well, I'm getting evicted soon, and I love you so much and I want to spend the rest of my life making you happy and—"

"It's not too soon. I mean, it is, I shouldn't want to. I should be against marriage and anything of the sort. I shouldn't trust in the entire institution. But I know myself. And I know you. And I want us both to make each other happy. And... please, propose. As soon as possible."

In the distance, their friends pulled into the parking lot and unloaded from their cars, dressed for a game. Trace and Pippa carted a picnic basket. Grady and Claire followed hand-in-hand behind, Freya bouncing behind and joining at their side. Zane and Asher and Sophie sprinted by, racing for the opposite end-zone. Scott, Zoe, and Evan carted bags of gear to the sideline.

Finn scanned the field, their friends and family setting up for a game. He scrunched his brow in question.

"This okay? I know you miss the game, and, well, I made some calls. I wasn't sure if you were recovered enough, but we'll go easy on you."

"I can't believe you did all this for me." Finn dropped to one knee in the middle of the field, in the middle of the chaos around them. "Everyone seems to think I don't know what I want. That I'm simply following the path of least resistance. But I know exactly what I want. I like Foothills. I like tending bar at my family's restaurant. And the moment you walked into my life, I wanted you. Will you marry me?"

"Yes." She dropped to her knees with him. An exhilarated laugh bubbled up from deep in her belly.

Tugging her against him, he poured everything into her, and she wrapped her hands around the back of his neck and held on for dear life.

"I am apologizing in advance for Sunday dinners with my family."

He groaned in a pitiful pout. "Only if we can put the game on. I'm not suffering Patricia and missing football."

"She's good with that. Besides, she sort of likes you now. Need a hand getting up?"

"I've almost worked my way back up to a complete set of fifty-forties, but yes, please, I could use a hand." He braced his hand against his thigh with one hand, took her hand in the other and they rose to stand together. He took her lips in his, sliding his hands around her waist. "What happened? Did she figure out I'm neither a player nor poor?"

"Nope. She was impressed with you driving out to her house and demanding she get her ass to San Francisco to stand up for me like she should have done ten years ago."

Clearing his throat, Grady interrupted, "I may have turned the TV on during your 'interview' with ESPN. She thought you looked pretty spiffy on camera and hopes you'll be a regular guest commentator."

"Fuck that," Finn sneered.

Evan jogged over and dropped a bag of balls at their feet. "Let's play some ball before sunset."

Pulling back, Finn didn't let go of Haley's waist but sneered at his brother. "Shove off. We're having a moment here."

Evan shrugged with his arms open wide. "It was Haley's idea, dragging us all out to get your lazy ass moving. Don't disappoint."

Finn released Haley, backing up a few steps, then took off across the field. His strides long, each footfall was light and mobile. Snagging the football from Evan, Haley adjusted her body and passed as high and far as she could. Cutting across the field, Finn snatched it from the air and hit the ground running, taking off for the end zone.

Thanks for reading!

Next up: 280 Days. One spontaneous night with her childhood crush was supposed to be enough for Zoe Halseth, but nothing is simple when Ryder Mallory is around... Visit carriet horne.com to find out more!

A Demon Hunter Romance

Plucky, yet badass demon hunters in this paranormal romance series.

1. **Six:** Fate sucks. Even demon hunters deserve a little normal.

2. **Wildest:** Bookworm demon hunter begrudgingly joins forces with a werewolf. Need I say more?

3. **Changed:** Who will hunt the hunter?

4. **Echo**: Badass military hero. Flirty, commitment-phobe demon hunter. What if she accidentally falls for him? Saving the world can be so complicated.

5. *And many more are on the way! Vann of course, Noah, Skye, Blayk... did someone say **epic**?*

Foothills Romance

Make yourself at home in the Foothills Romance series set in the Cascade Foothills of Washington State.

1. **All the Days After:** Former Navy SEAL Asher Sutherland can't seem to get a grip on his future, nor can he keep his hands off his sister's best friend.